BIRD LIFE

BIRD LIFE

ANNA SMAILL

SCRIBE
Melbourne • London

Scribe Publications
18–20 Edward St, Brunswick, Victoria 3056, Australia
2 John St, Clerkenwell, London, WC1N 2ES, United Kingdom
3754 Pleasant Ave, Suite 100, Minneapolis, Minnesota 55409, USA

First published by Scribe 2023

Typeset in Adobe Garamond Pro by the publishers.

Printed and bound in the UK by CPI Group (UK) Ltd,
Croydon CR0 4YY

Scribe is committed to the sustainable use of natural resources and
the use of paper products made responsibly from those resources.

978 1 761380 11 2 (Australian edition)
978 1 915590 03 9 (UK edition)
978 1 957363 54 7 (US edition)
978 1 761385 46 9 (ebook)

Catalogue records for this book are available from the
National Library of Australia and the British Library.

ARTS COUNCIL OF NEW ZEALAND TOI AOTEAROA

scribepublications.com.au
scribepublications.co.uk
scribepublications.com

For Sandeep

In life, in order to understand, to really understand the world, you must die at least once. So, it's better to die young, when there's still time left to recover ...

The Garden of the Finzi-Continis

In Ueno Park the pollen was blowing. It was alive on the warm air with a scent that was elusive and bodily, like the secretion of a vast clean organism, perhaps an oil emitted by the pores of the city itself. It floated in the air and teased the nostrils. It made one feel constantly on the verge of some sort of epiphany.

Girls walked through the park, in pairs and in groups. They wore sling-back sandals and short, tiered skirts in floaty fabrics. They were carrying poodles and chihuahuas in their oversized handbags. Up in the sky a dirigible hung, advertising Sofmap data storage.

Takenodai Fountain was at the end of the concourse. It was made up of a large, elegant rectangular pool ringed with gloriously flowering azalea bushes. The pool contained seven tall jets of water and dozens of smaller jets. These all spouted at odd times. The pattern of their eruption was erratic and playful, impossible to decipher.

On one of the park benches around the fountain, there sat a group of women from the nearby tourist office. They were having their morning coffee. They all wore a uniform of dusty olive-green and were as neat as flight attendants in their pencil skirts and wasp waists and garrison caps. They talked and laughed while the zelkova and ginkgo pollen blew, drawing the park together into a common intimacy. Pigeons fluttered in the dust.

On the park bench opposite, three young men were seated. Their postures differed completely from the tourist-office ladies. Two were leaning back in a caricature of boredom, legs outstretched, arms folded, smoking. Theirs were bodies in repose after physical labour. They wore the uniform of construction workers: wide-legged blue trousers made from heavy cotton drill, cut in a swaggering balloon from the waist and tapered back at the ankles. On the young men's bodies the style was somehow both old-fashioned and subversive. They also wore rubber-soled tabi boots and had branded beer flannels draped over their foreheads. The third member of the group was dressed in the attire of a different profession altogether. He was wearing a cheap black suit and had the wasted, concupiscent air of one whose night had bled into the subsequent morning.

A red plastic Coca-Cola crate sat in front of this suited young man, and he was knotting a piece of string to a thin forked stick. Next he got down on his knees and propped the crate corner up with the stick. He trailed the string back to where his friends were sitting. Then he took a balled-up Denny's bag from the park bench, pulled out a half-eaten hamburger bun, broke it, and sprinkled crumbs across the concrete. He placed the largest piece of bread directly under the balanced crate. Then he dusted his hands and knees, picked up the end of the string, and returned to sit down.

His actions had caught the attention of the women. They spoke to each other and looked across the divide and then back to each other and laughed behind their hands.

Thus the doomed venture unfolded. Not a pigeon came near. The suited young man rocked forward on the balls of his feet. He scowled and clenched his hands. The pigeons fluttered in the dust around him. They studiously avoided the bread and the bright-red trap he'd engineered. The pollen filtered down in drifts.

Further afield, children's voices wove together. Mothers stood in aprons and hats, arms folded, rocking back on their heels, never speaking. The water rippled around the fountain. The small dogs barked. Couples sat on their foldaway mats with their cans of beer and their eel-and-rice lunch boxes. A child wearing a frilled strawberry dress with matching strawberry bloomers stood and wobbled.

Here, in the middle of this benign scene, a woman walked by. There was nothing much to remark about her. She was a picture of middle-class, middle-aged femininity. She wore a fine cotton-knit cream twin set and a black skirt of many light layers. She carried a Louis Vuitton handbag.

The only surprising thing about the woman was that she wore only one shoe. She had removed the other and was carrying it in her hand. Her fine black Wolford stockings had clearly suffered in whatever misadventure had befallen the shoe. Each knee was a spider's web of snags where the fabric had holed and run.

It might seem impossible to walk with any dignity in this circumstance — one shoe off, stockings ruined — but the woman managed it. On her the holed stockings seemed an emblem of some insouciant fashion, a dereliction *miraculously transformed into chic by the alchemy of her disdain. Halfway down the concourse she removed the other shoe and padded lightly. She had spotted something.*

What had she seen? What was there to see?

The water trickled on over the metal sculpture. The small dogs barked. The child in her strawberry dress tentatively took her first step.

A young foreign woman was lying on the ground in the grass beneath one of the large zelkovas. Something about her position suggested collapse rather than repose. There was a backpack on the grass next to her, one strap still looped through an arm where she lay. Next to that was a large paper bag with the logo of the National Museum of Western Art. Her eyes were closed and her face was contorted in what appeared to be anguish.

It was quite an awful thing to behold, that anguish. Like coming across a person with their clothes removed in public. Passers-by had observed the girl — of course they had. The couples and families stepped politely around her. Encountering a foreigner in a state of collapse was not unusual at this time of year. It was spring, and it was Tokyo. The world was full of lightness and calm, blessed by the benignity of blossom.

The young woman on the ground was not, in any case, aware of anything. Perhaps she was caught in the throes of some personal calamity or injury. Her arm moved in a crazed, crabwise fashion to shield her eyes. The limb hardly seemed to belong to her. She was not aware of the other woman's approach.

The shoeless woman was moving at pace now, as light on her feet as a teenager. A few people threw a glance her way, but nothing more. The woman padded; the girl struggled. The distance between the two shrank step by step.

What was drawing them together remained unclear. But there was a great quantity of patience in the air. The pollen was floating; the dust was floating. Whatever came next would follow.

And so it did.

Suddenly, as if by some prearranged signal, the fountain spoke. The dozen tiny jets shot up from the edge of the rectangular pool, and then a second, more violent spray of water from the large jets shot up after them in a single loud announcement.

In perfect unison the olive-uniformed women and the young men all jumped. The Coca-Cola crate fell, catching nothing. The child in her dress and bloomers fell backwards. The pigeons, arrested in fright, took to the sky, filling the air with the battened clap of wings.

MAISON DU PARC

1

Dinah Glover arrived in Tokyo to take up residence in a block ambitiously named Maison du Parc. The building was surrounded by concrete and clad in more concrete, pink and stuccoed. It was long and squat, like the egg casing of a huge insect.

Dinah had come on a work visa sponsored by Saitama Denki University. The interview had been completed over Skype; the flights had been paid for. She was here to teach English to undergraduate engineering and science students.

Her predecessor, Phil, met her at the airport to show her the train system. It was easy once you got the hang of it; you didn't need to speak Japanese at all. When they reached their final stop, she followed Phil through a shopping district and down a long residential road. The neighbourhood was suburban and had a threadbare, dusty quality. There were a few empty squares of wild, weedy grass with high wire fences. A poster on bulging damp particle board showed a couple standing outside a new home. The woman held an infant in her arms.

'There was a typhoon last week,' said Phil, 'but you missed it.' They were at the apartment block now. A gravel-covered pathway made the clattering noise of Dinah's suitcase all at once very loud.

'Nice place,' said Phil. She couldn't tell if he was being sarcastic. His accent was Canadian. 'One of your suitcase wheels is broken.'

He was right. It had split into two neat rounds like an orange. Dinah lifted the suitcase into her arms like a wayward child and followed him up the stairs. They were narrow and rusting so that flakes of white paint dropped down through the steps to the ground below as they walked.

When they reached the right floor, the top one, the landing seemed very provisional and narrow and Phil very broad and stocky in his bad suit. The railing only reached his upper thigh.

Dinah walked inside past him, removing her shoes as she did. There was a kitchenette with a small fridge and small toaster oven. A small table in yellowish pine. A door on the left, and one on the right, presumably to the bathroom and toilet. There was a futon couch near the far wall, and that was the end of it. There were sliding glass doors along the back wall and a narrow balcony beyond them.

Phil made it across the apartment in three steps in his stockinged feet. He slid the door open, gestured.

'There's your park,' he said, without a hint of irony.

She went out and looked down. It wasn't a park. It was a square of gingery gravel. No grass; no green. A few old plane trees lined the periphery, and there was a strange concrete play area rising up out of the dust. Some park benches, all of which were empty.

She was glad when Phil left. He gave her the key and some paperwork. 'Good luck at SDU,' he said. Then she was alone.

The door to the apartment was made of metal like a submarine door. It made a ridiculously loud clang into the silent air as she left. The noise echoed around the whole building. She looked up at the other windows. It was very silent.

Dinah walked, which was pleasant to do after the long flight, the train ride.

The neighbourhood's other buildings were similar to her apartment block, in muted, washed-out colours — pink, blue, cream, grey. Upper balconies had bedding hanging over the rails, as if the façades were covered in patchwork.

She walked and walked. It was very quiet — nobody on the streets at all. Through the gaps in fences she saw paved courtyards, small

8

domestic gardens with assorted pot plants.

It was not simply that the neighbourhood was quiet. It was more as if, by some mutual signal, everyone in it had up and left. The silence was like an indrawn breath. She realised that she was walking quietly, listening. After a few blocks she came across a bike leaning against a wall. In its basket was a brown paper bag emblazoned with the words 'Mister Donut'. The bag was crisply folded and the bike's tyres were still spinning.

She turned a corner and almost bowled headfirst into an elderly woman. *'Sumimasen!'* Excuse me. It was one of her first Japanese phrases.

The woman was crouched over in a patch of grass next to the pavement. There was a black plastic supermarket bag on the grass in front of her, and she was wearing a floral housecoat and zip-up slipper boots. Using a metal spoon she was digging slowly in the grass verge. As Dinah watched, the woman extracted the dirt from her hole and piled it up in a neat heap. When she had removed enough dirt, she reached into the supermarket bag and took out a small seedling. The flower was a bright, almost electric, blue. For a second it seemed the only spot of bright colour in the whole street, possibly the whole neighbourhood.

Dinah watched. The woman nestled it down into the hole. She scooped carefully with her spoon, then she put back the earth that had been removed and eased it in around the plant's shoulders with great care. Like tucking a child into bed. She didn't look up at Dinah all the time she worked. When she had finished, the leftover soil and the spoon went back into the plastic bag. She left, slipping through a gap in the fence.

Dinah kept walking.

The train tracks. Then more apartment blocks. All concrete stucco like her own. A small supermarket. A drycleaner, a hairdresser, a few convenience stores. Some cafés and restaurants that looked somehow domestic, as if they were really people's homes that had one day been turned to this purpose.

She bought a tall can of either soft drink or alcohol from one of the convenience stores.

At last she had walked the full circumference of the neighbourhood and was back at her apartment block. The light was fading as she looked up at the windows. There were three floors above the ground floor. She counted nine apartments in all. Three on the bottom floor and two on each of the three floors above. All of the windows were dark, except her own, at the top. She touched the key in her pocket. It was true that she did not wish to go back up. Too quiet. The windows around her too dark and blind.

The next corner, then, and the park. There was a metal chain strung between two dark metal bollards, but there were gaps on either side, large enough for a person. The plane trees stood like gentle sentries.

Peering in she saw that the wide space of fine, biscuity gravel was larger than the view from her apartment balcony had suggested. It was completely empty. She took a leaf from each of the trees and stepped over the chain. 'One of each kind,' she said to nobody.

What was the story again? You picked the leaves for something. To prove you had been down into the underground world. Or did you collect the leaves so you could use them later? They would transform into silver or gold, if you brought them back up with you to the surface. There was something about being silent. You had to be silent. It shouldn't be too difficult to be silent here.

There were benches along the edge of the park and she sat on the first. From this position she could study the odd playground structure. The main element was a large dome of concrete, which had metal rungs embedded in its sides. It looked a bit like the hump of a prehistoric beast that had died and gradually subsided into the bath of gravel. It had a slide at one end; not far away was a small swing set. It didn't look very child-friendly but resembled a piece of modernist sculpture more than anything.

Dinah opened the can and took a long swig. It was grapefruit flavoured. Below that, thank god, was a clean, dry alcohol with no flavour. The bubbles stung her throat.

There was a grapefruit tree in the garden of the house she had grown up in. She recalled the way it had grown, right in the middle of the lawn, popping rudely out of the grass as if it had burst through in a single night. Her twin brother used to twist the grapefruit right off the tree and bite right through the skin and the horrible white pith so that the juice ran down his chin. That was the kind of person he was. They were her brother's fruit; she didn't even really like them. Something morose and sharp and rebarbative about the taste and the way their heavy oil hung around. She smelt it now, the sourness and sweetness. It asked you to go back to your body in some way, like plunging into very cold water.

Dinah sat on the park bench and took another sip. She felt the mercy of mild drunkenness. She finished the tall can and placed it carefully next to her on the bench. Then she turned her attention to what was in her hand. She inspected the leaves. They were large and palmate, a late-spring green. There was writing on the back, scribbles from an insect that had recorded its journey. She studied the message for a long time. It was in a different language to her own. She had known it once, but now its meaning was lost altogether.

2

Yasuko Kinoshita woke very early each morning to apply her make-up. She took the pursuit very seriously. She was not a person who liked to rush. The ritual began with moisturiser. During Yasuko's teenage years acne had flowered on her cheeks like bright blossom. There was still some scarring. She did not mind it — the stippled scars had become inextricable from her beauty — but she did wish to minimise the tinge of redness that remained. This moisturiser had been developed in a research laboratory for wound care in Seoul and was very expensive indeed. It seemed that with daily application some of the old discolouration was fading.

Next she applied a primer. Following that, foundation with a moistened sponge for more complete coverage. She used bronzer to contour her slightly wide nose bridge, then blusher to accentuate her rounded apple cheeks. If anything, the blusher drew attention to the scarring. But camouflage and candour are not necessarily contradictory.

The eye shadow that she selected was purple with good colour saturation and a fine glitter that by common standards was much too young for a woman of her years. She lightly pencilled in her brows. She finished by spraying on a light fixative and then the usual four coats of Fiberwig mascara.

Yasuko looked herself straight in the eyes while she worked. She neither flinched nor glanced away. It is true that not enough is made of the courage of the woman of a certain age who examines her own face so intently. Who treats it as material, simply. A canvas for transformation.

'Goodbye, lazy bones,' she called to her son, who was still in bed. He would not be up for another hour, just before his first lecture commenced. She slammed the door very loudly, to help him along the way.

Yasuko entered the station with a swagger. The attendant behind the windowed booths gathered himself as she passed. He straightened his peaked cap and pulled in his gut. He tried, via the densely gathered presence of his sad middle-aged body, to draw her attention. He had been in love with her for at least a year. By good fortune — both his own and hers — he was much too shy to act. Yasuko passed and climbed the stairs. She stood on the concrete platform as she had done so many thousands and thousands of times that they were all blended into one.

In that moment, everything shifted. Just for a second, the world broke loose from its bearings, and she was alone in it.

It was impossible to tell what had triggered it.

Perhaps it was the sound of the train approaching.

Perhaps the air filled with the spring that had been coming slowly, creeping over the trees and the concrete as it always did.

Perhaps the birds that were rustling in the eaves of the platform shelter, arguing over a cigarette.

Whatever the cause, the moment came with a whispering sound, a susurration. Yasuko heard it, of course she did — it was for her. She tried to ignore it. But it was too late.

The world outside continued, which was what the world always did. The train pulled in. Heavy with momentum. Carrying such weight.

Yasuko was not unfamiliar with such moments. She managed as best as she could. She pulled her eyes away from the disturbance of the birds. She girded herself to board. She gave strength to her shoulders. She hardened her eyes, flickering beneath the glitter. Resolute.

She sat, and the train pulled away.

On her seat, next to the upright pole, she sat very upright. She placed both her work tote and her handbag on her knee. She placed a hand inside her handbag to ensure that everything was there: purse, keys, make-up, notebook. There was a feeling of blur, a feathery sensation all over her.

13

She did not look out of the window, being at this present moment too afraid of what she would see. In the matter of a few seconds, even at her age and maturity and confidence, the world had thinned. Its texture had become brittle, repellent. Her own place in it had become provisional.

However, if she acknowledged this, that would make it real, so she did not acknowledge it. Perhaps it would pass.

At each stop more people got on. The travellers were mostly men at this hour. Businessmen going to work. Students going to the expensive city universities. Men, travelling solo and in packs. You couldn't avoid them. Lord knows she had tried in her life. It was impossible. Men were simply everywhere, with their suits and valises.

Really, Yasuko was so tired of them. Deeply tired. In her body. She was tired of all the extra, entitled parts of them that muscled their way in without even buying a ticket. The smell of their hair and their teeth and bodies. The sheer unnecessary physical heat that accompanied them. She was tired of being crammed into the available spaces between them, between their glances and their assertively placed hands and feet and the bodies with which they leaned.

Perhaps it was this irritation that helped propel her forward.

Yasuko did what she had learned to do in such moments. She inhaled and exhaled. She looked at one thing only. What she chose to look at was her white Louis Vuitton Murakami Monogram Speedy handbag. She examined the supple pebbled canvas of the bag and the satisfying chunkiness of the leather handles. She thought about the journey each component part had taken in order to be turned into an object that existed simply to be purchased by her and held by her and to give her pleasure. The bright logo pattern jumped cheerfully on its white field. Miraculously, it was enough. She felt her equanimity return. She sat in the relief of her handbag, its strangeness, its adequacy. She travelled all the way to work and did not once look up.

Saitama Denki University was a science and engineering university. The campus where Yasuko taught was located in Hatoyama, in the middle of Saitama prefecture. The university was not a very good one, but its English programme was fairly large.

The four Japanese English-language teachers had their own small office with a computer-printed sign in both English and Japanese. The four native English speakers were housed in a smaller office in an anonymous corridor above the administration block. The two groups had little, if anything, to do with each other.

By the time Yasuko reached campus, she had, in fact, almost recovered. Nobody was likely to notice anything.

Okinawa-sensei was already in the Japanese teachers' office. She pushed open the door and saw his feet on his desk. He appeared to be in hiding. His desk was barricaded with books and he was almost fully reclined in his chair. He had opened a large grey ring binder over his face like a mansard roof.

'Ohayo gozaimasu,' Yasuko said. With a flourish of irony. She fought the urge to laugh at Okinawa. How strange to go from despair to humour so quickly, but such was her life. 'Good morning!'

She stowed her Louis Vuitton handbag next to her computer and took her tote on her knee to find the papers she had marked the night before. The papers blinked at her, white and papery. She recoiled only slightly.

Okinawa lifted the edge of the ring binder.

'You scared me,' he said.

'What on earth are you doing under that ring binder?'

'Hiding. Mayumi-san's on the prowl. She came in before, but I hid under the desk.'

'You are ridiculous,' said Yasuko, and smiled at him and lifted out the papers, her notebook and workbook.

Okinawa had no wife and no children. He had no elderly mother, no siblings, and no dog. He may have had a cat, but even if he did he was the kind of fellow who would certainly not have mentioned it. He was a misanthrope, and entirely charming.

The door opened again with a jangle. Okinawa shrank further under his ring binder; Yasuko sat up straight in her chair.

15

It was not Mayumi, the English-programme administrator. It was Machiko and Chiaki. They had caught the bus to campus together and were gossiping intently.

Machiko and Chiaki were rather inconsequential beings. Each was pretty in her own way. As colleagues they had their merits, but you could not say that they had really entered into life yet. They were still fluttering around its edges. Typically Yasuko did not give either woman much thought. But this morning, still on edge from her upset in the train station, she smiled at them.

They were curious about her, she knew. Chiaki in particular watched her with avidity. One day she had even come up to her at the photocopier. Yasuko had felt the girl's gaze along the back of her neck and the top of her shoulders. Then there had been a sudden fizzing of speech from the girl, as if something had popped in her head and caused an explosion of candour.

'Yasuko, you are so muscular,' Chiaki blurted, almost making Yasuko laugh. The girl was so ashamed that she had continued on recklessly with another question. 'Do you work out?'

Yasuko extended her forearm and considered her own muscles and their hardness and the way the veins lay above them, as if estranged. She was muscular, had always been so, in fact. A small punishment was necessary.

'No, my dear. I am actually a man,' she said.

The brief pleasure of seeing Chiaki's face register the shock. Seeing that, for a second, Chiaki had believed her.

Now, as Yasuko watched, Chiaki tucked her top lip over her slightly protruding teeth. She was trying to be serious, but her eyes pushed forward, goggling. Even if Chiaki were being held at gunpoint, her eyes would goggle, her face would dance, she would be struggling not to laugh.

Machiko stood next to Chiaki in a halo of calm, with her fringe, her dimples, her pregnant belly. She spoke not a word.

Yasuko felt their eyes moving over her.

'Ohayo gozaimasu,' they both called. She answered with a nod and

16

smile only. At last they settled in their enclave at the back of the room.

'Mayumi's on the prowl,' said Okinawa. 'They've finally found a replacement for Phil.'

The native English lecturers and the Japanese lecturers may have had little to do with each other, but everyone in the office knew Phil. He was Canadian. Built like a hockey player. The students hated him, couldn't understand his accent, mocked him openly. Really it had been a blessing when he gave his notice.

'What's that got to do with us?' asked Chiaki.

Okinawa shrugged. 'She wants to introduce everyone to the new teacher. Something like that. They're in the staff cafeteria.'

'Oh,' said Chiaki. She looked at her watch.

Machiko, who was the gentlest and kindest of them all, turned to Yasuko with an expression of appeal. She sat down at her desk and blew air through her fringe. 'I have so much preparation to do,' she said. 'The baby kept me up all night, kicking.'

Yasuko shook her head in decision, which was what they all needed from her. Largesse blossomed within her.

'I don't think we need to worry about that,' she said. 'I'll sort things out with Mayumi.'

And so the danger passed. Things returned to normal. The world's strangeness was held back by the ordinary routines of the day. Which was, after all, what she had built them for.

Yasuko enjoyed her students. They were mostly young men, but were exempt from her contempt due to their precocious innocence. She enjoyed their youth, their absurd hair curled up in the outrageous cockerel plumes that were the current fashion. They did not yet know what they were made of. They did not yet know what the world would give them.

And so she teased them mercilessly. She loved to pinpoint their weaknesses and make them blush. She loved to flirt with them and scare them, and then turn and write on the whiteboard with their eyes on her.

'Stop gossiping, Daizo,' she called. 'Your daddy won't give you a job in his bank if you fail English. We all know that's your only chance of finding a girl.'

She heard the most confident boys laughing and in her mind's eye saw Daizo clearly even as she faced the board. His homeliness and sincerity; the way his hair stood straight up like a hedgehog.

'I know it's a challenge, but if you want to get laid, you must practise your vocab.'

At last the day was over. Somehow she had survived it, and now it was plain sailing, home to Jun.

Just past Tsurugashima, on her ride home, the internal door of the carriage opened with a breathless double hiss. The homeless man entered. Yasuko knew him, and sighed. The man lived on the Tobu Tojo line. He rode up and down, up and down all day. He was harmless enough. His hair was bird-nested around his head and his skin had been flayed by the elements into the appearance of ruddy health, lit up from within by the beacons of craziness and alcohol.

'Oh.' He laughed and swayed. 'Oh, oh! The pissing, cunting worker ants. The little trainee worker ants! The larvae!'

There were a handful of students in the carriage. The rest were women on their way home. Office ladies with dowdy skirts and worn-down shoes and plastic supermarket bags full of cucumbers and eggplant. Women heading home from their overbearing bosses to make dinner for their overbearing husbands. Everybody in the carriage looked down and examined their hands and watches or phones. They studiously turned the pages of their modest brown-paper-wrapped paperbacks. They were not afraid of or embarrassed by the man: he existed in his own space, and they in theirs. At some point he would get off at a station.

Yasuko kept her head down too. The homeless man's hands fluttered and swooped in the edge of her vision, and she clasped her own hands as if they might rise in sympathy.

She thought about her students. Daizo had cornered her after the lecture and asked her if she played chess. She sat with her back ramrod straight.

She left the train in Shinjuku and went to Isetan to look at the spring accessories. There was a wonderful calm in that and she felt her confidence had returned. The upset of the morning was over. She felt flirtatious, imperious. She even went to the basement supermarket to buy the dessert Jun loved most of all and never allowed himself due to some odd stringent rule of his own making.

At home, in front of their apartment door, she paused, then she turned the key and pushed it open quietly.

'Hello!' she called quietly, with the phrase one uses when coming to the end of the day's journey: 'I'm back with you!'

She walked into the living room. At the doorway Yasuko stopped in horror. During the day, Jun had altered, transformed. His legs and arms were too long for the small apartment. A sudden shift would dislodge something in the narrow room. A single arm-flap would break a window, cause the roof to lift off. In her chest under her ribcage, something sharp. As if a thread between them had pulled tight.

Then he turned his head and the outsized look disappeared. It was simply a trick of the light. She blinked. There was no doubt that it was happening again. The world flickered. One second it was on, the next off. She knew that she could not fight it. Already she could feel her skin twitching, refusing. She felt the guilt too that always attended.

There was nothing much to do. The sunlight had clearly faded while Jun had been absorbed in his book and now she reached up, in a small act of rebellious free will, and flicked the light switch so that the room flooded with light. Jun looked up in surprise and saw her.

'Okaeri,' he said, using the phrase of the one who has kept the home fire burning and celebrates the traveller's completed journey.

She tried to keep her face cheerful. She tried not to show him. But they were connected very deeply. As soon as he looked up at her, she knew that he saw it too.

19

3

There is a specific skill to sleeping on the trains. In her first few weeks at Saitama Denki, Dinah mastered it. Sleeping on a journey brings an element of risk. How easy to miss a stop. But Dinah had the knack. As soon as she boarded, sleep came up to meet her. She simmered in it gently, as if in a soup stock that was made up of the jolting of the train, the sounds of the PA system, the smells and murmurings of her fellow passengers. Then just as her final stop neared she felt herself lifting, rising, emerging into wakefulness. She managed it in both directions. Any station and any route, she slept and woke. Slept and woke. Whether she caught an express or a limited express service. Even just a local. It was a sign of the evolution taking place below the surface. Her body was adjusting to the new environment, growing new limbs and reflexes.

The university campus was far away. To get there took two separate train journeys. One from her local station to Ikebukuro and then one from Ikebukuro deep into Saitama, on the Tobu Tojo line. Much of the journey passed through a proper countryside of ancient mallow trees and kudzu and small shrines hidden in wild grasses as high as your hip.

The university station itself was situated amongst rich-green rice fields. There were people at work in the fields as the train passed, knee-deep in the silver water, leaning in toward their reflections. Behind them were long, low white factories that produced ball bearings, roller bearings, ball screws, and automotive parts.

At each progressive stop before the university station, the train slowly filled with students. When it reached the university station at last, each carriage was a maelstrom of bodies. The bus to campus left five minutes after that final stop, and there was a vast tide of students to fight through.

Dinah launched herself into the flood and out down the concrete ramp toward the bus. If you didn't hurry you wouldn't get a seat and you'd be standing all the way to campus. This was probably the worst part of her day. The bus driver was a maniac and took the corners like a race driver. She held tight to the poles, propped herself against any surface. How awful to fall into the lap of a student she would be teaching imperative verbs in the second period.

There were a series of hairpin turns as the bus navigated through the semi-rural sprawl, then the journey became gentler. The hills rose slowly and followed a gradual incline through larger market gardens and smallholdings. Then they entered pine forest, with occasional steep faces lined with latticed concrete.

Dinah always felt a sharp pain in her side at this point. She dreamed about pushing the button that would cause the bus to halt. Nobody would stop her, she thought. She'd simply pick up her bag and walk through the door and out into the forest.

After a long while of climbing, when it seemed possible that the driver had taken a wrong turn, the trees suddenly thinned and the road widened. A clearing. It was a bit like the story where the piper plays and the hillside cracks open. Inside was clear, level terrain, as if a giant had flattened it out with one hand, plucked out the trees one by one, and placed the whole university campus down in one piece.

On her way to the native English lecturers' office, Dinah passed the glossy wooden desk at the front of the administration block.

'Dinah-sensei!'

It was the English programme administrator Mayumi-san. Dinah had no choice but to turn.

'Yes!' she said and took the few steps back that politeness required.

'You should not wear black stockings like that, you know.' Mayumi gestured at Dinah's legs. 'Too hot. Pale ones like these, please.' She pointed to her own slender knees in their sheer flesh-coloured stockings. Dinah nodded. There was a dark bruise on the woman's ankle.

'It's important, Dinah-sensei!' Mayumi said.

Then she was released, but not really safe. Not really because when she paused just outside the door to the lecturers' room, Carla was talking. Dinah heard, with the sudden shock of intimacy, her own name. Then Dougal's voice, lower, a demurral, and then laughter.

Dinah stopped. She felt the blood running warm in her face. She blew air from between her lips. Something made her wait a few seconds before she pushed the door open. It was not her own embarrassment she wished to avoid, but Carla's, with its slippery, tiring texture.

'Hi,' she said.

The blinds were pulled down against the mid-morning sun, and the desks were covered with piles of folders, scrap paper, lunch debris, and plastic cups from the Doutour at the station.

Dinah did her best to avoid Carla's face and discomfort. Luckily Dougal was speaking in his broad Glaswegian accent, which was a comfort to her ears. What a clarity and poise it gave him in this odd, derelict room with the crummy office seats, the half-eaten mochi in plastic packets. Dinah took her seat at one of the desks and listened.

Dougal grinned and in a genteel fashion twitched the permanent-pressed crease of his cheap trousers and leaned back in his chair so that it tipped precariously. He took a swig of his imported Irn-Bru so that they were all given a proud view of his Adam's apple, specked with blood from a mercilessly clean shave. He had the air of a person fully at home in his body. Fully at home with the pleasure and disappointment it could afford.

'This job is very good. As jobs go,' he said, glancing around. 'If you play your cards right it's very easy indeed.' He looked across at Dinah. 'Give it a few months. You'll see.'

His chair tipped back further and finally came to rest against the desk behind him. Dinah waited, not breathing, to see whether the chair legs would shoot out from under him.

'But it's not the perfect job. How do I know? Because someone else has that job already. In Aberdeenshire.'

He paused as if waiting for questions. Nobody spoke, but Dinah smiled a bit to encourage him. Above Dougal's belt was a potbelly that protruded neatly, small and hard like one of those endless balls of rubber bands you could buy in stationery stores. He nodded soberly back at Dinah in acknowledgement and continued.

'They were renovating a railway station there, you see. During the renovation the station had to shut. Trains still went through but not to stop. But,' he said, meaningfully, and took another sip, 'because of some legal loophole, they had to keep the ticket booth open. And there you go. Someone has to look after that station. The luckiest man in the world, that man. Off he goes in his uniform every morning. Unlocks his booth. Sits in his chair. And what does he do down there all day? Nothing. Sweet fuck all. Listens to his wee radio, sips his brew, does his crossword, minds his own business. That, my friends. That is the dream job.'

For a moment Dinah imagined Dougal in the booth. She imagined him in the small silent room with the layers of concrete pressing down above his head.

'You're fucking mental, Dougal,' Carla said in her Australian accent.

'Yes, you're crazy, Dougal,' Dinah said.

The hours ticked down. They all taught their classes.

The job was unbearable.

It wasn't the commute or the long hours. Not the teaching or the threadbare carpets. She didn't even mind Carla, with her stares and whispers. It was Mayumi.

Mayumi had seen through her, and it had created a brittleness and tension that was becoming intolerable.

Mayumi did not understand exactly what she had seen. Dinah saw her stare sometimes, as she entered the admin block, as if teasing at the problem, worrying away at it like a loose tooth. If Dinah made eye contact, Mayumi flicked her gaze away. Her voice became louder and more convivial with the other staff.

Mayumi's initial solution had been simply to ignore Dinah. If she needed to convey a message — a change of classroom, a request that she supervise an exam — she passed it on through one of the other lecturers. For a few weeks this seemed adequate.

But Mayumi was still fretting. She managed her unease with concerted jabs. If a student wanted some extra conversation practice, or an academic staff member needed someone to edit a journal article, they would always arrive at Dinah's desk. Dinah knew it was Mayumi who sent them, as if the administrator knew how preciously she held the brief gasp of her lunch hour.

If only she could speak frankly to Mayumi. She would attempt to assure her, she thought, tell her she was not to blame. There is nothing wrong with your reaction, she would say. It is quite normal to recoil from someone who is not quite alive. If I were in your position and encountered myself, I would probably do the same.

At the end of the day you did it all backwards. The bus to the station, the two trains. But at the end of the day it was different, because it was suffused in relief. To celebrate she put on her earbuds and listened to Ella Fitzgerald sing the whole Gershwin songbook right through.

Nice Work if You Can Get It. While travelling backwards through the rice fields, through the low growth of industry and civilisation and toward Ikebukuro. *'S Wonderful. A Foggy Day.* If Ella finished singing before she was home, Dinah would start the album again, which relieved somewhat the silence of the silent neighbourhood, the silent apartment block.

Just a brief stop off at home. The white paint flaked down through the steps of the rusted staircase. Just to put down her tote, change her clothes. Through the quiet streets she went, and down to the river. It was wide and deep and lined in concrete with skeins of rust from the stormwater drains. Occasionally a shopping trolley was upended in the wash. Blossom floated on the surface, moving up and down on the muscular currents. Every few hundred metres a vending machine on the path. They seemed to keep an eye on her with their warm glow. Arigato gozaimasu, she said, as she retrieved her can.

And then back, to the park, the park. Back to the plane trees with their broad leaves, and the dust that had a gentle, friendly odour, almost bodily, a sort of protein calm, like the smell of your own arms after a day at the beach.

They had shared a room, she and Michael. Two narrow single beds and a narrow gap between. Their walls had white splotches of plaster on them. If you squinted you could make out different pictures. Michael devised elaborate fantastic stories for each.

Lunchtimes at school were spent together on the bank behind the field. None of the other kids ventured up there. Perhaps it had been out of bounds. They had dug in the dirt with sticks, and piled up monkey apples. She couldn't remember whether the monkey apples were weapons or imaginary food. Michael was always the one who made up the games. But she remembered the satisfaction of making the piles, seeing them grow.

For their first two years of school, they were in the same class. Then they were separated for the first time.

Once they were apart, her teachers treated her very differently. When Michael was being difficult the teachers spoke gently, solicitously. The more trouble Michael was in, the gentler and more solicitous they would be.

'Sorry, Dinah, but I was wondering. Could you tell me where Michael is today?'

Sometimes a student knocked on the door.

'Please, Miss, can Dinah come and help?'

It had been important to assume an appropriate dignity, putting her books aside carefully, silently. She remembered standing up. Very quiet, very stately. Walking out of the room and down the corridor, as if she were somebody grand in a story. Her clothing and hair had fluttered like pennants in the wind that Michael gave off.

She used to hear his voice in her head before it was audible. She sometimes caught a glimpse of the landscape he was in: dark buildings, fretted windows, rushing skies.

When she got to the class, he would be standing at the back of the room, perhaps holding something above his head. His face would be somehow wider across the cheekbones, blunt like a spade. The kids all standing around. Her heart filled with love for him, a perverse pride. She couldn't remember if people were scared. She just remembered looking at each other, saying nothing. She had known so much at that time, it seemed to her. Much more than she knew now. She remembered seeing the calm come over him.

'Okay, Michael,' she said gently. It was very easy for her to love him, because they were just the same. 'All over, red rover.'

His face unfroze and returned to its usual shape. He lowered his helm. His eyes softened and went back to their usual colour. She came up to him and put her arm through his and they walked out of the classroom together and into the corridor and to the top field.

When they got there, they lay down in the grass, which was long and unmown, because no one used it for sport. She didn't speak. Michael would have a headache, the sort that felt like a river inside had burst and was washing away the bank and taking too much with it.

Those times were what she remembered. Sometimes she would do something droll to cheer him up. She would pretend he was a visitor from another planet and had never seen any of their earth things before. 'These are trees,' she would say. 'Native to this land. Their fruit and sap are poison.' Or she would describe the teacher or the kid they'd sent into the classroom to get her. She would be merciless and scathing, to make him laugh. It was funny how prissy the kids were when they came and summoned her.

'What a milk drinker,' said Michael, which was his worst insult at the time.

The afternoons used to last forever, but usually a teacher would come up and check on them. She would see a short shape on the edge of her vision first, blinking and wavering and unreal against the light of the sun. She would sit up, reluctantly, and wait for her vision to come back, wait for the teacher to take his or her correct adult form.

'It's not my fault they take everything so seriously,' said Michael.

She sat in the park and remembered. She sipped from the can. She thought about calling her mother but decided it would be too late. Also, a pain. She could almost hear her mother's startled breath as she answered the phone, then the carefulness, which would be even worse. 'How is everything *going*? Are you having a good time?'

There was another game. It started the same every time. It was called It's only us now. Michael was the one who decided they would play.

It wasn't complicated. It went like this: It's only us now, everyone else is gone. There was no disaster or anything, no back story. Dinah and Michael simply plunged forward, into survival. Those were the best times, she thought. Just the two of them moving through the world. You weren't meant to talk to the adults, of course (all of them were dead), but you had to make some exceptions. There must have been pauses in the game for lunch and dinner. It had seemed to go on forever. And how quickly the adults' world had fallen away. How quickly everything had become temporary and unreal, apart from them.

They had stolen things. Food from the kitchen. Lollies and packets of chips from the dairy at the top of their street. If they woke early enough, milk bottles from outside other people's mailboxes. It wasn't really stealing. In the depths of the game, when they were deeply inside it, they would leave their beds and make places to sleep in the garden. Her neck would be itchy from the hairs of the tree fern that got down the back of her pyjama top. They ate grapefruit and drank from the hose.

'You think I make it all up too, don't you?' said Michael. She couldn't remember what he was talking about specifically. Maybe they were in their bedroom. Maybe in the garden. She could remember that their faces were very near to each other. She liked looking at his face. She knew it better than anything in the world.

'Of course not.'

She had discovered something, not something that Michael had taught her, but a rare thing she had learned herself. You could say yes or no and mean both things. Yes, you could say, that is true, or yes, it is not true. No, it isn't true, and no, it is true. Because she had learned this, her world and Michael's world were able to draw up to each other slowly and never collide. They were like two cars in next-door lanes at the traffic light. Sometimes the neighbouring car moved off and your car seemed to be slipping backwards. You got a feeling in your stomach that was almost like falling. But that was all. In all the real ways, the ways that mattered, you were safe and would be safe forever.

Dinah sat on her usual park bench.

'Where are you?' she asked the trees, the dark. Nobody else was in the park. Never anybody else. She had entered in the usual way, via the gap at the edge of the chain that hung between the two metal bollards on the street. She walked to the edge of the sand and touched the metal of the chain at the park's far side. It was cool on her skin, swaying. What she saw was that you could go further in, into the darkness.

'When will you come back?' she asked.

4

Yasuko first came into her powers when she was thirteen.

There had been a homeless man who lived in the park in their neighbourhood. He had a small lean-to shelter made of cardboard and blue tarpaulin, and every day he swept the whole park, as if this was the price he had to pay for the neighbourhood's tolerance of his small establishment. He had a cat that was as threadbare and stoical as he was, and he cared for it by buying cans of tuna from the konbini and letting it sleep inside the lean-to with him, sharing his carefully flattened cardboard palette.

One day, not long after her thirteenth birthday, Yasuko was crossing the park. She was familiar with the homeless man and his cat; her father often bought him a cup of miso or a bowl of udon from the station. They nodded to each other as she passed. Today, however, the cat looked at her. She noticed immediately that there was something different about the way it looked. It had more than its usual air of narrow cunning. Then she felt a rippling nausea and slowness. It was as if everything was happening all at once, but doing so at a tiny fraction of its typical speed.

The first moments of her gift had a heavy quality, almost a dullness. It was the quality of inevitability. The cat's face moved, twitched. Yasuko flinched.

When the cat spoke to her, the voice it used was her own voice, as if this might moderate her shock.

'Silly girl,' the cat said. 'Why don't you pull your socks up? You look like a slattern.'

The air was suddenly electric. The buzz of everything, the particles alight. A rush of saliva filled her mouth. She spat into the dust of the park.

Should she reply? What did you do when an animal spoke to you? 'What do you mean?' she stammered.

'I mean, just look at yourself.' And then it laughed.

Even if she had wanted to reply then, she would not have been able. She had lost the ability to form words. The next few minutes were a blur. There was the laughter only. The light, hissing laughter of a secret opening up. She turned her face away, afraid. Then gradually she looked back toward the cat, and the park was filled with golden light.

When she got home it was very late. She had no memory at all of the journey or what had happened in between. She was covered, somehow, in dust. Her mother was appalled. She was sent straight to bed. She heard her mother and father talking behind the closed door.

Really, the beginning of her powers had not been promising at all. The exhilaration had come later. In bed that night the light returned, like an apology. It was golden, shining. It shone across everything, and she saw that she would be called to use this in some important way. That was her first night without sleep.

The world is very beautiful. It was given to her fully at this time. She saw it all. There was so much to take in that some days she did not even get to the school gates. The trees swaying in the wind spoke to her; sunlight dappled the ground. There were patterns everywhere; all were filled with meaning. She walked through the park and heard the chirrup of small frogs and the tadpoles' stress as they pushed out their new legs into the silted water. Transformation is pain, their noiseless voices whispered. You have to give up your thin skin in order to change. She thought that she would like to move between the elements, though she did not yet know how.

When she did make it to school she was able to hear what people were thinking. This was not, in fact, something she would have chosen. But it turned out you could not choose your powers. When she looked at her friends she saw everything. What they had eaten for breakfast, what they felt guilty about, whom they were in love with. She wished she could ignore it. Why they no longer ate breakfast what they felt when they were alone why they were afraid of their brother. There were simply too many voices. It was difficult to disentangle them.

'Are you sick, Y-chan?' her friends asked. 'Why are you acting so weird?'

When she went to the bathroom her reflection was altered; she almost did not recognise herself. Her hands were clenched and her teeth set, her lips pulled back from them like a horse. The bright, proud flags of acne bloomed on her cheeks. She bit her tongue intentionally and tasted blood, and she didn't break eye contact with herself while she pissed.

Those heady first months. She was full with the new knowledge coming into her body. It revealed itself with a kind of violence: a pattering heart, the concussion of light, grass blades that slowed and spread into fat green sails. She sent this new knowledge out into her body with her breath every morning. And she knew, all along, that something was coming, the reason for all of it. She was filled with excitement.

She had stopped sleeping entirely. It was because of the power flowing through her. She felt it pulsing through her whole body, then returning to rest in the channels of her right arm. Sometimes when she lay in bed, she felt tears creeping from the corners of her eyes. They were tears of sympathy and understanding and generosity. She felt that she would do something wonderful, something that would be remarked and noticed. She lay in bed waiting. She would open her arms and the power would flow out, out, out, into the world.

She would do something. But what was it?

5

The twitch in her eye, the pigeons rustling in the eaves of the station. She had been going to do something, but what was it?

She had done nothing. She had done nothing at all.

'Have you seen the new teacher?'

It was lunchtime. Machiko and Chiaki were sitting on the chairs arranged in a semicircle by the tambour cabinets. In a gesture of defiance — though against what, or whom, exactly? — Chiaki had her feet up on the coffee table, amongst the decade-old engineering magazines. Machiko was breaking apart her disposable hashi in order to tackle her konbini salad. Yasuko sat at her desk. Usually she ate alone.

Today Yasuko's eyes were throbbing with strain. She had managed, she thought, to keep her mood hidden from Jun. And that was all it was, in fact, a bad mood. She had been cheerful all the previous evening. She knew that it would recede eventually. The world would take back its shape. But for now she had a headache. She wished that she were at home.

Machiko shook her head. 'She can't be any worse than Phil,' she said. She carefully poured her sesame dressing.

'That goes without saying,' said Chiaki. Then she stared at Machiko. 'You know, that's not really enough to eat,' she said.

Machiko's salad consisted of half a boiled egg on a bed of lettuce. This was covered in a half-hearted sprinkling of sesame seeds.

'I'm putting on weight,' said Machiko. 'I still have ten weeks to go.'

'That's ridiculous,' said Chiaki. 'Of course you're putting on weight. You're pregnant.'

A sensation of pressure moved up Yasuko's face. She was wearing her Fendi leather skirt, her pale-pink cashmere sweater.

It was an unusual sensation, the pressure. It had moved along the side of her nose and up into her eye cavity. It settled in her temples. She touched the skin at the bridge of her nose. She could feel her pulse pushing back beneath her finger.

She rose slowly from her seat and walked to the office fridge. She held the door open and withdrew her glass bento. The cool air touched her face and the light from the fridge was smooth, rounded, and white like an egg.

A stately calm came to the room as she walked back from the fridge to her desk. At the last minute, she did not sit back down at her desk at all. She moved toward the half-circle and took the chair next to Chiaki. She perched on the edge of it and folded one leg elegantly across the other.

'My dears,' she said, by way of an announcement. The impulse in her to do something, to jolt the room a little. She was not entirely in control.

Machiko sat forward with a look of warm surprise on her face. Her movement pushed the chair and it made a loud squeak against the lino. Chiaki blushed furiously. Almost inadvertently she had swivelled her entire body toward Yasuko, though she kept her eyes fixed on her own food. As if looking directly at Yasuko might scare her away.

'What are you having for lunch, Yasuko?' Chiaki asked.

Yasuko looked at the bento in her lap as if it were an object somebody had placed there a long time ago. In comparison to the tiny salad boxes of her colleagues, it was huge. It contained fine julienned vegetables — carrot, radish — and konnyaku noodles, all slick with oil. There were slices of pale meat in with the vegetables.

Yasuko looked back up at Chiaki. Another second passed.

'Pigs' ears,' said Yasuko, her voice very clear.

'Oh, how interesting,' Chiaki said. 'I don't think I've ever had that.' There was a hint of nausea in Chiaki's face, a resolve to continue speaking, no matter what. 'Where do you buy them from?'

'A Korean supermarket in Kabukicho.' Yasuko opened the lid. She smiled. She thought she would throw Chiaki a tidbit. 'I'm so hungry. I had no dinner last night.' There, it was almost a conversation.

'Why didn't you eat dinner?' asked Machiko.

Yasuko looked at Machiko.

'Well, you see, yesterday morning the scale went past the line I have drawn on it, and when that happens I miss dinner.'

Yasuko had the pleasure of seeing Chiaki's eyes widen ever so slightly. She knew what she was thinking. What was the number on that line? O hallowed, sacred line. Arcane; deeper than privacy.

She sat back. Machiko was eating her salad in silence. Chiaki's attention was a small beacon turned directly on her. Eyes moving intently over her outfit, her shoes, her stockings, when she thought Yasuko was not looking. She was almost unbearably transparent.

'Yasuko, that is such a great skirt,' said Chiaki in a casual tone. 'Where did you get it?'

'From Uniqlo,' lied Yasuko, just for fun.

Chiaki's eyebrows tightened as she struggled and failed to understand how Yasuko had found such a skirt between the drip-dry blouses and mom jeans at Uniqlo.

They sat in silence a little longer. Yasuko found that she wished to steer the conversation.

'Machiko,' Yasuko said. 'Machiko. When is your little girl due?'

Machiko looked startled.

'Well,' she said. 'I'm due in the middle of September. But actually, we do not know if it is a boy or a girl, yet. My husband didn't want to find out.'

Yasuko smiled and tilted her head to indicate it had been merely a playful guess. She should be more careful. 'That's best I think,' said Yasuko. 'I felt much the same when I was pregnant with my son. There is too much information about these days.'

Her statement settled in the room, changing the light. The two younger women drew in closer. Things would be different now; there was no way they could not be different. She had never mentioned

Junichiro in this room before. The two of them looked somehow incredulous.

Was it really so hard to imagine her as a mother? Yasuko wondered.

She saw their faces and saw they were questioning this new information. Had she really performed all those tasks, the ones they'd observed on television as well as first hand from their own mothers? The ones that they reviled and yearned for also. Had she really worn a house apron and stood in the dust at the park and taken her son to English lessons and Little League? Had she cooked nikujaga and helped him with his homework?

'You have a son, Y-chan? But you never said!'

Yasuko smiled. She nodded. She could see that it was the opening the pair of them had longed for, Chiaki in particular. They were women together, sharing their secrets, and they would feel able to speak also, to confess, to unfold all of their struggles.

Some hunger of her own, some desire for the safety of companionship had caused her to speak. She wished to draw them toward her. She had a son.

'His name is Junichiro,' she said. 'He is turning twenty-one this week.'

'But how lovely. A young man. Quite grown,' said Machiko.

'Are you buying him something special?' said Chiaki.

'A watch, I think,' said Yasuko. 'One like mine perhaps.' Chiaki's intent gaze registered Yasuko's Cartier.

'You can't prepare yourself for motherhood, of course,' Yasuko said. 'I didn't like Junichiro much at first. He was very ugly, you know, all curled and pink like a baby mouse. But it won't be like that for you, Machi-chan. Just look — you will be a natural mother.'

Machiko's eyes crinkled with gratitude, and she folded her hands gracefully over her bump and patted it, as if she had at last been given permission to do so.

'Of course what no one tells you about motherhood is the worry,' she said.

'Oh dear,' said Machiko. 'I don't know if I am ready for such worry.'

'Well, perhaps I misspoke,' said Yasuko. She smiled reassuringly at Machiko. 'It is not worry really but a kind of grief. It is a grief that begins when they are born and that begins *because* they are born. It starts because each breath they take contains the world in which they never lived at all. And also, the world after they have ceased entirely to exist. As soon as they take that first breath, that is what is loaded into your shoulder bag. Every future moment, including their death. What can you do, except carry it? Nothing. There is nothing else to do. People are very good at telling you all about the magic of motherhood. I'm sure they are correct. But in my opinion it is that awful realisation in which you are truly born as a mother.'

Was this what she had hoped to share? She shook her head. She looked at Machiko, who was sitting with her mouth open, which gave her the look of a ruminant animal. Yasuko broke the silence with a little laugh. 'Ah, but don't be upset, Machi-chan,' she said. 'You get the nerve for it quickly.'

Machiko sat back. She put her salad box to one side and breathed out, as if bracing herself.

Yasuko stood up. She was feeling much better, she realised. She slipped her hands inside the waistband of her leather skirt and slid it around her body 180 degrees so that the back of it was at the front and vice versa. Both women stared at her, transfixed, as if she were defying several physical laws all at once. The skirt was impeccable, soft, and creamy and cut from a single flawless hide. Chiaki saw the mono-grammed waistband and flushed.

'Why do you do that, Y-chan?' Machiko asked.

Yasuko looked at her very gently.

'Oh, you have to, with leather skirts, you know. If you don't turn them, they'll stretch. Even if they do come from Uniqlo.'

On the train home Yasuko gave herself a good talking to. She should not torture those two young women. It was not her job to teach them about the world. They would find out soon enough.

There were two schoolgirls in the seats directly opposite Yasuko. They were wearing the same uniform. The midshipman's collar. Navy neckerchief. Knee socks. She had worn an almost identical uniform herself, long ago. A girlhood lived in readiness for a sea voyage. The two heads were inclined, dark fringe to dark fringe, so that they could read from the single phone. They spoke in hushed voices. The train jolted, and everyone moved from side to side in rhythm. The omamori charm that hung from the phone in the girl's hand moved on its silken thread in the same dance.

Adjacent to the girls sat a large salaryman in a large black suit. He was bigger than the two of them put together, and the large metallic briefcase between his legs pushed his large thighs out to the next seat on either side so that the girls had to huddle closer together. They did not mind. It was natural for them to be close. From where she sat, Yasuko could see the salaryman was reading the phone screen over the narrow shoulders of the girls.

Shiki, Asakadai, Wakoshi.

She saw a woman and her son get on to the carriage. The boy was beautiful, very calm, the way he turned his eyes on his mother and looked up at her.

Because she could not do otherwise, she thought of Jun.

Giving him his first baths, the terror of that. How were you meant to do it? The small body that was separate from hers; the anger that was her own. She had made the water too hot and then too cold. She had held him too tightly. They had both cried.

And sitting on the floor with him, piling the blocks one on top of the other so that he could knock them down with time itself moving slowly, gently, around her feet, up over her legs, until it reached her knees. Looking across the landscape of tatami knowing that at any moment it would come up from the ground and carry everything — mud, concrete, rebar, stray cats — everything in a vast rushing soup. It would take her with it and there would be nothing she could do.

But the wave had never come. Nothing big or grand like that, in the end. Simply the slow every day of it, which you had to face because there was never any other choice. That was what you learned. And then suddenly the years had passed.

In the first, near-destitute years in Tokyo, after they had arrived, he used to sit in the little seat on the front of her bike, as if it were a celestial barque and he a small prince. He had sat in the front basket in his softly wrapped small body and had faced the traffic without fear and watched it part in front of him.

The clear, precise line of his profile and the perfect round of his head, as if he had been cut from paper with nail scissors. His finger pointing ahead in the direction they were to go. He was a small fish swimming through its native brine, so assured. Little imperious voice:

'Mama?'

'Mmm?'

'Can we go to Mister Donut for breakfast?'

'Of course.'

Three glazed crullers on an oil-spotted paper-lined tray. A filter coffee with creamer spooling into it. A small hot milk. The smell of cigarettes, heated vinyl, powdered sugar.

The homeless man entered the carriage at Wakoshi. It was very late for him. Everybody turned to their books and their phones, breathed shallowly so as to avoid his dense animal odour. The man was probably younger than he seemed. Sixty. Perhaps mid-sixties. About her father's age. He was wearing the blue shirt and ballooned drill trousers of a manual labourer, and he was laughing and muttering under his breath, holding the swinging vinyl straps and moving from each one to the next like a child on the monkey bars at school. His arms were ropey with muscle, and the odour he gave off was both thick and piercing.

He came to a stop in front of the young boy and his mother. The man took his weight fully on the bars and rocked forward on the balls of his feet. Yasuko looked down. His feet were bare and horned with calluses. His toenails long, like a lizard.

He seemed fascinated by the young boy.

'Little larvae! Squirming baby!' he said. 'You should be out playing! Why do they have you in uniform already?'

The boy kept his head down, holding his English workbook. His hands shook on his knee.

Yasuko's phone was on vibrate in her handbag. If Jun messaged her, she would feel it straightaway.

6

I've Got a Crush on You, sang Ella Fitzgerald. The only thing that Dinah could tolerate listening to was Ella Fitzgerald singing the complete Gershwin songbook. The music so completely occupied its own foreground and background that it made no demands on her. It helped her to feel that she existed somewhere soothingly outside of time.

Dinah caught an earlier train than usual, so as to avoid the students. The university station, when she arrived, was mercifully empty. She leaned over the open upper deck and breathed in the smell of concrete and pollen. To the north was a great motorway and the enormous ark of the mall.

There was a group of foreigners down below. They were walking in the direction of the McDonald's in their black suits and white shirts. A blonde woman, two men with short hair. It was Carla, Steve, and Dougal. She leaned over the barrier a little further, right out into the air. She knew she ought to call out, greet them. She should call in a bright unobjectionable voice and ask them to wait. But she didn't do so, and by the time she reached the bottom of the stairs, they were out of sight.

She got a seat on the student bus without any difficulty.

In the lunch break she bought a salad from the campus konbini and ate it without speaking.

Carla and Dougal were shooting the breeze. Steve ignored them both. Steve was the only one of the native English lecturers who had actually trained in ESOL. He wore awful striped shirts with white collars, and braces as if this proved he took his job seriously. He had a Japanese wife and a child and spoke more Japanese than any of the other native English lecturers. Occasionally he tried to approach one of the Japanese lecturers, who kept to themselves and had their own separate room. Each time, it was almost unbearable to watch.

The first time it had happened, Dinah, Steve, and Carla had been walking to a lecture through the admin block. The three female Japanese teachers were a little ahead. The one who was pregnant, with the smile and the dimples. The tall, slightly gawky one with the fringe. And the slightly older woman — whose face she felt she had never seen properly.

Steve cleared his throat and said something in Japanese. His tone was jocular and somehow patronising at the same time. He addressed the one in the middle: Chiaki, she thought.

None of the Japanese women had heard, however, and so they kept walking, chatting. Steve called again. And then he had done the almost unthinkable. He had actually caught at the young woman's jacket to seize her attention, and in doing so almost tripped on the carpet. It was at that point they had all turned in confusion. Chiaki's perplexity. The other two women standing at an angle to her as if for protection.

And Steve had asked his question. The brashness of that. Laughing, in his bullying way.

Chiaki had listened right the way through. Had nodded, as if considering. Then she responded to him, in English. That might have been humiliation enough. But then she blushed. It was absolutely inescapable, the realisation. It had clearly come to Steve in the same moment it reached each of the others — Chiaki was absolutely mortified for him. By some natural grace of manner, she was exquisitely mortified by the horror of his speech. And they were all aware of it. It was impossible to avoid.

If Dinah had been in the mood for schadenfreude, she would have enjoyed it. One quiet morning when she and Dougal were the only other ones in the room, Dinah had heard Steve say, quite clearly, amidst the junk food and malaise, as if he had confused the staff room with a subreddit thread: 'How old do you think a child has to be before you can leave their mother?'

41

She and Dougal had looked at each other. They were both thinking the same thing, she knew. What an asshole.

You Can't Take That Away from Me. Instead of leaving the train at Ikebukuro on her way home, Dinah travelled one stop further, to Shinjuku. *Fascinating Rhythm.* Why shouldn't she? She got caught up in the crowd and in not feeling anything. It was a relief to be surrounded by people. Also she had caught a whiff of the most delicious smell.

What a strange thing to be captured by. What was food, anymore, to her? She ate white bread from the konbini with Bonne Maman jam. She bought packages of sashimi and sushi from the supermarket, a six-pack of aloe yoghurt. She carried food home in a thin five-yen plastic bag and ate it quickly at the pine table. In the bowl in her apartment were two or three enormous, tasteless apples. If she were hungry on the way somewhere, if she couldn't avoid it, she'd buy a tuna mayo onigiri and hide it behind her hand, eat in neat bites so that the dry seaweed wrap stuck to her lip and ripped a snag of it clean off, spilling blood.

But this smell was delicious.

Caramel, she thought. But not a sickly kind of caramel. A wholesome caramel with fruit. Perhaps almonds underneath. Pastry that made her think of a warm kitchen. She longed for it, sharply.

You say 'potato', sang Ella. She went looking.

At first she followed the crowd. The pleasant vertigo of allowing herself to be carried along. She enjoyed the deftness of her own movements, manoeuvring, avoiding other bodies. The sheer proximity was almost exhilarating, preferable by far to returning to her silent neighbourhood, her empty apartment block. She moved without urgency. The smell became stronger. She navigated through the underground world. She passed windows with headless mannequins in the latest spring outfits and signs that directed her to Lumine Est department store where she could purchase them. She passed passages that led to more platforms, more trains. Then halfway down the concourse she saw a cluster of small storefronts — restaurants and cafés mostly. One of these was quite evidently the source of the glorious smell.

Glass counters lined in sparkling chrome, and the girl behind the counter dressed like a French pastry chef. The queue stretched and wound back on itself to allow travellers to pass. Ella Fitzgerald's voice came into sharp and sudden focus and for a second the inertia was unbearable. Dinah thought she might be sick. She heard the unctuous glide of the saxophones, the hiss of the old recording, the way the notes broke into pieces and became incomprehensible, improbable. How had Ella endured it? Those saxophones, that blaring brass, those blind precipices where the tune gave out and returned to noise?

Standing there, faced with the situation in its entirety, Dinah saw her grave mistake. There was no way she could see it through, this project. It was obvious. She could not wait in the queue. She could not reach the front of the queue. She could not point to what she wanted, ask for the price, hand over money. Ridiculous even to think of herself carrying a pie home to her apartment. Eating it? Why had she made such a mistake?

Dinah pulled her earbuds out. She swerved back into the concourse, nearly hitting someone. She started walking faster, almost running. She had ruined it for herself, she thought, the Gershwin. Of everything, that was what she most regretted in this moment. It hadn't been much, but she had lost even that.

She walked and walked. She walked all the way back home, down the long street that seemed to join the whole city together. Because she was afraid it would make things worse if she delayed, she replaced her earbuds and forced herself to listen. Mercifully the music became a blank, anodyne backdrop again. The worst had not in fact happened. She put Ella on again and made herself listen once more, right the way through.

The piano arrived when they were ten. It had been discussed beforehand and should not have been a surprise. But still it was. They had arrived home from school, she and Michael, and swung the door open and

43

there it was, in the hallway. Like finding that a horse or a sheep or a goat had wandered inside. It was ugly and ungainly. It had too many teeth.

'What are we meant to do with this?' Dinah asked Michael. But it was clear enough that Michael knew what to do with it.

He had placed his fingers on the keys and pushed one slowly, so that it moved in silence.

When he let it rise up, there was the sound of a bubble coming up to the surface, popping. She had stood, listening. Waiting, even though she didn't know what she was waiting for.

Michael had placed both hands down, heavily and seemingly at random, on the piano keys. Where there had been nothing, nothing at all, there was a sudden huge noise. It was a chord. A dark chord ringing through the house.

It was such a surprise.

It had made her *see* everything. The unpainted plasterboard on the walls. The cast-iron bath outside the kitchen that was waiting for the bathroom floor to be fixed before it was installed.

It was all such a surprise that Dinah had laughed even though she was filled with dread. Then came the sound of the chord ringing off, crumbling into the silence.

'Where did you learn how to do that?'

Michael took his hands off the keys and pushed his foot down on one of the pedals at the bottom of the piano. Just like that, the sound was dead, as if it had never been.

'I have to level with you, Dinah,' he said.

Dinah hadn't wanted him to level. She hadn't wanted him to continue talking at all. He was smiling, like it was a grand joke and she was in on it.

'This piano is for me.'

Once the piano had arrived, Michael left school early every Monday and Wednesday afternoon and went to his lessons. To prove that things were really on a roll, after a few short months that first teacher, Ms Somebody-or-other said that Michael needed another teacher because she only taught up to Grade Eight. It wasn't modesty on her part, she said, but should be obvious to anyone with an ear, which of course she had, that Michael would need an exceptional coach. Sooner rather than later.

And that was how they had all ended up standing in front of a house in the fancy part of town, with their mother holding her handbag in front of her like a shield.

'What are we doing here?' Michael had asked.

'Well,' said their mother. 'Ms Carrell said this man wanted to hear you play.'

'Can I stay out here?' Dinah asked. Nobody answered.

Michael turned over the pages of his music and her mother looked at the paper on which she'd written the address.

'Can I stay out here?' she asked again.

This time the door opened while she was speaking. A man with a middle-aged stomach and white hair came out.

'Yes, you may,' he said. Then, 'You must be Michael,' to Michael, and shook his hand and then her mother's hand. His eyes were a very light blue and clever, like a baby's eyes. He was German, or was it Polish? And had worked at the music school at the university in Christchurch before retiring.

Her mother and Michael went into the house. She sat outside.

Outside there had been a bench seat with slats of wood, slightly rotting, next to the built-up concrete wall of the garden bed. Everything went small and still, shrunk down to the ticking of her watch. She studied the moss and saw how it was made up of tiny individual fronds. It was a very different kind of garden to their own. She examined the succulents that grew along the edge of the concrete like little enamel brooches. She watched insects. She felt jealous of them, all going places with a specific purpose. The hour stretched and she was inside it, shrinking down and slowing.

After a while the door opened. The man held a coffee mug with juice in it and a paper plate with three different kinds of biscuit.

'I didn't know which you would like so I brought one of each,' he said in his accent.

She nodded. She should have said thank you, but didn't.

'What is your name?' the man asked. She told him. 'You are very alike, you and your brother,' he said. 'But you must hear that often. Twins. Very unusual.'

He waited for a response, but she didn't give one.

'Do you play an instrument also?'

She shook her head, and his clever blue eyes watched her.

'What do you do, then, Dinah?'

'I don't do anything,' she said. She held his gaze.

'You are the protector of your brother, I see. You look out for him. I think I understand.'

She had not liked this conversation, and hadn't liked that the man presumed to know about her and Michael when they had only just met.

'Is he any good?' she said rudely. She wanted to push the man off balance. But he simply exhaled and stood up.

'Yes,' he said. 'Could be.' He spoke to her as if she were an adult. Then it was his turn to be rude. 'And in such a place as this.' He had laughed and looked around the garden, and back at the dark-wood bungalow, as if he had never seen anywhere so strange. But she knew he meant New Zealand, where they lived.

'There is no accounting for it. Though whether he has a career ahead depends on many things. It is very demanding. Not everyone has the temperament for it.' He pronounced every syllable of temperament with even weight. 'And it takes luck. Is he lucky, do you think, Dinah? Or are you the lucky one?' He smiled at her. 'I must go back in,' he said.

She shrugged. From the open door she heard runs of notes, flexing and looping and straightening effortlessly.

'Goodbye,' the man said and went back through the door.

She said nothing. With the door shut she could no longer hear anything, which was good.

She had eaten the biscuits while sitting with a straight back on the seat, as if someone were watching her and giving her a mark out of ten. Then she had built a barricade for the ants and used some of the biscuit crumbs as an incentive for the line to climb. They were small and she could have squashed them at any second if she wished, but instead she made them a passageway, a maze out of twigs and dirt with more crumbs as the reward. After another half hour her mother and Michael came out.

'I hope you haven't been sitting on that damp wood the whole time,' her mother said. But her heart wasn't in it. She looked terrified. She put her hand on Michael's shoulder as if to steady him, or perhaps herself. Then she gave a sort of shake, and they all walked to the car.

The car had started first time, and on the way home the clouds were moving too fast. The sunset was breaking everything in two, pale blue and white on one side, and on the other a dark orangey red that bled into purple. It was far too grand for Oamaru, that sort of splendour. You could imagine angels with trumpets emerging, or a hand like God's in their *Children's Bible*, pointing at something. She didn't know what to do with that sort of beauty. It became blurry when she looked at it anyway, until she scrubbed her eyes with the back of her hand and looked away.

Dinah sat in the park. Somebody from the council had mulched around the plane trees, and the air was full of the ammoniac smell of chipped bark. A cat had joined her, following her in from the street in the hopes of food. It was a scrappy-looking ginger tabby, with a triangular face and narrowed eyes. She stood up and it darted away.

She walked the border, the periphery. The swinging chain barricaded her from the darkness. She returned to her usual bench. She did not look back at her silent apartment. The street lamp burned down on her, and it felt like safety and home enough.

'All the adults are dead,' said Michael. 'It's only us now.' The air was warm, very warm, the temperature of her own body. She took off her light jacket and bunched it into a pillow, then she turned over so that her front was protected by the seat of the bench, and her back was curved against the night, and she slept.

7

The food market at the bottom level of Seibu department store is one of the very best in the city. There are dumpling vendors, sticky trays of eel bento. There is Maison Kayser's immaculate patisserie, and an elaborate selection of green tea and omiyage, the gift boxes you can buy if you have travelled to one of the regions and forgotten to bring home a souvenir for your colleague or neighbour. There is a wonderful machine that injects red-bean paste into goldfish-shaped waffle moulds.

It was one of Yasuko's favourite places in the world, but she was not here to purchase food. She was on an errand and walked through quickly. The bad feeling was still with her. The world one-dimensional, flat. But it would be bearable. She could continue on.

Yasuko took the escalator up past cosmetics; past fine scarves, wraps, and foulards; past two floors of women's fashion and one of men's. She stopped at the Cartier concession on the seventh floor. It was cool and opulent in caramel velvet and gold trim. The woman behind the counter knew Yasuko well, as she had made this trip on a weekly basis for several years. She was a serious person, the saleswoman, with a serious nose. That dignified ugliness that in France they call *jolie laide*. Yasuko nodded to her. They had a civilised understanding.

'I was hoping that I would see you today,' said the woman.

Yasuko nodded. She was too experienced to give away emotion. The woman had any number of regulars pressing her about the next delivery.

'Oh yes,' she said. 'You could set your watch by me.' A little joke. 'Of course. I would not want to miss my chance.'

The woman was smiling, but her eyes were serious, deep as pools. 'Of course. We appreciate your vigilance. And it is your son's birthday very soon, is it not?'

'Yes it is,' she said. 'This very week.' Yasuko looked at her own watch, as if to remind herself of the date. The white-gold bevel caught the light. She waited, without giving the woman the pleasure of seeming to wait.

But the sales assistant was coming forward, her whole body inclining over the counter. 'That is what I thought,' she said. She spoke in a low voice, and now Yasuko could see that what she had identified as the sales assistant's usual cool restraint was really excitement. The woman spoke with a charming eagerness, as if she had been released from the formal bounds of their relationship.

'That is what I thought.' She reached her elegant hand forward as if she wished to grasp Yasuko's own. She lowered her voice even further. 'They have come in,' she said.

Yasuko caught her breath. She did not speak for a second.

'No,' she said. 'Not really?'

'Yes. Yes. The timing is perfect.'

'And you have the platinum? You still have it?'

'Of course, Madam. I held it here for you. For your son.' She spoke low, conspiratorially. 'Two gentlemen have been in, just in the last half hour. But I did not let it go.'

Yasuko nodded. She moved her hand in a brief flutter against her leg, as if in doing so she might discover the seams of the moment, that it was not quite real.

'If you will wait one moment, I will retrieve it.' The saleswoman was glowing. She was really no longer ugly at all, and Yasuko caught a brief glimpse of her home life. The handsome quiet husband, their suffering childlessness.

When the woman returned, she was carrying a display box. 'Madam,' she said with great dignity and a note of shyness. 'I invite you to examine the piece.' With flat hands she placed the display case carefully on the glass counter and stepped back, like a child presenting an artwork.

Yasuko stepped closer. She looked at the watch, the masculine version of her own. She knew the perfect weight and balance of it already. As if she held it in her hands. It was correct, perfect. It was a wonder that it should finally be here, and at the right time. What did it mean? The saleswoman who had, with her patience and kindness, engineered this wonder, was now waiting in her turn for Yasuko's reaction. She stood with anticipation. Her head was slightly bowed.

Yasuko drew her purse from her bag and stood up straight.

'Well,' she said. And she knew before she spoke that she would be cruel. 'I suppose it will do.'

It was almost invisible, but Yasuko had eyes for it and therefore caught the woman's momentary flinch.

What was it in Yasuko that made her do such things? Pride, of course. Though there was nobody but Jun to ever truly see her. The saleswoman was impeccable in the face of it. A professional. She said nothing. Too late to take the watch back and sell it to a Roppongi banker. She simply smiled at Yasuko and nodded, and received her payment in cash and took it on a silver plate to the back room, where presumably she counted it with care. That was her job, after all.

When Yasuko left the concession, the saleswoman followed her out to the juncture of the carpet and the scuffed tiles and bowed deeply and handed her the enormous carrier bag.

Yasuko nodded, coolly, with disdain. She would not be coming back. She looked at her phone. There was no message from Jun, so she texted him. 'I have a surprise for you,' she wrote.

Yasuko walked out into the wider shop floor. Past the luxury watch concessions. She walked across the floor, past the handicrafts and kimono. She walked to the lift bay and took the lift to the top floor. She did not know where she was going. She checked her phone. She walked out of the lift.

In the down-at-heel zone between the lift bay and the roof, where the air-con did not work and the rent was cheap, she passed a wig shop, a stamp seller. She continued walking up the ramp toward the sliding doors and the open roof terrace. She was full of strain. She saw the pet shop then. She paused, thoughtfully, on the ramp. Through the glass she could see small pure-bred puppies, the kind coveted by wealthy teenagers. Another cage with a tangle of kittens. She stood outside, looking in, observing the small, dumb creatures. Thoughtfully, she tapped on the glass. She listened, waited. Through the glass she saw a young man with a blue apron pause in his task of piling boxes of kibble and look at her.

She smiled to placate the shop attendant and continued on up the ramp. Through the sliding doors she went, and out onto the concrete plain. The heat was breathless, and there was the whole sky stretching pink out toward Akabane. She looked toward the children's play area, on the north side of the terrace. It was closed, and the plastic ride-on animals looked weary. Then she looked at what she really wanted to see. On the south side, a collection of shacks cobbled together with plastic sheeting. A complex arrangement of outdoor shelves. Buckets. Hundreds and hundreds of buckets.

She felt the silken thread of the carrier bag against her palm, and she turned and went back down the ramp.

Jun had saved her life.

A long time ago. But still, it was right there. Right at home under her skin. Right there, if she stopped and scratched the surface of what was in front of her, to find the memory.

She had picked up her small infant son from his warm, safe bed and held her finger up against her mouth to tell him: quiet. He was half asleep and his body was limp and warm against hers. She put his dressing gown around him. By the time they reached the end of the drive, he was fully awake and wanted to walk by himself. The only shoes she had packed for him were the ones with the soles that lit up when he walked, so she had carried him further, along the street until there was no way they could be seen. Then a taxi to the station. The taxi driver had stared at them hard but not said anything. A train as far as Tomakomai. It was very early in the morning when they arrived.

She saw a glowing sign. It was red and yellow, with a white font.

It blinked at them. The plate-glass window was clean, and even from 100 metres away she could feel the warmth and kindness of that place. When they arrived she slid into the booth and Jun sat opposite her. The gentleman behind the counter came out with his pitcher of brewed coffee. He smiled at her and even though they had not yet ordered, not yet paid for anything, handed a plate to Jun on which sat a single chocolate glazed cruller.

By the age of fourteen Yasuko had been able to feel the currents of the city moving beneath her feet. Power was not an easy thing to own. The world was sharp, and everything had a texture that brushed up against her. The sun was like a hard flat stone in the sky.

How acute the world's violence had been. Blades of grass seemed to sprout up out of nothing, penetrating the soil with their sharpness and thrust. Every solitary thing was humming, vibrating, shaking in the wind of life that was both concentric and hyperactive. The drops of water on the grass were both crystalline and jelly at once, flowing, flowing, and you could not arrest them. It was exhausting. She still wasn't sleeping.

Her father was cunning. He pressed her for details. 'Why are you waking so early, Yasuko-chan?' he had asked.

She had been more cunning still and said nothing.

In her mind's eye she watched him. This was a new skill. She watched him when he was at ease, as if this would allow her to better understand. She watched him stand at the low tap in the tiled bathroom and bring clouds of foam into being from beneath his arms, from his crotch, the cleft between his buttocks, before dispatching them in quick ribbons across the concrete floor. The soap he used was an English brand — Knight's Castile. When combined with the smell of his wet hair, it had a forlorn smell.

As a little girl she had bathed with him. She remembered the bath dipper and that she had used it as a boat, sailing her fingers from one side of the tub to the other.

She watched now as he leaned back into the hot water. He placed the flannel over his eyes. His body displaced tiny bubbles and algae and the cockroaches scuttled and regrouped beyond the bath's edge.

Each morning she walked to school via Nakajima Park. She had taken to sitting for some time each morning, next to the still depths of Shobu Pond on the winter-brown grass. She listened in on the whispers of insects. In her middy blouse and pleated skirt and knee socks and no coat in the depths of winter, she was lit, warm, from within.

Inside the pond the fish rose up in order to speak with her. She waited for them. The oldest carp pushed its snout above the surface, and the water divided and ran down in twin rivulets over its back and across its whiskers. The streams of water returning to the pool made it appear to be crying. She sat forward.

'We have been waiting for you,' said the fish.

Yasuko leaned further forward, ready. 'What do you need me for?'

The fish returned to the pool and circled there. Yasuko waited, bending her thumbs down with the fingers of each hand until the joints protested.

When it resurfaced, the fish spoke in irritating riddles.

'If you keep sharpening the blade, you'll blunt it. If you keep filling the bowl without drinking, it'll overbrim and stain the tatami.'

'What does that mean?' Yasuko asked.

It answered with another question: 'Do you know how to work hard, and how to lie low?'

Yasuko had nodded yes. Yes, she did. She knew already, at fourteen, the ways of passing that girls learn. How to train your body to be silent. How to be invisible. She nodded yes. The soft hills of her thumb joints were blent with quiet fire.

She was ready for a task, for sacrifice. She would work harder than was necessary, would forgo sleep and food. The carp rose up higher and shook its head. The water dripped from its trailing whiskers again. In the depths, other carp were roiling. Dumb, she supposed; voiceless, those.

'Everything is waiting. Everything is bringing forth. You must make room for stillness, not attempt to create it in yourself. Are you ready?'

She had nodded again. She knew the carp was quoting from the I Ching. She had borrowed her mother's copy from the bookshelf.

Her father took a great deal of interest in her at this time. 'The key to happiness,' he said, 'is to choose a job in which you continue learning.' When he returned from his lab, his clothes and neatly trimmed beard smelt of chemicals.

Her father had let her sort the lenses for his microscope. He sat her down in the corner with a shoebox full of slides, which she put into order by date. She dusted the journal volumes. She enjoyed her mother's hesitation outside the door when she called her father to dinner. It was only right that the two worlds should be separated, because her mother's was plain and uncomfortable while her father's was one of magic and transformation. He was a crystallographer. A scientist of snow. Under the microscope the small fragments of crystal revealed their structures: they leapt up and scattered.

'You are my favourite child, Yasuko-chan,' her father said.

'I am your *only* child.'

'Yes, but even if I had more. Even if I had six or seven, you would still be my favourite. I can promise you that.'

'Why?'

Laughter. 'Because you are so clever.'

He pointed at the pinboard above his desk: 'Look, Yasuko.' There was a photograph that showed a hazy circle, darker at the edges. Inside the circle was a series of broken dashes in the shape of a cross. At the very centre was a bright hole. The image was blurred, as if it had been caught moving at great speed.

'Do you know what that is?' he asked.

Yasuko shook her head.

'That is a photograph of the first X-ray image of DNA. The scientists who made it later won a very big prize, the biggest of them all. It was taken from a crystal that was built from protein taken from human tissue. It is one of the most important photographs of all time.'

Yasuko looked. The bright halo in the centre was like a wormhole or rabbit hole that you might tumble through.

'Nobody thought much about that molecule at first, but the crystals showed us that it carries all the instructions for your whole body. Like a code. Can you imagine? All the qualities that make up who you are. This tiny little molecule is why you have straight black hair, and why you are so fond of pastry.'

'I get that from you.'

He laughed. 'Yes. Exactly.' He pulled her up to show her more closely.

'Is it like the crystals I looked at under the microscope?' she asked.

'Yes, exactly like. But we can build crystals out of other things. They let us understand everything in the world. Any question you ask. Why is your blood red? Why does sunlight make plants grow?'

She nodded. She wondered if now was the right time to tell him what was happening.

'Do you know, my love, why I keep this photo on my pinboard?'

Yasuko shook her head, no.

'It is to remind me, whatever I am doing, that there is more in the world than I can easily understand. It is to remind me that I always need to keep looking.'

8

After Dinah's second night in the park, her whole body ached. She woke with a feeling that was akin to shame and returned to the apartment to shower for a long time. The bark smell from the park was starting to become her own smell, untouched by showering. It was distinctly non-human, but also anti-human somehow, repellent. She checked her arm, the skin of her stomach, to see if there were traces of it there.

In the teacher's room Dinah straightened her shoulders.

'Dougal,' she began, 'whereabouts do you live?'

Everyone in the room shifted around a little.

Dougal picked up his phone. He checked it first, then looked at her. He was a kind person. But it wasn't enough anymore. 'Ageo, not far from here. Why?'

'Oh just, sometimes, I think I'm the only person in my whole building.'

'We all live in the same apartment block,' Carla said, pre-emptively, waving a hand around the room, though it was hardly relevant.

Dinah wondered how to explain. She could not tell them about her empty apartment building. She could not tell them about the unmoving curtains. She could hardly tell them about the silence, or about sleeping in the park and how its smell was getting inside her. 'It's just a bit strange,' she finished, weakly.

'No,' said Steve.

'I'm sorry,' said Dinah, 'I don't understand.'

'I said no. That's impossible.'

'I'm not sure …'

'Where do you live?'

'Itabashi,' said Dinah. 'Near Ikebukuro.'

'Well, there you are,' said Steve, as if this proved his point and there was no need to discuss it any further.

Dinah looked at him, waiting to see if more was coming. It was.

'Look, Itabashi is on the Saikyo line, right? That's almost central Tokyo. Prime real estate. There's no way a whole block of apartments would be standing empty. It wouldn't make any sense. My wife works for the council, and she's always coming home with stories about how desperate people are, the kind of key money they'll pay. Do you know how much money someone would lose, keeping a whole apartment block empty?'

'Yes,' said Dinah, though she had no idea, 'but …'

Steve raised his eyebrows.

'Well,' Dinah continued. 'I've never seen anyone, at all. The whole time I've been living there.'

Carla, Dougal, and Steve were all looking in different directions.

Steve shook his head. 'They're probably foreigners, all on different shift schedules. Some of the big conversation schools are open twenty-four hours, you know.'

'You're lucky,' said Carla. 'Our place is so crowded. They're all fresh off the plane and loud. And the halls all stink because nobody sorts their rubbish properly.'

Dinah nodded. There wasn't anything else to say.

At five to four, Dinah got up, straightened her shirt, and checked her teeth in her phone camera. She combed and lifted her hair with her fingers, then she went to teach her final lecture of the day.

One didn't like to acknowledge that Steve could be right about anything.

However, that evening, when Dinah turned the corner into Maison du Parc, there was a rubbish sack sitting to the left of the mailboxes, just next to the front stairs. She stood and looked. Certainly, there could be no doubt. It was a large clear plastic rubbish sack and filled with rubbish that was indisputably not her own.

Dinah cleared her throat. The sound echoed, and she looked up again at the blank and faceless windows. Somehow, by some improbable logic, the apartment block was even more silent, emptier than ever before.

From the shadow beneath the stairs, something emerged. It was a dark shape that in the light became a huge black crow. The crow moved further into the light and pecked at the rubbish sack. This was evidently what it had been doing before she disturbed its work. As she approached, it turned its head to one side and looked at her with a coy expression. Could a bird be coy? It seemed so.

Dinah lifted her chin. The bird hopped a few steps closer and opened out its enormous black wings. This was clearly intended as a display of capability rather than preparation for flight. After the demonstration was complete, the crow refolded its wings, an action eerily like a shrug. It turned back to its task, which was steadily, systematically, enlarging a hole in the bag about the size of her fist. With every stab, a pool of dark liquid bled from the bag onto the concrete path. She was not a threat to the bird. No threat at all.

Dinah felt a hardness in her throat. A kind of indignance. It was *her* home. She was tired, and thirsty, and she wanted to get to the stairs so she could get to her apartment. She wasn't afraid of the bird, but it was very much in her way. She walked forward. The increase of proximity barely registered. She took another step. The bird fluttered back a little but did not cede any further ground.

This time she swung her arms with an exaggerated movement as she stepped forward.

It was humiliating. The crow just looked at her with its black eyes, looked deep at her as if she were nothing, nothing to budge for. The steady gaze gave her the sensation that her whole body was made of cardboard. But with one more step she was past the crow and she reached the stairs and walked up them. The keys were in her hand. They were shaking more than she could control and she fumbled the lock.

Down below she could hear the bird stabbing with a renewed energy. *Thwack, thwack.*

She opened the door. Shut it, hard, behind her. She walked to the sink and poured herself a glass of water. It tasted like the air; like a decoction of the air. Numbing, maybe poisonous. She stood for a while.

Dinah put the glass carefully back on the bench. She let her heartbeat return to normal.

The rubbish had not been there when she left for work. She knew that she would have noticed. She had been listening and waiting, for how long now? Waiting for the twitch of a curtain when she returned home, listening for footsteps on the stairs, for the tinny echo of a radio through the walls, for a voice or cry. There had not been any rubbish since her arrival.

Dinah made a bowl of instant ramen in order to steady herself. When the water had boiled she peeled the lid from the plastic bowl and removed the noodle cake. Then she poured the water in over the sachet of flavouring and the dried noodles, up to the line, and pressed the foil lid back into place using the tab as a lip to hold it down. She placed the disposable chopsticks back on top of the bowl to keep the steam in. Her hands were still shaking.

Immersed in her task she did not notice her phone vibrating. It rang and then it rang again. She looked and it was her mother calling. She wanted to ignore it but knew that would be the wrong thing to do.

'Hello,' she said. There was a rushing noise first, the noise of distance and delay. Then her mother's voice.

'Dinah?'

'Hi.'

Rushing. Silence.

'I'm sorry I haven't called,' said Dinah, speaking clearly. 'How are you?' It was not at all a fair question to ask. But it was very difficult to break the habits of a lifetime. Very hard to avoid such questions.

'Oh yes. All well here. You?'

Dinah laughed. Batting the question back was only just. The conversation could continue like this indefinitely, a volley of impossible questions that they both refused to answer.

'Fine. The job's awful.' She let herself pause, respond honestly, though not completely. 'But kind of a relief too. It's good just being somewhere I can turn the corner without thinking of him.'

That, of course, was entirely dishonest. Just the other day, on the way to the supermarket, she had passed a black van and glanced into the reflection of the pristine black glass, and Michael had been there looking right back at her. The angle of his head, the tilt of it. His arm in the reflection was bent up and cradled in the other as if it were injured. The jolt of joy she had felt was so strong and so quick that everything around her slowed down. It all became so slow that she was able to watch meaning rush back into everything, like a seizure.

Then the image in the darkened car window had resolved itself. Michael's back and neck became her own back and neck. The crooked-up arm became her own, laid across her small leather cross-body bag. The loneliness was like a blow to the stomach, but she had kept breathing through it. She didn't say any of this.

'Oh. Yes, I can see that. Yes, I can understand that,' said her mother.

They sat in silence. Dinah could visualise the kitchen where her mother was sitting. She would be looking out the window at the trees in the garden. It was mid-afternoon there, evening here.

'Speaking of memories, I went up to Pembroke Primary the other day.'

'Why on earth did you do that?'

'Reading recovery. I'm still helping out.'

'Oh.'

'I bumped into Mrs Woolley.'

'Oh yes?'

'She remembered you.'

'Really?' Dinah sat up. She stood and looked through the kitchen window, rising on her toes so she could see down further. There was a darting movement, she thought. A flash of black.

'You mean she remembered Michael,' she said. She opened the door and looked back down over the stairs. The crow was still there. It had moved away from the rubbish sack. She craned her neck and could see it clearly. It was rubbing its beak one way on the concrete, then turning and dragging its beak along the other side. It reminded her of something.

'She talked about that time, do you remember, when he told everyone he'd been abducted?' Her mother's voice was full of cheer, far too cheerful. 'Remember how the police talked to everyone? And then the news crew came, and he told *them* the whole thing too. It was so embarrassing. I felt like such a bad mother.' She laughed.

Dinah was only half listening. She knew she should rebut her mother's comment, but she was fascinated by the crow's steady, intent movements. What did it remind her of? The dragging, the turning. She thought for a while and then had it. It was the movement a butcher made with a blunt knife, turning it this way and that on the knife steel. The damn thing was sharpening its beak. She almost laughed.

'Dinah? Are you there?'

'I don't know if those stories help, though,' said Dinah firmly. 'There are so many stories from primary school.' Then she ignored her own advice and said with the flourish of someone playing the winning hand. 'But what about the pastilles!'

'Oh my god,' said her mother. 'I forgot the pastilles.'

Dinah saw the enormous cardboard box of sugar almonds, and Michael handing them out. Piles and piles of little cellophane bags, the tiny eggs in all the pastel colours — aqua, pink, white, pale yellow, baby blue. Michael at the centre of a huge crowd of kids with their hands outstretched, reaching.

'Where did he get them?' said Dinah. 'I can't remember. Did he steal them?' She leaned forward again. The crow was still there. It was tugging at something.

'He borrowed them. They were Catholics, weren't they, the Thorpes? I think they were meant for church, at Easter.'

Dinah shook her head. Michael had always been borrowing things.

61

She looked back at the crow. It had half-disappeared under the stairs next to the ground-floor apartment again. She could see its back and tail feathers still, but the front half had disappeared.

'Mum,' she said, 'I have to go. I'm sorry. I'll call you tomorrow. I have to go.'

Dinah put her phone down on the kitchen counter and returned outside. She jogged down the steps. She stood and looked again at the rubbish bag, and at the dark gritty stain that was seeping out to discolour the concrete of the path. The crow's dissection had revealed banana peels, cans of tuna, a bottle of Absolut Vanilia vodka, disposable chopsticks. It was the most intimate thing she had seen for weeks.

She looked back up at the apartment building. She scanned each of the two apartments that were visible on each of the floors. She had peered into each of the windows on each level. She had knocked on the external doors. She felt certain there was no one living in them. But it occurred to her now, having seen the crow disappear, that she might be able to access the other side of the ground-floor apartments, the side where the sliding doors faced the park. It was all at once imperative that she do so.

The ground-floor apartments were not designed to be entered in this fashion. There was not much room between the external wall and that of the neighbouring apartment block. At the corner a tall steel paling fence bounded the narrow area that was the equivalent of the upper-floor balconies. She found, however, that she was able to get her shoulders through, and by climbing a little, manoeuvre her body between the edge of the concrete and the fence. She was inside the first courtyard.

She stood warily at the corner for a few seconds and then leaned forward and peered through the glass of the sliding door. The layout was identical to hers; the same wood-patterned laminate flooring. It was completely empty. Not even any furniture. She recoiled a little.

Maybe someone from a neighbouring building had dumped the trash. People did that; she had heard of this form of minor domestic terrorism. She walked across the courtyard, squeezing around a dust-covered washing machine. There was a low concrete wall separating her from the next apartment. She boosted herself up from the washing machine and dropped down.

At the next apartment she went through the same motions. She stood as close to the edge of the door frame as possible and then turned and leaned in to the glass quickly. Through the glass these rooms were also stripped of furniture. She sheltered her eyes and put her face in closer. There was something on the floor: a suitcase. Clothes were strewn around it. She pulled back. There was something disturbing about the suitcase. The scene was of someone who had been interrupted in the middle of packing. Yet what made it uncanny was the complete lack of urgency. She wondered how long the suitcase had been sitting there, waiting. Dust motes floated idly in the air. Even the inside of the apartment looked dusty. She knocked gently. Nobody came.

Slowly now she climbed the remaining barrier and reached the final apartment. This time when she peered through she was shocked to see that the room was furnished. Sparsely furnished, but furnished nonetheless. There was a folded futon bed directly in front of the glass. Behind that was a small yellow-pine table. On the table was a bowl. She moved in closer. A pair of chopsticks were balanced neatly on top of the bowl. She leaned in, wiped some of the dust off the window. It was a bowl of instant ramen. The lid had been peeled and then placed back. The chopsticks sat on top to hold it down. The brand of instant ramen was the same she had chosen for herself for dinner from the convenience store. She could have been looking at her own apartment: there was nothing to distinguish them. She tapped on the glass as if to alert herself, lest she be waiting inside, just out of sight. What would that be like, to come face to face with oneself? She felt suddenly dizzy, as if she might faint.

'Hey!'

She jumped. She didn't know where the voice had come from. It could have come from the floor above, or from inside, or perhaps from somewhere else altogether. It echoed inside her head, but she didn't stop to enquire because her whole body was already in motion.

Dinah launched herself upward and through the gap between the metal fence and the concrete. The gap was tighter here than at the first corner and for a second she found herself stuck, but she wedged her foot in and pushed higher and managed to pivot her shoulders and she was through. Out in the dusty ferns at the edge of the park. She rose from her knees and walked in a toppling fashion toward the road and then twice around the block to calm herself.

So, she was not crazy. Or perhaps she was crazy. What exactly was the measure? She could not be sure anymore.

After a while she walked back to the park. There was no other action she could think of. Obediently she took the correct leaves from the sentry trees. One bronze, one silver, one gold. She sat on the park bench so that she faced the gathering dark.

What were you meant to do with all the stuff? She had travelled halfway across the world, but it was all still there. The shape of his cheek, which was the shape of her cheek. The feeling of talking and knowing the inside of the other person's head. What were all the memories for? She didn't know what to do with them. It was all surplus, a raw substance like sebum that had been overproduced and clogged everything. No space for it; nowhere to put it down.

The trees were thicker and bushier, and taller. There were more and more leaves each day. And it made no sense, because Michael was gone and would not come back again.

9

Routine was a kind of second-order magic.

It was the second Tuesday of the month and therefore Yasuko woke early and took a train to the Aoyama district post office. She called 'Ohayo gozaimasu' to the staff behind the counter and took out her small silver key to open her private box. She removed the plain brown manila envelope that was addressed to her and slid it into her handbag.

Since she had disembarked in the city seventeen years ago, carrying her young son on her back, Yasuko had not once spoken with her father. She had escaped him, it seemed, completely. Yet about a year after her arrival, the envelopes had begun to arrive. They were addressed to her newly rented PO Box and used her maiden name. They arrived from the postcode of the old Sapporo neighbourhood without any note or return address. The same amount each month, in fresh, clean bills. Of course it was her father's doing. Who else would do such a thing? It was utterly useless to ponder how he had discovered the address. He was a powerful man, after all. The first envelope had sent her into a spin. But after three months with no further contact, she started to breathe again. Here was the material fact: he had not come in person. She had chosen the PO Box expressly because it was a good distance from her own neighbourhood. She did not relax entirely, but she relaxed a little. Was it possible that her father was no longer a threat?

Nevertheless she had not touched the money for a whole year. She had placed the envelopes in the corner of the same drawer that held the red-lettered notices for overdue payment. Then one day she had taken them all, every last one, and travelled to Isetan Shinjuku and spent the entire haul in the same shop. That had given her great pleasure.

She walked to her favourite sushi restaurant, a hole-in-the-wall joint in a narrow corridor shaded by the opulent boutiques of Aoyama. It was full of construction labourers returning from the night shift. She pushed the button for ikura don at the vending machine, fed coins into the slot until it spat out her coupon, retrieved it, and walked to the counter. When her number was called she collected the bowl. Salmon roe on a bed of blameless white rice. One green shiso leaf, its anisic mint pointing to the grubby walls and the chef behind the counter. She took a plastic glass of the free barley tea that was dispensed from a thermos near the counter. She sat hunched over the bowl like a teenage boy, bringing the ikura to her mouth and crushing the eggs with her tongue.

The envelope in her handbag came from a place like a cage and brought with it the sound of scratching. However, she retrieved it from her bag and placed it next to her, like an unwanted guest. She had expected the envelopes to stop when Jun turned eighteen, but still they came, pointed and imperious. Now and again she took a glance at the familiar writing. Even the kanji was self-righteous. Her maiden name and her PO Box number: neat, unimpeachable. Written with a thin nib on the smooth paper, probably the one she gave him when she was twelve. A small barb. She heard the sound of scratching against wallpaper. But she thought of Jun and she turned the envelope over and slid her finger through the seal and broke it and counted out the clean 10,000-yen notes.

She thought of a fish turning in the water, rising up. A tingling in her palms and at the base of her thumbs.

She called, 'Thank you for the food,' and received a grunt in return. Then she stood for a second in the doorway, sliding her hand back into the envelope to feel and separate a single note from the stack.

At the nearest convenience store she bought two tins of tuna. The compulsion moved through her. She knew she should not do it. But nevertheless she walked toward Aoyama cemetery. When she neared the edge she stopped. The vast terraced park hovered in a shallow morning fog. From both ends of the bottom terrace, the cats streamed toward her. They swarmed without touching. She spoke to them, swept the air above them with her hands. She waited and waited and she walked with her head tilted one way and then another, as if listening. She opened her mouth to speak. 'Can you hear me?' she asked.

Why did she do it? Why when she knew what she knew already? She should have learned her lesson. The hunger always returned when she was weakened. And she was certainly weak at present. The world had been jumping in its skin and showing its seams. Of course she knew the signs had no meaning. They were not the return of her gift, but a hook and a line that would pull her down into misery. She had given in to this lure many times when Jun was a child, unable to resist. Then her hope and hunger had been too strong. But these delusions, as she had learned to identify them, had not occurred for a long time.

You must not allow it, she thought. Jun will leave. Yet still she took out the cans of tuna, removed their ring pulls, and placed them on the ground.

She thought of the last morning of her first life. She thought of a morning marked by sun that entered through dark cloud.

'Stay alert, child,' said the fish. 'It is happening today.'

She thought of how it had happened.

Her childhood self, in the full flush of her power, walking to school. The nerves of great excitement. Great anticipation.

Back when the world had spoken to her. Great meaning in each of the signs that day.

When she turned the corner by the school's spring-wire fence, the sun had come out from behind the buildings and hit her. It shone so straight, as if the whole world above her head had been cut off, replaced with a realm of darkness, and what was left to dwell in was horribly askew. The wind had moved with intent; the clouds rushed and slowed. She heard the bamboo creaking with pained omniscience. Her best friend Mei had called to greet her at the school gate, and Yasuko had walked straight past.

Everything had been too large to keep in her vision all at once. Or in pieces. Like the dark around one of her father's slides when you looked into the world of the microscope. Someone tightening her focus.

In the classroom, sitting next to Mei, she had seen the red string that was tied around Mei's plaits that morning. She had seen the whiteheads on Mei's nose, and the skin on her legs, which was papery and dry with scratches showing on it like writing. There had been a cruelty in her blood, and the high incitement of power. She was separate from it all.

It had happened while she was putting away the textbooks after algebra. She tripped and fell against a desk. As she rose to her hands and knees, a mouse ran across the floor. It stopped short of its escape into the skirting boards and paused on its back legs, to look right at her.

There had been a hot sticky feeling on the brow above her right eye. No one in the class moved. The mouse spoke to her alone.

'You must carry the shopping for your mother after school today,' it said.

'Why?' she asked. There was dread in her belly.

'Because she is going to die.'

'Friend Mouse,' she said. 'Please don't let her die.'

But then everything started again and it was too late. A desk lid banged, someone shouted, the teacher reached out and then dropped down on knees and hands to Yasuko's level. Someone was pulling her up, against her will. The mouse fled back under the classroom skirting boards on legs light as twigs, a balloon of air in its bones.

She went to the infirmary, where the nurse pushed the edges of the cut together roughly and sealed it with a butterfly plaster. She felt nothing. In the office they called a cab for her, and she travelled in it back to her parents' house.

The thing was happening at last. The waiting was over. And now she knew what it was for. The purpose of her powers. She would save her mother.

There was a feeling of amassed energy in her stomach and the tips of her fingers. It lodged in the thenar eminence at the base of her thumb, where her gift lived. She stood at the door trembling and knocked. If she had had a choice, she would have chosen something else. She would have asked the mouse to share the answers to the big test, or who would be the next prime minister. Yet as she breathed through her wonder and fear, one thing struck her. She finally had something worthy to share with her father. There could be no doubt of her power.

She stood outside her father's study and called his name in a flat-footed voice — once, twice, thrice. She remembered his face at the door when he opened it. The great gentleness, his surprise and his love.

She told him what she had learned.

Yasuko looked at the cans on the ground, the cats milling. She felt anger rising at their silence and knew that she must leave. She must leave. She stood up. She dusted herself down. She started to walk back in the direction she had come. Slowly at first, then more quickly.

She heard her father's voice in her head and it made her hands tremble.

But she kept walking, back down Aoyama-dori. She thought of Jun's face, and that gave her strength.

She was striding now, back to Jun, back home.

Striding. She felt people turn to look. She was on Aoyami-dori again. Then Omotesando-dori. She turned her head in her going, and the boutiques soothed her. Loewe. Givenchy. Celine. Perhaps she would go in, but no. She would go home to her son.

She remembered the transformation of her father's face.

'What do you mean, Y-chan?' he had asked. She saw it again, flick-ering between expressions. Hope there for a second, as he considered the possibility that she was only joking. Then it settled back into horror. After all, what child jokes about their mother's death?

She pleaded with him. She spoke calmly and then in tears. When his face did not change, she held him by the knees. He must believe her, she thought. He must. We are one and the same. Her heart insisted

— we are one and the same. Trusting him in this manner was a grave mistake. But where she had gone wrong first was in thinking he could have prevented anything.

Her mother did not know about this quiet battle taking place between Yasuko and her father. It was clear between them that she should not be allowed to overhear. They ate dinner that evening in silence. Yasuko did not raise her eyes or speak. Later she visited her father in his study for the last time. This time she took care not to mention the mouse, the animals that spoke, the wonder of her powers. Instead she spoke calmly, as if things between them were just the same as ever.

'Don't you think,' she said, 'we should go to the hospital just in case?'

'In case of what?'

'Well, just in case she *is* ill. Perhaps there is a test she could take?'

'A test? What sort of test might that be?'

Yasuko shook her head; she didn't know. 'The doctor would know,' she said. She felt very tired. The room around her was humming.

'The doctor. I see. The doctor. We would go to the doctor and ask him about the test. But what do you suggest we tell him? For that matter, what should we tell your mother, when we take her to the clinic?' Her father looked at her with a disdain so deep she could not see the bottom of it.

Yasuko was silent.

'I did not hear you,' her father said.

Yasuko shook her head again.

He came toward her. She shivered. Still in his suit and the scent of the university lab on it. How she had loved that smell.

'Perhaps, if you think harder, you can think of a more intelligent explanation.' He looked at her. He was holding the door open, just a crack. 'Has your mother complained to you of some pain, or some discomfort? Or maybe you have noticed something. You have always been a very observant girl. What was it that gave you this idea?' He waited, without looking at her.

Yasuko stood where she was. She knew when she was trapped. She couldn't lie to him. She reached inside herself for the strength to offer it up again. 'There is nothing else,' she said. 'Just what I told you. But you have to believe me.'

Her father nodded. 'I think that you should go to your room now,' he said. His expression was fixed, and the coldness went deep into her.

The next morning she could not stop weeping. When her mother called her to breakfast, Yasuko was unable to answer. Grief and power filled her in equal measure. Weeping seemed all she could do. She would weep an endless stream of tears.

Her father came into her room wearing his suit and carrying his valise just as he did every morning. Perhaps he had forgiven her. But he looked at her and shook his head.

'I am very ashamed,' he said.

She had slept that first day in her room. Time stretched. She heard her mother open her door and then shut it again. She heard the front door open, shut. She slept and woke and slept again. She had done all that she could do. Perhaps everything would still come out alright. Her mother would be fine. Her father would forgive her. Perhaps it was simply a test. The fish had asked her if she could lie low, so she would show that she could do so. She would show that she was very patient. She slept.

What woke Yasuko were the voices in the hall. Her father's at the top of the babble. She heard his sharp exclamation. A shout. A cry. A sob that could have been either grief or anger. She closed her eyes. There was the sound of loud banging. Somebody banging loudly on her door.

She did not need to speak to anyone to know. She closed her eyes and felt the tears edging out of them. The trickle was slow, warm, implacable, as if her face were nothing, just a surface to be crossed.

And so the room became her home.

Her father did not enter. She heard him speaking about her — the phone table was in the hall not far from her room. On the day of her mother's funeral, she heard the footsteps and polite enquiries. Her father's sympathetic voice. The priest chanting the sutra.

He looked after her very well, all told. Three times a day, when she woke, there was a tray of food inside the door. Usually a bowl of her father's broiled salmon for breakfast. A bowl of miso. Sandwiches for lunch, from the konbini. Egg and mayo on white bread. A single piece of fruit. Perhaps a mandarin. A sliced pear. She refused most of it. She found she could only eat white food. Rice. Sometimes an aloe yoghurt, plain rice.

For the evening meal her father often placed a single marinated plum in the middle of the rice bowl. The plum sat like an aggrieved sour sun on its white field, leaching its pink. On those days she ate nothing, simply pushed the tray to the side and waited until it was collected like all of the others. It was beyond her control that saliva had blossomed in her mouth as she looked.

The cold of loneliness was the hardest. She dreamed that she was trapped beneath a thick green wall of ice. Her father walked around on the surface, oblivious. His footsteps caused creaks and pops as he tramped above. His face was rippled and occasionally his lips moved but no sounds made it through. She listened for the animals. They would find her, she thought. They would reach her. She had delivered the message and as a result she was suffering. Surely they would look for her and offer help.

There were noises certainly. They began in the first few nights and continued, loud then soft. Irregular and unpredictable. They usually came at night. Tiny scurrying sounds in the wall like a mouse trapped between the beams and the plaster. Perhaps the very mouse who had shared the vision of her mother's death. She called out, her voice cracked and strange to her ears. 'Are you there?' she called. 'What do I do? What do I do next?'

She listened for a response, but nothing ever came. She pressed her ears to the wall. The sound of scurrying became a flapping, full of anger. Not a mouse; a bird. Trapped in the wall cavity. Flapping its wings in self-punishment.

She called again and again. 'How can I help you?' 'Why won't you speak?'

Perhaps it was part of the test. She waited. The hollow tapping became the sound of her father's footsteps. She listened. She waited. Listening and waiting was better than the alternative, which was to acknowledge that after the brief advent of her powers, their destruction of her life, they had now deserted her.

'I will die,' she said to her room. 'I cannot bear it. I will die if you don't say anything.'

But there was nothing, only silence.

On a starvation diet, hope will live a surprisingly long time, but even so, it cannot endure forever. Throughout her long period of captivity following the death of her mother and her father's disownment, no animal spoke to Yasuko. She received no sign, no word. The world was silent and without meaning. When she listened she could no longer feel the city's magnetic lines pulling like bright cords along her own body. If she strained her ears she could not hear her father's desperate bitterness, his shame. When she closed her eyes there were no colours, no lights. She could not feel the hasty unfurling of the leaves outside the window. She had been in her room almost an entire year.

If anyone had asked her whether she would trade her father's approval, her mother's life, she knew without a doubt she would have chosen the powers. She would have chosen them. But as it happened she had been given no choice.

There was no change. But one morning she got out of bed.

She almost tripped. She had not eaten properly for a long time and was weak. She tried the door to her room and it was not locked at all. It opened. Her school clothes had been placed in a neat pile beside the door, ready for her. She blinked in the bright light of the hallway. There was the sun. Still there, continuing on in spite of her suffering: blank and awful and unseeing in the white sky. The whole of the world, blank and flat, and as thin as the cotton lawn handkerchiefs her mother used to pin inside the sleeve of her kimono.

She picked up her school skirt and stepped into it. She pulled her middy blouse over her head, right over the night dress that smelt of her body and its hunger. The skirt hung right down over her hips, but it didn't matter.

73

She walked upstairs. Her father was there, at the kotatsu, as if nothing had happened.

'Good morning,' he said. 'Do you feel you are ready to go back to school?'

No one is tested beyond what they can bear, but Yasuko Kinoshita had been.

'I'm fine. I'm ready to go back to school,' she said.

Dead for the first time at the age of sixteen, she sat down to eat her breakfast.

Yasuko stood in the courtyard. She was breathing heavily. She looked up at the many floors of the apartment building above, the many windows. She wondered if Jun was up. She hoped so. He might be stretching his legs, cupping his first cup of coffee, looking out. What would he see when he looked at her? She did not know. It was the last mystery. Her heart rose up, thinking of him. It was filled with love. She smiled up at the sky and then lowered her head and walked in, straight ahead, through the door.

10

Dinah was fine. She was sleeping in the park most nights. At five am the thing she did was to return to the apartment. This gave her about an hour to lie under a sheet on the futon, and then to rise almost as if she had spent the whole night in bed.

For some reason this hour was the trick. It seemed to be keeping things steady. When she got up from the futon, with the semblance of having been there all night, she showered for a long time. A cold shower in the heat. She did not always sleep. Cats clustered under the trees. Very occasionally somebody wandered in. A woman had entered with photographic equipment and spent a long time setting up her tripod, taking a very long-exposure shot of the play equipment. Dinah had pretended to be reading, then to be speaking on the phone. It was only when the woman had cleared everything back into her JanSport backpack and given her a stare of assessment and finally gone on her way that she'd been able to lie back down on what she now thought of as her own bench.

11

It was certainly a challenging time. Yasuko could no longer pretend otherwise. Her head ached with the strain of it. Perhaps one of the worst she had passed through. But she would come through it again. What choice did she have? Jun had been clear enough the previous time — oh, many many years ago. He was never one to forget.

Each day that she returned home from work was an achievement. And each day that she entered the apartment, she was filled with relief that she had done so. Because Jun himself was Yasuko's reward. He was waiting for her in the apartment.

If Jun suspected she was struggling, he did not let on. They talked idly about the same old things. He cooked tarako spaghetti and used every pan in the apartment. He poured her a gin, and they sat on the couch. At ten pm they went to the window.

Down below on the ground floor outside their apartment, there was a paved courtyard. Every night at roughly the same time, a gentleman came down to walk his dog.

They had happened upon this routine by accident. Perhaps Yasuko had been hanging up clothes on the balcony and had spotted the pair down below. She couldn't remember the details, but however it happened she had known instantly that it would appeal to Jun's sense of humour. They were very alike in this regard.

It was the incongruity of the pairing that struck her. The dog a small white thing with bows affixed to its ears so that they resembled schoolgirl bunches. The dog's owner, on the other hand, a middle-aged man who always wore a cheap leisure suit in some pastel colour.

The owner seemed made for derision. His hair stuck up every which way and his clothes looked slept in. He had a saggy face with twitchy eyes. He had just the look of the sort of man who always tried to start a conversation. The sort who kept a bottle behind the counter at the local bar and ate peanuts for dinner.

It had become part of their evening routine that they watched, from behind the curtains. The man came every night. What kept them watching was the dog's odd and entertaining habit. A few minutes into its walk, after a circuit of the courtyard, it would begin tugging at its leash, lunging and barking, straining upward. It was the weird repetition of this trait that entertained them. Perhaps also that the owner seemed surprised by it every time. He would put on a perplexed expression and exclaim and hold up his hands in irritation at the dog. The whole thing was a sort of dumb-show entertainment.

It was part of the game that they come up with an explanation for the strange behaviour.

Jun's theory du jour was that the routine was part of a drug deal.

'Look!' he said, triumphantly, as they watched. 'There, I told you! He's tapping that fence. It's some sort of signal. He is organising the drop-off.'

Yasuko's prevalent theory was that the man was having an affair. The dog was his mistress's pet. If he wanted to get lucky, he needed to take it for a walk each night. He was impatient for it to take a shit so he could get back to the bedroom. She did not venture to explain the dog's behaviour.

Jun shook his head. Yasuko shook hers.

'Look,' Jun said again. Yasuko looked.

'Wait for it …' They waited.

All at once, the dog began tugging on its lead, leaping as if it wanted to garotte itself.

'Clockwork!' And they both laughed, behind the curtains. She felt a little better.

His eyes were on her face. She knew it, but she was very strong.

Nothing would go wrong tonight. And tomorrow was his birthday. It had become for some reason a milestone for her, this date. If she were able to reach that date without giving in, then she felt certain there would be a reprieve. Things would return to normal.

The next day, after work ended, Yasuko had the pleasure of watching for Jun on the platform of Ginza-itchome. She could always spot him immediately in a crowd. Like a magnet between them. The tilt of his head, the slight hunch, the light that shone around him and marked him out as more important, more real than all the other bustling commuters.

'Happy birthday, my darling!' she shouted across the platform. She took great delight in seeing all of the silent passengers jump.

They walked along the street with an air of holiday. She had been correct: the reprieve had come. They knocked and waited at the unassuming door of the best tempura restaurant in Tokyo, and Jun caught her eye as they proceeded behind the very serious maître d' and sent her into a fit of giggles. They ate the best tempura in Tokyo and she smiled at him. His hair was almost black in the low light, and she did not think about anything at all.

When he went to the bathroom she asked the waiter for a clean napkin. She placed the box containing the watch in front of Jun's cleared place and spread the napkin over the top. When he returned he removed the cloth.

He was his mother's son and knew straightaway what the box contained. He looked at it steadily for a long while.

'Okaasan,' he said. 'I have something I want to talk about.'

'Let's forget about that for now, darling. Open your present.'

'You haven't done anything silly have you?'

'Nothing!' she said, with great happiness.

'Okaasan,' he said, and his voice was a warning. 'Something tells me I don't want to open this.'

'Don't be so foolish, Jun-kun. It is a present. It is your birthday.

When would you expect a present if not on your birthday?'

He looked at the small box without taking it in his hands.

'You are always buying me things,' he said, though not with the note of gratitude that one might expect.

'Please,' she said.

He seemed for a moment to relent, to take pity on her. Carefully he opened the fine leather box. When it snapped open it made the sound of expensive engineering. She saw in her mind's eye what he was seeing. The elegant crocodile strap. The burnished face that would never cease to keep correct time, even if submerged to 100 feet, even if subjected to the shock of nuclear war, that would continue to conceal the fine crystal oscillator that regulated the tiny gears that turned the cog that turned the hands that pulled the sun away from its shroud of night and exposed it mercilessly again and again.

Jun did not speak. She waited for a few minutes. She pretended to sip her drink.

'It is magnificent. Truly. Thank you, Mama,' he said.

Yasuko smiled and nodded. 'That is a relief. I don't think they take returns.'

His face was very serious suddenly.

'Can we talk?'

Yasuko felt the blood rush lightly in her ears. She thought she had done quite well over the last few weeks really. All considered. She had resisted and she had concealed. In the past she would have been flattened; she would have struggled to leave the house. It had been years and years since she had been so afflicted. These points flashed up for her, as if she were preparing a defence. She cleared her throat and did not risk looking up at her son, but spoke as if her heart were light, as if she were entirely carefree.

'Of course,' she said. 'Primarily we are here to enjoy ourselves, and to eat a ridiculous amount of tempura. But talking is accepted. What is it?'

'Nothing much really. Just that Kenta has taken a room on campus. I was thinking about it again.'

Yasuko exhaled, and the tension eased off. It was an old topic of his, this whim of renting a room in one of the residential halls at his university. He reached a certain pitch each time and then subsided. Usually when he saw how much they would charge him for the privilege.

'Well, of course. That would be fine. Though, as I said before, I think it is foolish to throw money away on accommodation when you can live rent-free not far from campus. Kenta's parents are very wealthy, are they not?'

Jun nodded.

'And you and I, well we are the sort who don't need much to get by.'

'Oh yes. Nothing much,' said Jun and picked up his birthday gift. 'Just a few little knick-knacks.'

Yasuko laughed. She smiled coquettishly. 'Well. This is a celebration. This is a celebration of you reaching manhood, and of me keeping you alive for that long.'

Jun shook his head, and looked again at the watch. 'I adore it. It's really far too much. Thank you.'

And so the birthday dinner was a success after all. It was just like old times, the two of them. Laughing, talking. The wings flapped in Yasuko's head, and she steadfastly ignored them. They ate a ridiculous amount of tempura. She drank another glass of shochu. Finally it was time to pay. She added a generous tip for the waiter who had helped her to hide Jun's present. She stood, waiting for her son to return from the bathroom, and placed her hand on the counter to steady herself. The dark wing rose in her mind.

She felt the familiarity of anger. It wasn't fair. Not fair at all. She had worked so hard. Hadn't she worked hard enough? Hadn't she done all she could to placate things with normality? When would she ever get free of it? She turned from these thoughts as she had learned to do and looked at what was in front of her. She held her hand up as if scrutinising her nails and examined the grain of her skin, opalescent with skin cream.

It did not work. Nothing was working. She could not pretend, she thought, that it was working anymore.

When Jun returned she forced herself to smile at him, though she could see everything too sharply: the bones under his face, the light reflecting off the new watch. He held it up to her. He had put it on in the bathroom, taking those few moments of privacy to configure how its gravity had altered his bearing.

She took his arm in their customary fashion, and they walked out to Ginza-dori. It was a joke they had, this gesture, a mock gallantry, yet this evening she was grateful for his steadiness. The strain building at her temples.

How quickly she had seized on these signs the first time they had arrived. How quickly she had assumed they heralded the return of her powers. When in fact it was a kind of bitter trick, a false prophecy. But even self-knowledge was insufficient.

'Stop,' she whispered under her breath, in the taxi. Jun did not hear her.

Through the window Yasuko saw the crows in the trees, their gathering malignancy. She turned away from them.

'Stop!' Jun called as they went up Meiji-dori and passed Mister Donut. 'Stop!' and the cab driver, long-suffering, did so. Jun went in for doughnuts. When he returned he passed the box across to her and slid across the vinyl bench seat so that they were next to each other. He placed his arm through hers.

They came to their neighbourhood, and they emerged from the taxi. She moved through the cloud of her disappointment. She walked to the sliding doors of the apartment. She pushed the drapes around them so that they could not be seen, but to ensure a good vantage point. She squeezed the arm of her beautiful son. She looked out at the silent, blank world.

They waited, and tonight like all the others the man emerged from the main doors and onto the courtyard, a foreshortened figure with his even-tinier dog. Today's shell suit was turquoise and white. The dog and the man began their circuit under the tall fluorescent lights. The air was warm. Maybe there was still cause for hope. She had not lost him yet.

'Wait for it,' said Jun. And they waited. She listened for something, anything, that would save her.

The dog jumped, leapt against its restraint. It barked.

'There's nothing *there*, you silly mongrel!' called Jun. Lightly. Not enough to carry down to the ground floor, just enough to make her laugh. But she didn't laugh.

She looked down to the dog as it leapt and pulled. Her head was aching. The dog. What was it doing? They had laughed and laughed at this dog in the past, but perhaps that had been foolish. Maybe it saw something beyond its rope, in the dark streets that led toward the great river of the motorway. Perhaps if she was more patient, she would see it also. Her mistakes and failures swelled together and rushed toward her. 'Do you know how to work hard, and how to lie low?' She felt them swell into a great sob. What had she done? She had failed, but perhaps it was not too late. There could not be nothing left in the world for her. There could not be.

'You know, Jun,' she said, clear, cold. The voice of her illness, rising. 'Maybe there's something we could learn from that dog.'

'What on earth could we learn from that dog?' Jun asked, still laughing.

She should stop talking. Her own voice rising, rising, like a tide. Like a wing.

'Maybe it sees something that we can't see. You know,' and she heard her father's voice, and it made her press on. Anger. 'Perhaps there is more in the world than can easily be understood. Perhaps we must always keep looking.'

'That's funny,' said Jun, 'because I have come to the opposite conclusion. I really think that all our theories are just a joke. It's just a mad old fellow with a mad, mad dog.'

The dog barked and she heard its pain and entrapment, its hunger to be free, completely.

She stood up sharply, as if she could cast everything off.

Jun waited a little longer then closed the curtain with what was a dismissive movement. His expression seemed to her to be flat and unresponsive, even cold. For a brief moment she saw his face from a great distance and the coldness went right through her. It was so lonely, like ice. She kept her eyes focused ahead. She couldn't bear it.

'I don't know,' she said. That was all. It all felt too late. She had done nothing. She had done nothing at all.

'Jun,' she said at last, cautious, but about to jump. 'I am scared.'

Jun looked at her carefully. She should have taken the warning.

'What are you scared of?' he asked. He said it almost casually, as if they were just talking about their days, their plans, the funny thing that had happened at work or at university.

She had a choice, but she was too tired to take it. She looked at him with an appeal to his love, to her sacrifice, to all that she had given him and all that she still, somehow, needed.

'I am scared that it is happening again,' she said.

Jun stood next to her. He was very quiet.

'But I will be fine,' she said, filling the gap. 'You don't need to worry. I'll be okay.'

Her reassurance was not enough. It would not be enough for him. Not even enough for her. But even at the last moment: rebellion, defiance. Why should she always be the one who was weak, and he strong? She had been so powerful, once.

'But you never know,' she said. Lightly, as you should always speak when picking up an object of great danger. 'Perhaps this time my powers will come back.'

She said it so quietly that she could not be certain that he heard it. But Jun's hearing had always been very sharp.

'Oh,' he said. Then he walked past her into his room. He ducked around her in a graceful feint so that no part of their bodies touched.

12

In the teacher's room, between lectures, Dinah shook her head from side to side. There was a little something extra there. An additional substance, a new quality of buzz around everything. It was not unpleasant. She moved her head experimentally to feel it again. Sort of entertaining, that spotty, blank sensation at the sides of her vision. And also a sense of shrinkage. Things slowing down without warning, and voices echoey, tinny with presentiment. The world after all was only this, only this room. Only this carpet and the air conditioning, the clock and the heavy object she had been asked to carry by Michael. The morning shadows slid across the walls like paint.

She taught her second class. What of it? A feeling of predictability or déjà vu. As if everything were just a little bit out of sync with itself.

In the ten minutes before her final class, she walked back to the administration block to photocopy some materials. The distance seemed to stretch. As if the lattice pattern of the concrete was a ladder and she was pulling herself up one step at a time.

In the admin block she warily approached the vast industrial photocopier. She used her full arm strength to lift the machine's heavy convex lid. She pushed a button and it vibrated into life. A shimmer of heat across her vision. The photocopier a wildebeest or a rhinoceros, camouflaged on the grey savannah of carpet. She rested her head against its bulk.

Papers spooled into the tray. Then she heard the machine give a cough of demurral. There was a beeping from somewhere deep inside.

The machine coughed again; it spat out a few further pages then came reluctantly, judderingly to a halt. She half-heartedly opened each of the portals and feeds that were visible to her. No clot of chewed papers. No spooling in the rollers. Nothing. She pushed the green start button again. Nothing.

She looked across to the cubicles of the admin staff. She felt a sense of panic. The admin staff cubicles were cosy, somehow, like miniature domestic shrines — teapot, framed photograph, personal mug, house slippers. The comforting routines of email, a hot drink, refilling the water bottle. No call to stand up in front of 150 eighteen-year-old men.

One of them must help her. But what would she say? She was dizzy, even standing there. She didn't think she could make it across the carpet to speak to anyone. Just please don't make it Mayumi, she thought.

'Photocopier trouble?'

It was Mayumi. Of course.

'It's jammed,' she said. 'I have a class in five minutes.'

'Of course. It is a horrible creature, this machine,' said Mayumi calmly. She examined the great lumbering side and the LED screen. Then she moved to the manual feed tray and unhinged the cover. She did it slowly, did everything slowly. Dinah watched. Mayumi levered the relevant section open, splaying the creature and revealing its inner workings, its secrets. She found a single concertinaed page.

'I'm sorry. I thought that I checked in there.'

She waited for the reprimand, but it didn't come.

Dinah moved her head a little, feeling the odd sensation. It seemed that it might somehow protect her from Mayumi. She actually smiled, slowly. 'I'm afraid I'm a little late,' she said.

Mayumi looked at her watch. 'You have just enough time. I have a spare book. I will bring you the copies. Here.' She took the textbook from the photocopier and placed it in Dinah's hands.

Dinah took the book from her and walked toward the lecture theatre. It was really more of a large room than a theatre. It contained sets of tables in pairs, divided by aisles that she could walk between to coach the students. The format for each lesson was always the same. You just followed the textbook. Dougal was right, after all, it really was an easy job. A warm-up exercise, then paired practice, and she would finally choose a group of students to present their role-play at the end. This was usually an opportunity for much hilarity.

She opened the book.

Somehow, even while she had been photocopying, she had managed not to notice the topic of today's class.

Lesson 12: Brothers and Sisters. There was a picture of a cartoon house with trees and a lawn outside and a group of people standing in front.

'I'm sorry,' she said, as she stood in the middle of the room. 'Just a moment. I have forgotten something.'

Then she turned and opened the door and walked back up the corridor. 'Just a moment,' Dinah said to herself again, though nobody at all was listening.

She walked to the bathroom and opened the door. She put the toilet lid down and her head in her hands. Just for a moment. She must be doing something wrong, she thought. Things were meant to get easier, but instead they were getting harder.

With a calm inevitability she saw all at once that she been in the room forever, the weeds growing up through the floor, through her arms and legs, her armpits and pelvis. The feeling of undoing was a sweet sort of ache. She longed to give in to it. She took a deep breath of air-freshened air. She washed her hands and neck and walked out into the corridor to return to the lecture.

In the corridor, just in front of the door to the theatre, stood Mayumi. She was holding a pile of papers. Dinah could hear the class through the door. Their whoops and laughs echoed down the corridor.

Mayumi stared at her. Her face was a mask of horror. 'What are you doing?' she hissed.

Dinah seemed to have forgotten how to speak. 'I forgot my pencil,' she said.

'You do not need a pencil. You need a whiteboard marker. And your textbook. That is my understanding.'

'I'm sorry. I needed a pencil. For the roll.'

Mayumi was breathing heavily. 'Dinah-sensei. You must not leave the classroom in the middle of the lecture. Ever.'

'I'm sorry.'

'This is in the contract that you signed. The students have paid for these classes. Each minute is paid for. Do you understand?'

'Yes, of course.' Dinah came closer, to take the papers from Mayumi. 'It was just a moment. It won't happen again.' She bowed apologetically and attempted to move past Mayumi to open the lecture theatre door.

Mayumi's voice came again. This time in a sort of shriek. 'Dinah-san!'

Dinah almost tripped.

'Your blouse!'

Dinah looked down at her body. She was wearing a very plain white shirt. She had bought it from Muji. Buy One, Get One Free. She had done so. She felt her eyes prick with tears. She looked back at Mayumi, whose face was rigid with distress.

'What's wrong with it?' Her voice sounded very ordinary. It was almost a relief to be surprised.

Mayumi was breathing even more quickly, as if the whole thing were simply too much for her. 'The back,' she said. Even saying this exhausted her. Dinah craned her neck. She turned the blouse as far as she could. She saw nothing.

'What?'

'There are stains all over. Grass! Mud! All over! It is unacceptable, inappropriate attire.' There was a kind of joyful release in her face, as if she had finally found something to do with her hatred of Dinah. 'You must go! Now! Make sure it is washed properly before you return. I … I will cancel the lecture. I will send a warning!'

Dinah backed past her, keeping to the wall. It did not make any sense. She had changed her blouse.

'Go!' said Mayumi. 'It is unacceptable.'

Dinah walked out, past the desk, then out into the clearing, where the student bus was waiting and would carry her back to the train station.

The sun beat down. Pollen floated in the air. She boarded the train back to Ikebukuro, and at Ikebukuro she boarded a train on the next platform, without looking at the destination. She saw the name of a station she remembered and got off.

On her first day in the country, she had travelled from Narita to Ueno. She had been on autopilot, in the double haze of jet lag and grief. Phil had shown her which tickets to buy, which way to go. At Ueno they had left the station briefly, had bought a bowl of rice and fried tempura before boarding the next train. She had looked out and seen a huge park. A proper park.

She got off the train and followed the stream of people. Up in the sky a dirigible hung, advertising Sofmap data storage.

13

Yasuko had woken with the taste of sugar in her mouth.

It was a good sign, she thought, as if she had been returned to an earlier life, a younger body. She had drunk too much, too late. She had said something she shouldn't have. But the worst was over.

Yasuko had risen and dressed and applied her make-up with the same discipline as any other morning, then she had walked down the hall to see her son.

Outside Jun's bedroom, she stood for a while. She waited, counting. Then she tapped with her nails on the wall.

It wasn't a knock, not exactly. It was simply something they did. In the way of two people who knew each other better than any others anywhere, who had lived together for so long that every form of silence was familiar. The tap was the patter of a shared mood, their own sort of language. An acknowledgement of the other's presence when you didn't quite feel like speaking. Tap, tap, tappety-tap.

From inside Jun's bedroom she heard a light rustling sound. Then she heard the light tapping that was his answer.

Her heart rose with relief. She had thought, perhaps, that she had offended him last night. Her memory was hazy. She knocked properly this time, firm and peremptory like a mother who was coming in, and she pushed open the door.

Jun's room was always clean. She joked about it with him. She teased him. Where are the balled-up gym socks? Where is the seinen manga? Where are the piles of papers, the cup ramen? Where is the mug with its inch of milk coffee grown cold and thick and pale with mould, its own slow, creeping form of life?

Today, cleaner than ever. The old blue sun-faded duvet cover. The neatly ranged paperbacks. The souvenir Lakers basketball hoop on the back of the door, and the foam basketball Velcroed neatly in place next to it. The room was completely empty. He was gone.

The tapping sound came again. It was coming from somewhere in the room. Coming from outside the window.

Why did her heart rise even though it was impossible? For the same reason we understand words even with half the characters missing or misspelled, or we see a face in random markings on a piece of wood.

Yasuko stepped calmly across the room and raised the blind as if she would greet her son on the third floor, under the window's eave. As if he would be sitting there with a crooked smile and his long legs improbably folded. This is what she understood: the noise was his message, was his voice, and he was speaking to her.

She pulled the blind and released it. It shot up to reveal a pigeon sitting on the windowsill. The pigeon was dusky grey with a purple décolletage. Its wings were shoaled like a dirty estuary. The bird tapped at the window with its beak tap tap tappety-tap and then it flew away.

Yasuko stood up and left the room.

She did not check her phone, nor look for a note, because she didn't need any other signs to tell her what her body knew. Jun had indeed left her. As truly as if the earth had opened and swallowed him up.

With her whole body she resisted what was coming. But it came anyway. It flicked like a whip, merciless and forked, curling the moment into its own end. She had known that he would leave. She had known it was coming, but everybody thinks they'll be the exception. How terrible it is, suddenly, to exist in a story.

She reached out with a hand. Not to steady herself, but gently, as if to touch somebody. As if to touch her son, in fact, or just the top of his head at five or six years old, if he were standing in front of her close enough to be touched.

She almost felt that hard warmth of his head. She thought about the rightness and correctness of his shape. How whenever she saw him, his profile, his brow, something in her rang with the rightness. She thought of the skin at his temples, and the unprotected crown when seen from above.

For a moment the memory's richness made her feel it would all be tolerable, that she would be able to extract everything she needed and live inside this richness forever, that it would be more than adequate compensation for the pain.

But then the next moment came, and the one after that, and she knew it would be too much for her to bear.

14

On the outskirts of the National Museum of Western Art in Ueno, there is a garden with evergreen shrubbery and bamboo. It is full of statues, all in the same heavy black metal. The famous statue in the centre is an enormous male figure. It leans forward and rests its elbow on its knee. The back of its hand is bent to make a small platform, and upon that platform it rests the weight of its chin.

Dinah stood alongside the figure for a good few minutes. She did not properly study it. Instead she looked at the sky; at the clouds; at the trees, which were giving off a distinct odour like chlorine. She felt the breadth of the statue's legs, though, their power like a physical substance. You didn't need to have studied art history to know the statue and what it represented. The famous hunch that is actually a kind of torture. Why would anyone make a tribute to that sort of pain?

Dinah continued walking. She found an enclosed sort of courtyard where there was shade and she could sit. The courtyard contained another statue, quite different to the others. This one was formed to look like a big black door. She walked closer, peered in. The door's thick blackness was, she saw, a mass of tiny fairy-like figures. Closer again, to inspect them. Tiny people. Beautifully sculpted, as fine and intricate as insects. But people. Young and old. Beautiful and ugly. Lovers embracing, and mothers holding young children. All of them being sucked into the gate. As they went they were flayed and twisted and pulled forever from what they wanted to keep. She felt another surge of anger, as if she had been tricked into looking at something obscene.

A righteous surge of self-pity too. She would be justified in making a complaint. But to whom would she complain? And what would she say? *Fucking Rodin. Who thought Rodin would be a good idea?*

Dinah walked away from the statues and into the lane between it and the museum. Everything was cardboard. The heat went into her. She had never been so hot in her life. There was a truck backed up to a large set of double doors. It was huge and green and had the words *Tokyo Symphony Orchestra* on it in white. The doors were open due to the heat. Inside was a chipboard floor and trailing electrical cords: a temporarily erected sound stage.

If she had not been so engrossed in the statues, earlier, she might have realised what had been in the air in the park all along — floating up high with the pollen and almost indiscernible, like a gas.

Music. Strings marching along in a genteel fashion. The notes were light, frothy, full of air. And somehow amusing, like a giant wire whisk lifting and turning an enormous bowl of egg whites. A single, redeemingly human voice rose above.

By the time Dinah realised what she was listening to, it was too late. Against her will she walked closer to the doors and looked inside to the bare stage. A man was standing there. He was short and broad and strange. He wore a tee-shirt and cargo shorts and a mask. The mask was covered in feathers. He stood like a ballet dancer, poised and light-footed in spite of his weight, and he sang. The notes were like bubbles popping: *Pa — pa — pa pa — pa- pa- pa.*

A second, female voice joined his, offstage, a response. A duet.

Dinah knew the melody very well. It was her brother's favourite aria from his favourite opera. If he put it on at home it meant he was in a good mood, a great mood. 'How is it possible,' he would say, out of breath with singing, 'that something can be so beautiful and so ridiculous at the same time?'

Dinah walked back down the path, through the statuary garden, through the rotating doors, and into the museum. She stood in the gift shop. Her hairs rose and her skin prickled in the sudden cold of the air conditioning. People politely moved around her as if she were a rock in the middle of a river.

She found some postcards of the Rodin statues and paid for them, as if this act of normality might placate something. But it was already too late. Bright spots hung and floated and scattered away when she looked. Soon thereafter the whole world became flimsy like tissue paper. The strings of the carrier bag rocked against her palm, and she walked out and away, somewhere. Her footsteps were clownlike — oversized, clumsy.

She was blind as she walked, and did not know where she sat, but she sat somewhere on the grass and felt the black wing rise in her head and the true shape of the beast approach. It had borrowed its colour from the foliage rustling all around her. Heavy and malign and lumbering it came to club her with its arms of spring green. There was nothing that she could do.

15

The morning her son disappeared Yasuko left the house and walked. The world was still full of ordinary things: the dry cleaner, the apartment buildings with their futons hanging over the balconies, women carrying their purses, the optometrist with the free machine to wash your spectacles. Crows. Plane trees. The smell of melon bread. It all continued.

There were many ways in which you could misplace a child. So many ways that you could carry them faultily.

You could be on a moving travelator at an airport and step off it, onto the carpet, and watch your child travel on and on. Or while carrying them downstairs, you could catch your foot on the hem of a garment and fall. You would be falling together, head over heels, for a very long time. Perhaps you would never hit the ground. The whole thing would take a very long time.

There was the disappearance of neglect. It was possible to forget that your child existed. You could leave him in a cardboard box like a guinea pig. You could leave him in the back of a car or in the train. You could forget to feed him for several days. During that period the child would change. When you finally remembered, with a quaking, nauseous, inevitable jolt, the child would have changed utterly. He would smile up at you from a misshapen face and flattened body: an undone, spoiled enterprise. He would speak words that should not be spoken — awful, precocious, unwhole.

You could fall into despair about having lost a gift so young, and the horror of living in a world stripped of meaning. Or you could emerge from that place and eat, and wash yourself, and care for him. And that was what she had done. She had fed Jun and raised him. She had worked from the beginning of the day until the day's end and her own aching certainty of demise. He had bent her will back and forth as if he had known that its iron strength would, in that action, become weak enough to break. She had nursed him and dressed him and biked him to kindergarten as he sat in the front carrier, a prince surveying his domain.

It was remarkable, really, that given all this, her son had now left her, had really gone. She felt it in a definitive way, in her bones, where she kept all her knowledge.

She heard voices calling down at the bottom of the building, echoing up toward her balcony. Just human voices. Just the ordinary world, going about its ordinary business.

She walked through the city all day. By Shinobazu Pond, Yasuko leaned deeper, her head closer to the smooth skin of the water. 'Please,' she said, gently.

The fish were moving, rising. A pattern became clear in their movements. They were circling toward her. One of the fish came up. It rose so far that its snout broke above the surface, and she felt her face move without her control. Yasuko sat forward.

'I have come to tell you,' she said, 'that my son has left me. I would appreciate your help.'

The fish's snout sat suspended, still, out of the water. Then it turned. It did not speak. The carp subsided back into the pond's mute gloom. It left behind a pattern of cords and tension in the water, the surface pulled smooth like a keloid scar.

It was futile. She had known that it would be. After all of these times, why should today be any different?

There was no pain. All she felt was a sort of numb cloudiness. She thought for a second of a picture in one of her father's books, something

96

that happened to divers when they rose too quickly, a crystalline flowering in the blood. She nodded. That was that. She had missed the whole day of work. How late it was. She stood and looked up at what remained of the day. The sun dull above the towers of Ueno's shopping district. A white sky. Its patience greater than hers, greater than anyone's.

She walked, slowly at first, then with greater speed, back across the bridge, back past the museums, and toward the station. She passed the fountain and the concourse where the courting couples walked and sat. The park was filling. A trio of young men walked toward her, one of them carrying a red soft-drink crate.

When she was halfway down the concourse, she stopped suddenly, arrested by her shoe. Her heel had become caught in the earth between two concrete pavers. She hopped, off-balance, found her footing, then yanked. But she had misjudged both the force of her movement and the stubbornness of the earth. The slender heel held firm. She wobbled once, twice, and went over, shedding the shoe, putting out her hands instinctively. Her Wolford stockings erupted into a spider's web of runs.

It was in that position, on her hands and knees, her cheeks burning with shame and injustice, looking at the fountain, that she saw the peacock.

On the pale-grey concrete the bird stood, its immense tail spread out like the cape of a tired monarch. People walked past: a young foreign woman in business clothes, an older couple pushing their adult child in a wheelchair. A group of high-school boys. They each passed without a glance, so close that they could have stroked its feathers. But none of them did, because it had appeared solely for her.

When her powers returned, Yasuko wondered that she could ever have mistaken the earlier episodes as the real thing. She wondered at how much she had forgotten. Her stomach moved up into her throat. Her heart opened like a fist and started to speed. Hope waved to her like a handkerchief, far off, almost beyond her range of vision. She recognised its sharp white colour and the uptick in her bloodstream. She felt the old intoxicant drip of ego. Everything sharpened, as if she had turned a lens. No, she said. But it was impossible to fight the tide of mercy that crept up her throat and into her face. It was only right, after all that she had had to put up with, the work that she had put into making her life.

From a crouch on her knees, she spoke. Under her breath but loud enough to be heard. She was afraid. She had forgotten the terror.

'Please,' she said. 'Leave me alone.'

The peacock walked idly in her direction on its clawed feet. It turned its head on the periscope of its neck and blinked so that she saw herself briefly reflected in a dark eye before the life-occluding shutter of its lid lowered once, twice.

'We know you are suffering,' it said. 'We have been watching you.' The opulence and richness of its plumage was awful. It spoke without opening its beak.

'You are not alone.'

Absence had marked her life for as long as she could remember. The shape of something hard and heavy that had pressed down, and the bloodless grass after it had been removed.

She wanted to show her anger. She wanted to resist. But in the end she was like a wronged wife who gives up her oath of silence at her husband's first kind word. She looked warily at the messenger, and she felt the rush of relief that was headier than any drug. It slipped along her veins. Even in her grief she felt the pleasure that was her whole body being returned to her. She could feel her skin. She could feel the nerve endings all along her heels, her knees within the intricate web of her stockings, her fingers moving against the gravel. It was all at once given back. She could not bear to look around because she knew she would see the clouds moving with alarming purpose. She knew that outside the station, every blade of grass would hold a further message. She leaned forward on her hands, helplessly. Even the pain in her skin was a delight. A trickle of blood curled down from her knee.

And she saw that, of course, the two things were connected.

Jun had left and her powers had returned. That was the trade-off; that was the reward.

'Is that why you came back?' she wanted to ask. She did not say it out loud. At the height of her suffering, she knew that, if called on to make a choice, this time she could not say which she would choose.

'Have you really come back?' she asked instead. 'After all of these years?'

'Oh yes,' the bird said. 'We are going to help you.' Its eye was fringed and blank. 'Remain alert. We are sending you a girl.'

'A girl? What good is a girl? What kind of girl?'

But already the bird had reared, and its wings flexed like the muscles on a swimmer's back. It moved into the air.

MICHAEL

1

Afterward — it might have been half an hour or three hours — when the migraine had receded, Dinah was able to open her eyes. She looked straight up. The light was moving over her without character, animus, or agenda. The world had settled back into its proper place. In the dusty arms of the tree above her head, two small parakeets or lovebirds hopped. She felt a sense of relief, almost of affection, at the passing of pain.

Dinah sat up, arranged herself. She looked around.

She was sitting on a grass slope. There was a magnificent fountain in the middle of the broad gravel concourse ahead. Around it pigeons stalked and pecked idly in the dust. At the edge of the gravel pathway that led back to the entrance of the park, there was a young man dressed in a black suit and tie, a tote bag over his shoulder. He was sitting on a bench and smoking with an air of intense thought or disappointment.

As she watched, the young man took a few deep drags on his cigarette then dropped the butt, ground at it with a chisel-toed shoe and stood. He walked forward a few steps with intent. Then he stopped. There was something of the dance in his movements, as if he were listening to an invisible beat. His actions were somehow related to the pigeons that milled around him. Was he trying to scare them? Dinah wondered. Surely that was something that only a child might do.

The birds tolerated the fellow's presence, but they were not about to let him get close. Each time he neared they moved away casually in half-flutters, as if such behaviour was something they saw all the time and was insufficient to get stirred up over. Then all at once, as if from a private signal, the young man swerved and ploughed right through their group. The pigeons scattered into the air like iron filings from a magnet. He flapped his own arms, hooting as if deranged.

When the birds returned to the ground, Dinah saw that a single pigeon had been separated from the group. The young man narrowed his attention to this lone bird. He moved with it. At a distance but with steady pressure. When it scooted toward the concrete wall, he scooted too. When it turned he turned. When it cornered he cornered. When it stopped he stopped. Always he was just behind. On the next feint the bird dodged and walked in Dinah's direction. Perhaps she seemed some sort of safe haven. There was mange around the pigeon's eye and beak. A feather floated from its belly down past its knotted grey legs. There were oily patterns of pink and pale grey and dark grey and white. Its beady eyes turned as its head swivelled silently.

Behind the bird Dinah saw the young man coming up low. He reached with two loosely cupped hands and in a quick thrust grabbed the pigeon around its breast. The bird fluttered, but it was caught. The man tucked it into his chest for purchase then calmly renewed his grip around its body and wings.

Dinah felt angry.

'What are you doing to that bird?' she asked loudly in English.

The young man shook his head to show he did not understand. His eyebrows were thick and his hair combed into an angular whipped bouffant. Dinah saw the sweat standing on his face and nose in beads. Then he walked down the gravel concourse. She followed him with her eyes. He walked a few metres only. Then he came to a stop at another bench under one of the large trees.

There was nothing of elegance in any of his movements, and yet the whole thing had clearly been well practised. Sitting, and using his legs to gently pincer the bird's body, the young man shrugged his shoulder so that the tote slid into the crook of his elbow. Then he withdrew a second bag from the tote, a string bag like the ones French people use to bring home the baguette, the onions, the copy of *Le Monde* from the market.

Dinah watched in silence, not even striving anymore to understand. The man held open the string bag and in one swift movement pulled the bag up and over the pigeon and opened his legs so it flapped, flapped, but was caught. As if this were an entirely normal activity. Then he laughed: a rude noise of merriment. He stood, putting the bird in the bag under his arm, saluted the fountain, and walked rapidly away.

Dinah blinked.

At just that moment a woman stepped forward, on the concourse.

She appeared to be walking right toward Dinah. With a sense of wonder Dinah watched her come. She wore a cream knitted top and a skirt that could only be described as a confection. It fell in a set of tiers and ended in a froth of black netting just above her knees. She wore black stockings that had snagged and run with great profligacy. Tucked under one arm, in just the same fashion the young man had carried the bird, she carried a handbag so ugly that its ugliness conferred a sort of distinction. Under the other were her shoes.

There was something miraculous about the woman's presence, Dinah felt. The suddenness of her arrival, her beauty, the fullness and completion of the way she appeared, standing against the light. As if each garment had been carefully selected, a vocabulary that Dinah did not understand.

Dinah stood up a little clumsily. The woman's face was heart-shaped. Broad cheekbones and a pointed chin. Her hair a tawny animal black-brown. Her make-up impeccable. The skin of her cheeks bore the pockmarks of old acne scarring, and the bold swipe of her blusher seemed to intentionally draw attention to this, as if the scars were an accessory to her beauty. She bowed her head in a way that was both demure and insolent.

'Are you feeling better?' she asked.

'Yes,' said Dinah.

'I have been waiting just over there to ensure you recovered. Is it a migraine?' Her voice was light and full of charm, and she spoke with a slight American accent.

'Yes,' said Dinah.

'I am a fellow sufferer. I wanted to ensure you had recovered enough to travel home. My name is Yasuko.' Then she paused. She began to laugh. 'But we know each other.' It was a gentle laugh, sweet and full of mischief. 'What a strange world this is. We are colleagues.'

Dinah recognised the woman. She was one of the cohort of Japanese English lecturers at SDU. 'How funny,' she said. She felt moved and embarrassed at the same time. 'Thank you for staying with me. That was very kind.'

'Oh, no, not kindness at all. It was pure selfishness on my part. I have a use for you.'

Dinah nodded. There was a floating quality to the heat. She nodded to show that she was happy to be made use of. 'Anything,' she said.

'Well,' said the older woman. 'I was going to buy myself a cup of coffee, and I hate to sit alone. Would you care to join me?'

Dinah nodded. Then Yasuko led and Dinah followed. They walked together, out of the park.

On the ground floor of the station plaza, to the left of the East Exit, was a glass-fronted restaurant with the cheery red-and-yellow sign of Mister Donut.

'Please,' the woman said.

Dinah allowed herself to be moved forward and inside. A strange feeling had come over her. It was calmness. For the first time since she had arrived in Tokyo, perhaps long before that, even, she felt at peace. The feeling seemed to be coming from the woman's presence. Her eyes sparkled. It was as if she knew Dinah, knew everything about her, and had forgiven her for everything. She had taken her in hand.

'Sit, sit.'

Dinah sat. The leatherette was bright orange, and the tabletops glittered with gold mica. The air smelt of filter coffee and powdered sugar. The woman disappeared and then came back. She had a brown plastic tray and, on the tray, coffee, cream, a plate of doughnuts. She arranged everything with an air of amused cultivation.

'Aren't the names pleasant? Cruller. Chocolate-glazed. Cinnamon old-fashioned. A kind of poetry. The poetry of doughnuts.' Again Dinah felt a sense of floating. As if the whole thing were a gentle joke to which only the woman was privy. But her face was also careful, serious. As Dinah watched, the woman sat and picked up a doughnut with great concentration. She bit into it, then she looked up.

'Dozo,' she said. 'Eat.'

Dinah looked at the plate. She realised that she was very hungry. When was the last time she had eaten solid food? She had been living off aloe yoghurt and cup ramen. She picked up a whole doughnut and took a bite. Her mouth was flooded with the gift of sugar. It was wonderful. A new chemical channel sparked open between her brain and body.

'What caused your migraine?' the woman asked, very matter of fact. Again Dinah had the strange sense that the woman knew everything. It was all running in a current down below, and the words were a sort of shared code, a way of navigating that was a clever art in its own right. When she caught the woman's eyes, she felt it. Almost a crackle. She had not felt that in a long while.

Dinah swallowed.

'The music,' she said, 'in the park.' As if it were very simple. Perhaps it was very simple.

'Is the music in here a problem?'

Dinah listened. There was a light spangle of Muzak, an orchestration of a Celine Dion song.

She laughed. 'No, that's fine,' she said. 'The music in the park was one of my brother's favourite pieces. So.' She did not finish.

The woman didn't say anything. She nodded.

The man behind the counter smiled at Dinah, and she smiled back. He was thin and elderly, and wearing a puffy hat somewhere in style between a chef's toque and a train conductor's peaked cap. There was a great dignity in his wearing of the cap and, in fact, the entire uniform. His posture was very precise, very erect.

'Tell me about your brother,' the woman said.

Dinah looked up. The music in the café seemed to quieten.

Something was happening. She looked at the woman's eyes. She blinked.

'Tell me,' the woman said. 'What does he do?'

There was nothing she could do except answer, so she told the truth. It was not the whole truth, but how else does one manage in this world?

'He's a musician,' she said.

'A magician?' the woman asked, with a light laugh. She fixed her with an intense gaze.

Dinah smiled, but then saw that the woman was not in fact joking. 'Oh, no. A *musician*.'

'Ah, I see. Well, that is almost as remarkable.'

Dinah smiled in agreement. She was still dazed by the migraine, by this whole strange encounter. It was not a lie, not really. Her mother had talked about this. How hard to tell people you barely knew. A stranger on the street. A teacher from school. But the truth was, she said: you don't have to tell everybody everything.

'A professional musician?'

And so, because of the space that the woman's kindness and the gift of sugar had made in the day, in her pain, in her grief, Dinah heard herself continue on in the lie. It was just easier that way. 'Yes, a pianist.'

'I see.' The woman picked up another piece of doughnut and held it between her fingers with a mixture of humour and grace. Her eyes were clear, a direct luminous brown.

'And you, do you share his gift?'

The man behind the counter turned to remove one of the coffee jugs from the hotplate. He carefully held the filter jug in front of his body and walked out from behind the counter and into the café. He stopped at each occupied table, and people passed their cups to the end of the table to be refilled.

For some reason Dinah felt that she must answer Yasuko's question before he reached their table.

'No, not at all,' she said. 'I was just the one who listened, and watched.'

Yasuko cocked her head to one side, as if assessing her. Then she smiled and sat back a little. 'I would say that listening and watching are very important gifts in their own right,' she said.

The restaurant owner paused at their table at a discreet distance. Yasuko took Dinah's cup and passed it to the manager. With great dignity he bent from the waist and refilled it. Dinah felt the dark shape of the migraine rise and fall again in her peripheral vision.

She thought about dancing around the house to *The Magic Flute* with Michael at thirteen. They were drinking wine from coffee cups, stolen from the cask on the top shelf of the pantry. The dark was coming up from the garden, and they had not turned on the light. It made the house seem feel full of mystery.

'Why do you love it so much?' she had asked.

'Because it is the best,' he said.

'Why is it the best?' Breathless from the dancing.

'Because there is nothing tragic in it. The tragedy has been burned off. Vaporised. Like sun on wet pavement.'

'What burned it off?'

'Beauty,' he said. 'Beauty did.'

'But isn't beauty tragic too?' It sounded right. And someone needed to argue with Michael. She had decided it was her job.

'No, no,' he said. 'Beauty is pure humour. That's why it's the best.'

Yasuko was stirring cream and sugar into the cup. She handed it back to Dinah. The manager moved off.

'Is your brother also in Japan?'

Really it would be too complicated to explain. The floating warmth that seemed to exonerate her. In a certain way, it was true.

'Not in Japan, no,' Dinah said. 'Still in New Zealand.'

The sun was going down. It was reflecting on all of the mirrors of the station plaza. The genial light filled Mister Donut, touching the booth, the Formica, the spotless counter-top, the dignified manager who was at another table now gently tipping the filter-coffee jug. Pink and gold. Warm and soft. Pink and gold and warm with the kindness of sugar.

Dinah waited, as if the woman were testing her resolve, but the silence was sufficient. The warmth was sufficient. They sat together and ate and watched the sunlight move across the room.

At last Yasuko placed her hands on the edge of the table.

'If you are fond of doughnuts, I know an excellent place in Shinjuku. You must let me take you some time.'

Dinah nodded.

'I would like that,' she said.

'I am very glad that I met you today.'

'I'm glad too. Thank you for being so kind.'

'It was my pleasure.'

Dinah had known the early evening light would not last indefinitely. Nevertheless she lingered as she picked up her bag, her work tote, her blazer. She moved slowly, as if delaying the moment that she would leave this golden light, the warmth of this strange woman's attention.

'Well, I should really get going,' she said. 'But thank you very much for the coffee. The doughnuts.'

Yasuko nodded. Dinah thought there was still a possibility that she would delay the departure from this halo of warmth. But the moment passed, and Dinah shouldered her bag and stood and nodded a thank you to the manager and offered another wave to Yasuko and walked through the café toward the door to the station.

She had almost reached it when she heard her name.

'Dinah-san.'

She stopped and turned back. A little cautious, as if she might have imagined the summons.

Yasuko was standing up, smiling. There was something seductively gay about her smile. 'Dinah-san!' She beckoned. Dinah took the few steps back toward the table where the coffee things were still gathered.

'Yes?' she said, trying to keep the gladness from her voice.

'I am so silly,' said Yasuko. 'Where do you live?'

'In Itabashi.'

'So you travel from Ikebukuro to campus? I have never seen you on the train. I change at Ikebukuro also. We should travel together.'

'Oh,' said Dinah. 'I would like that.'

110

2

What does one do? If forced to choose? Perhaps it is not necessary to do so straightaway.

I have not been a perfect mother, she said to herself, silently. Speaking to her son. When you were small I resented you. Babies are pure selfishness. I wanted to leave the world and my failure far behind. But that is not what being a mother is. There were times when I gave in to weakness, certainly. But for the most part, I swallowed my disappointments down with great patience. Surely that is worth something.

Yasuko did not wish to think about the times she had given in to weakness. She thought instead of dark mornings, the streets shining with water, the bike like a boat and the small boy at the prow. She thought of the bundle of his warm body in the mouse-grey sweatshirt. She thought of doughnuts on a white plate.

She thought she was entitled to *something*. A phone call at the very least. She sent Jun a text message. Then another. But he remained silent.

She paced the apartment. She listened.

The city was speaking to her. A pulse beating beneath the day. Far below, below the floor of the apartment block, below the concrete foundations, below the cables and cords and tunnels of the city's infrastructure. It came up through her body and it coursed through her muscles and right to the tips of her fingers. When she clenched her fist she heard her powers crackle. Stronger than she remembered.

She closed her eyes. There were children outside, calling. She heard the couple in the neighbouring apartment to hers, their tension and

111

sadness, their wordless frustration. She could hear the wife crying silently in the shower.

She stood, eager. She strained her ears. There were animals talking. Noise at first, then meaning. Slow, but steady. Pigeons under the window eaves. A dog in the courtyard below.

The world shone around her. It shone for the first time in thirty years. She walked to the window and drew the blind and looked up at the white sky. For the first time in thirty years, she met the sun's eye without blinking and knew that she would not look away first.

When you walked for a long time, the people on the streets ceased to be people at all. They became rhythm only, tides and currents. When this took place, one was no longer part of the thousand things of the street but almost as a piece of wood adrift on a vast sea. You were as nothing, momentarily. It was like falling at first.

Yasuko stepped forward; her stomach plunged, like being on a Ferris wheel or rollercoaster. A boat at sea, cresting a wave.

Then, like magic, obstacles melted away; schoolgirls dropped hands to move around her; smokers pulled their cigarettes back into the protectorate of their bodies.

She reached the curb. Because she had summoned it in her mind, a taxicab appeared, as if out of nowhere. She knew where she needed to go and told him. The driver grunted politely, and the cab pulled out — gently — into the stream of traffic.

She messaged Jun again. What would one do? If forced to choose?

'I hope you are okay?' she wrote. 'Please let me know. Have you gone to stay with friends? Let me know if you need money. I love you.'

Then she sat back and let the taxi take her through the city.

She saw everything. It shone in the pure intensity of her sight. She saw the taxi driver's beaded back-rest and the lace-frilled tissue-box cover. The tinted glass thermos filled with pu-erh tea. She knew without looking that under the passenger-side visor there would be a photo of a woman held in place with two rubber bands. She saw it. She looked at it. It moved her immeasurably. The woman's face was broad and her cheeks were rosy. She wore a quilted jacket. She held an equally well-padded baby in her arms. The wonder of the curved cheek, the new eye. Love: that strange thing.

Yasuko's phone vibrated. She took it from her handbag and read the message.

'I am fine. I am sorry I left without talking to you. I hope you understand. I need some space. Are you okay?'

'Never better,' she wrote.

On the roof of Seibu she stood and surveyed the concrete plain. She looked across at the children's playground and then toward the ramshackle lean-to shed at the far end of the roof. She looked at the shelving that spread around it outside, with its immense collection of tubs and buckets. She saw it all anew, this strange encampment at the top of the expensive department store.

She laughed with anticipation and relief.

It was so comforting, so familiar to be back. To be back and this time with her powers intact.

She walked through the shelves of untreated wood and breezeblocks of hollow concrete. As she walked, at ease, she looked into each of the tubs and buckets. There was no uniformity to the arrangement at all. The tubs were plastic, rubber, terracotta, glass, ancient polystyrene painted to look like marble. The buckets were variously plastic — like the kind a child might take to the beach — and heavy-lipped industrial steel.

Fish peered back at her. Big ones and little ones. Fish with neon lights in their bellies. Plain goldfish like the ones you won in plastic bags at festivals. Snails, clinging to the sides tenaciously. Tadpoles, in various stages of transformation. Turtles with red ears like creatures made privy to the shameful secrets of the entire world.

Oh how pleasant it was to be in just the right place. She could hear their whispers, the mild electrical currents of their existence, but she did

113

not stop to listen at this time. Instead she walked to the largest of the ramshackle buildings and stood in front of the doors so that they slid open. She pushed past the heavy plastic. It was the sort of curtain found in the meat or butchery area of a supermarket, but instead of keeping in a frigid cold, it protected a deeper humidity.

Inside was a rainforest of plants, both real and artificial. Woven plastic mats that covered the concrete floor. At the far end of the office a vast partner's desk in ancient, beautiful mahogany, and behind it a man with completely white hair.

The man did not look up as she approached. He was reading, the laggard. She could not help but smile. The old black crew-neck jumper in tissue-fine merino wool. Celine or perhaps Pringle. The jumper sleeves pushed right up to reveal a single nested dragon on each of his forearms.

The book he was reading was huge, with tissue-thin pages. He licked one of his fingers, turned the page. '*Don Quixote*,' he said, without looking up. 'Have you read it?'

Then at last he looked up and with an elegant action pulled the sleeves of his jumper down over his forearms. He sat back in his chair to regard her. He did it slowly, as if time was something from which he had graduated, as she had.

'Of course,' she said. 'Which translation are you reading?'

'Ushijima.'

'Ah, well. Everyone has their favourite, of course. But in my opinion only Ogiuchi's captures the true spirit of the original.'

He blinked, but only a little. She looked back at him with a bland smile.

'How can I help you, Kinoshita-san?' he asked.

'I was hoping to purchase something, Seito.'

He looked at her for a long while. She bore his gaze resolutely, calmly. She smiled at him. She felt her mouth twitching. It was pure delight to be in control again.

'Well,' he said. 'I don't want to disappoint you. But last time ...'

'Oh, last time,' she said. She scoffed at last time. Last time had been pure desperation. Last time had been despair.

'Yes, but Kinoshita-san ...' She felt almost sorry for him. She could see his struggle to find the correct words, his desire to avoid offence. 'Last time, your son was in touch. He told me not to sell to you anymore.'

In fact she had not known that Jun had done that. But it did not figure. It was simply information, and she put it away for future use.

'That was years ago,' she said.

He nodded, a slight flutter to his eyelids.

She looked steadily at him. How familiar he was. She saw everything, almost without looking. She saw the index finger of the hand that had been removed to just above the middle joint, the little finger entirely missing. She saw the arrangements he had made with disappointment. His dignified hair.

'That was years ago,' she said again. 'And you should know. He has left home.'

'Really? Jun-san has left home? I will light incense for you.'

Yasuko could not be doing with his sympathy. Her patience with niceties had passed. She could smell chemicals, carefully titrated. It was the smell of obsessiveness. It was the smell of order and knowledge. It reminded her of her father.

Yasuko shrugged. 'Save it for your own funeral, Seito,' she said. 'I'm a busy woman. Do you have any beetles or not? If you are not willing to sell them to me, I will simply go to the pet shop next door.'

He hesitated. He was not sure what to do, so she continued speaking.

'I would like to buy one of those large ones. I don't know the correct *scientific* name, I'm afraid. But you know the kind I mean. The ones with the horns.'

She saw the beetle quite clearly in her mind, and wanted it very much. She saw dark wood, soapy with age. She saw the beetle, and heard her own voice speaking to it, asking the questions. There was a tremor in her calf, but she carefully tensed the muscle until it stopped.

'If you are sure it is alright,' said Seito. He was a little cowed now, contrite. 'If you are sure that *you* are alright?'

That she could not stand for. 'Do I look alright to you?' She raised her chin and straightened her Gucci skirt. She smiled and met his eyes, dipping her eyelids with modest humour. She felt her skin crackle. She could hear children calling in the playground across the concrete terrace of the roof. She felt the calm balance of grief, knowledge, strength — a full sense of the strength at her fingertips.

He looked at her. His gaze was serious and assessing.

'Well, yes. You look very well. Very well indeed.'

'Between you and me, Seito,' she said. 'I have not felt so good in a long time. In fact I have a secret to share. My powers have returned at last.'

Seito's eyes were steady. 'Yes,' he said. 'I can see. Well, then I should not stand in your way. If you really want a beetle. Do you still have the equipment?'

'No,' she said. 'Jun threw the last one away, that terrible child. I will need a small terrarium and some substrate. And food, of course.'

'Of course.'

He stood up. He was wearing his usual uniform. The very old, very clean Levi's 501s. The deck shoes so down at heel that they looked like slippers. He took a small balsa-wood box down from the shelf and went out of the room.

He was gone for several minutes. She could hear the beetle even before he returned. She could see it in her mind's eye. A shift in the matter of the room, its small intelligence suddenly alert and suddenly aware of her own mind, listening. The beetle was sitting inside the box, its antennae aquiver, its hard carapace dark and mottled. It was so beautiful.

'What do I owe you?' asked Yasuko, reaching for the box already.

'Nothing,' he said. 'Consider it a welcome-back present.'

Seito walked with her to the edge of the shack's door and the plastic threshold.

'Come with me,' he said then, and held his arm in a gentle crook so that she could place her own hand upon its ledge. 'I want to show you something.'

116

They walked out onto the concrete plain of the roof. There were two shipping containers just beyond the cluster of shelves. He walked toward the first, which had a door in its side. He opened the door and gestured that she should enter first, so she did so.

Inside the container it was dark. There was the rhythmic inertia of fluorescent strip lighting waking into life, and then the hum of black light. Beneath the hum she heard the stir of life and patience. In response to it she felt her own breath come slower and her heartbeat slow. She felt the peripherals of attention drop away until she became simply a listening, watching thing. The air was dim and dense with wisdom, and over her whole body her skin rose and prickled in deference and perceptivity.

There were fish tanks along the walls of the container. They were the expensive sort. Inside each tank large goldfish oscillated gracefully and vacantly, like actors studiously avoiding the gaze of the camera. They were large, almost as large as carp. They had distended growths above their eyes that made some of them look like bulldogs, some like lions. They were florid, efflorescent. Their tails were like spun taffy, like Murano glass.

'I have missed you, Kinoshita-san,' he said. 'Who else could I show them to?'

'They are remarkable,' she said. And it was true.

Seito stood gazing at the tanks. His face was filled with the light of the individual fluid worlds. Each tank was a small stage of improbable beauty lit for shipwreck, courtship, or devastation.

'Aren't they?' he asked, with the soft paternal voice of somebody admiring a baby. 'Aren't they beautiful? And yet grotesque. There is something in that, isn't there?'

She turned away. 'It is a new hobby of yours, then? Do you sell them?'

'I sell a few. I have put them into competition. Mostly it's a hobby.' His hand wafted in front of the glass as if he wished to stroke his creations.

'And how do you get them to develop like this?'

117

'People have been breeding goldfish for these growths for many years. They are tumours, you know, the excrescences, but benign. I don't think that they cause the fish any pain.' He looked at her with his intelligent, knowing eyes. 'We would never know, though, would we? In any case certain people say that pain is necessary for the cultivation of beauty.'

Yasuko nodded. She wished that Seito would leave. She wished to be alone with the fish. But he was waiting to escort her back onto the concrete.

They stood at the door, bathed in the glow.

'It is a difficult choice that you are faced with,' he said to her. 'I see that.'

Yasuko looked hard at Seito. She was very fond of the man. She thought of all of the many times she had visited in the past. Her suffering must have been crystal clear to him each time. An individual of his sensitivity must have quickly seen the pattern: the false ecstasy of her gift's return, the frenzy as she gathered up her props. All followed by the drawn-out weeks of denial and then despair. Her skin prickled with embarrassment at what he had seen. Yet he had never treated her with anything but respect.

And she was certainly grateful. But she felt a measure of resentment that he so quickly, so acutely grasped the very core of the problem that she now faced. A difficult choice, he said. A difficult choice. She bridled against this notion. Why was it always her who must make the choice? Why should it be all or nothing? Why should she be expected to give up everything all over again?

'Who says I have to make a choice?' she said quietly. 'Who says there is a choice to be made at all?'

Seito shrugged. 'It is simply my experience.'

She glanced at his hand, the taxed fingers that were the price he had paid for giving up one world and attempting to move into another.

But perhaps things would be different. Perhaps she could keep her powers and her son also. She was grown now, more powerful than before. She had lived in a blank and silent world for so long that she had been forced to master certain skills all of her own.

She stood next to Seito, thinking hard. After a while she spoke.

'Well, yes. But perhaps there is another way.'

3

Dinah was walking up the steps in Ikebukuro station to reach the north section of the Tobu Tojo platform. It was 7.13 am. Would Yasuko be there?

Yasuko was already there, on the platform. It was as if she had emerged from a different world. She was perfectly dressed, immaculate and girlish in her costume. Her eyes were very wide, and again it struck Dinah that the woman was making a good-natured mockery of it all — the ugliness of the station, the orderliness of the queue, her own pristine beauty — all of it.

Yasuko turned and saw Dinah and summoned her with a careless wave, and Dinah's heart lifted, as if someone had tied a few balloons to it.

Yasuko was at the very front of the queue, right by the edge of the platform. She was taking up the space next to her, Dinah's space, with an enormous Cartier carrier bag. Dinah walked toward the dimpled yellow plastic line.

Behind them an angular gentleman in an ancient silver-grey double-breasted suit sighed loudly and shook his head in impatience at this overt queue-jumping. Yasuko inclined her head a little to Dinah, took her hand and guided her to her spot as if they were partnering in a waltz.

'This arrangement is most satisfactory,' said Yasuko as they stood and looked over the scar of the tracks. 'I really feel it is our duty as women to piss off as many of these creatures as is humanly possible. Don't you?'

Dinah bowed her head a little. Yasuko turned and made several small, incremental bows to the queue behind them. She moved a few degrees each time in order to scatter her faux courtesy evenly.

'See how happy it makes them!'

The man behind and his queue partner were both sucking their teeth in disapproval.

'Never as comfortable or as fulfilled as when they are disapproving of somebody. I really feel we must constantly oblige them, don't you?'

'I ...' said Dinah.

'Quite. It is an act of kindness. They feel so shored up in themselves that they will all have a truly splendid day.'

She gave a last little bent-fingered wave to a man a few places back who was glowering. Then, reluctantly, as if separating herself from a loving audience, turned the full beam of her attention back to Dinah.

'But, most importantly. How are *you*?'

It *felt* like a beam. Corded energy, light, humour, something else. It pulled everything into shape. Dinah felt herself grow taller. Her nose straightened. Her shoulders fell back as she took her place more firmly. She had thought that perhaps she had imagined it, the strange interlude in the doughnut shop. The strange space it had afforded her from her guilt and grief. But as soon as she stood next to the woman, it returned. She could not have explained it if she had tried.

'I am very good,' she said. And it was true. She was much better. She had slept all night in her bed. Even the apartment block, which had begun to feel like a place of danger, now seemed benign.

The train arrived; they boarded, taking adjacent seats just inside the door. The journey began.

Yasuko turned again in her seat with the ease of customary friendship. Dinah felt the same feeling she had felt in Mister Donut. A current beneath them, some deep subterranean knowledge, and the words floating above. She thought of Michael playing Mozart. The steady, measured consciousness of the left hand, and the right hand embroidering the air above. Frippery. Beauty. Humour. The thought came to her and went, and it did so without pain. That in itself was a small kind of miracle. She leaned in to the woman's voice with a grace that was borrowed and yet, remarkably, all her own. She smiled.

'In American movies when men are speaking about their taste in women, they say: *I am a breast man*, or *I am a bottom man*. Correct?'

'Not "bottom". That sounds too formal. You'd say *ass*, I guess. So, *I'm an ass man*.'

Yasuko nodded gravely, a model student.

'In any case, before we continue in our friendship, I should share something very personal.' She looked seriously and ruefully at Dinah. 'I am a leg woman. More accurately, a thigh woman.'

She inclined her head to indicate. Slowly Dinah turned to her right. A young man was sitting on the seat. He was a student, at least half Yasuko's age, though it was very hard to say how old Yasuko was, exactly. He had, she saw, unusually strong, thick thighs. They were showcased in pale light-wash denim, in which there were not simply rips, but carefully frayed holes cut out, like slots in a mailbox, right the way down the leg. You could see thick dark leg hair through them, right down to the calf. The appearance achieved was almost contemptuous in its violation of the norms of leg coverings. As if the young man enjoyed his own body so much that it was a simple act of generosity to share it in this way. Dinah blushed, looked down at her lap, then back at Yasuko, who winked.

Outside there was clear farmland and an increase in rice fields. At each stop more students got on.

When they reached the station Dinah braced herself to battle the tide of students.

'Where on earth are you going?'

'To catch the bus.'

Yasuko shook her head incredulously. 'Thank goodness we are travelling together.' She pointed to a sign in front of the McDonald's. '*This* is where you catch the teachers' bus. We only ride with the students in a dire emergency.'

The teachers' bus had padded seats, little permanent-pleated curtains, and a driver with a peaked cap and wrist-length white polycotton gloves.

They sat together. Yasuko took a small paperback book from her bag. It remained on her knee and she looked out of the window to watch the suburbs of Kita-Sakado pass.

Dinah studied Yasuko's face.

She had lied about Michael, that he was still alive. It had been a lie of omission. Understandable, in the circumstances. In the golden light of the doughnut shop, in the moment of rescue, it had been almost possible to believe that Michael was still alive. He was in Auckland perhaps, or maybe he had taken up the scholarship after all. He was in London. Practising in a small room lit by the energy of his brain. Starting his recording career. First the chamber works, building to the solo repertoire.

But in the light of the morning, the lie revealed itself as still a lie. Yesterday it seemed to have drawn the woman and her together. Now she felt certain that it would keep them apart. It was there when she looked out at the bright green of the grass and the cold grey of the concrete. It felt like something physical. A minor impediment that marred the whole. A splinter in her finger, a scratch on a record, a streak on a clean window.

Why did she even care? She hadn't spoken to anyone else about Michael. The woman was unlikely to ask her any more questions. Her lie would recede.

But somehow it did matter. It seemed to matter very much. She looked at Yasuko. Her profile against the window was sharp and correct, its beauty somehow greater in the hard light, without the glamour of the sunset. There was something very moving in the bravado of her cheeks and the finely milled shimmering blush on top of the scars.

Dinah felt the oddness of compulsion. She would confess her lie. She would efface herself. She would admit to this woman that she was not a whole person, but a creature handicapped forever. It seemed the right, the necessary, tribute.

'Yasuko?' Dinah said, about to begin. But she was interrupted.

'Mister Donut is my son's favourite place in the whole world.'

Yasuko said it apropos of nothing at all.

123

Dinah waited for what might come next, but it seemed a self-contained statement. Yasuko smiled, then she nodded and placed her hand on Dinah's arm. Dinah could see the individual pores on her face. She blinked in the sudden flare of proximity and trust.

Out the window was a river whose sides were formed out of concrete. Two old men were fishing, several hundred metres away. They wore bucket hats and khaki vests.

'I have been taking this bus route for several years,' Yasuko said. 'It leaves at the same time every single morning. I know each of the landmarks by heart.'

She leaned in confidentially to Dinah. She pointed cheerily, like a tour guide. 'See that house over there?'

Dinah nodded.

'It had a bad fire about a year ago. That was a dramatic morning. They have repaired it since. But you can still see the blackened eaves.'

Then she reached across to point through the opposite window. 'That's my favourite farm. Look, that chestnut horse is always there. And there's a pond over by the farmhouse with koi in it.'

Something was flickering in her face. She looked at Dinah as if measuring something.

'But I have something much more important to show you.' She turned back and indicated her own window. 'Start watching.'

Dinah looked out of the window. 'What am I looking for?' she asked.

'It's a test. I'm confident you will pass. I think that you will know it when you see it.'

Dinah knew that she wouldn't. It had been Michael's eyes that found the story in everything, the gold thread shining up out of the dust. When they were together she could see it too. But without him there was just too much stuff out there. The world was full of it. Surplus. She could look and look for a thousand years and not exhaust it all or understand any of it. The rows of bedraggled onion heads. The tyres stacked for animals to drink from. The grey stone shrines with their red frilled neckerchiefs. The houses with their dark-tiled roofs.

She was filled with a sharp and unreasonable disappointment. The interlude in Ueno Park, then, the strange intimacy of her connection with this woman, it had all been nothing. It had just been the aftermath of the migraine, an illusion, the by-product of exhaustion and loneliness.

Dinah readied herself to manage the social awkwardness of this altogether-odd situation. She prepared herself to smooth her own irrational disappointment. She was good at that. She would go back to her own, silent train journeys. The woman could return to her own routine. Things would go back to normal.

But then with a flash of certainty she saw what Yasuko wanted her to see.

She pointed. 'There,' she said.

Yasuko laughed. 'Yes?'

'Yes. There. That bus,' said Dinah. She knew that she was right. There was something special about the bus.

Yasuko nodded with smug approval. 'I told you you would see it. Didn't I tell you that you were gifted at watching.'

The landscape was so flat and sparse that the blue bus was visible even from about a mile away, travelling toward them.

'I see this same bus every time I am on board,' Yasuko said.

They continued to travel along their parallel journey, and the distance between the buses narrowed.

'You might be wondering why that bus is so important. Soon you will know. Now. Look.'

Yasuko pointed to a corner ahead. Dinah looked as directed, down the street that joined the two parallel roads. The blue bus had turned and was travelling down. So close.

'Look, quick,' said Yasuko, and Dinah looked. Yasuko pointed to a woman and a boy standing at a bus stop, waiting.

It was a simple, everyday sort of scene. A boy and his mother. The boy was leaning his weight against the woman. She was encircling him from behind with her arms. The mother was wearing an apron, and the little boy was in a school uniform: navy shorts, a white shirt with a red neckerchief at the collar, a large leather backpack shaped like a bowling bag. Dinah glimpsed the tableau for a bare second before their bus passed.

She smiled at Yasuko. 'That is lovely,' she said.

'I have been watching them for about a year. We always cross paths at the same time each morning. It reminds me of my son and me. When he was young.' Her voice was warm, but it had changed, there was something dark in it. 'A testament to punctuality, isn't it?'

Dinah nodded. They were rising up the hill to the university. Pines on each side, and the roads retained in patterned walls of concrete similar to the banks of the river.

'They are mine, those two,' said Yasuko. 'I am somehow so fond of them that they feel like family.' She looked back at Dinah, and the warmth was again renewed. The current that had passed between them in the coffee shop had returned. Dinah saw that it was not an illusion, not a fluke. It was something else entirely.

'Seeing as we are friends, now you may share them with me, if you like.'

4

And so Dinah moved from the native English teachers' room to take up an honorary position in the Japanese English teachers' room.

When she bumped into her other colleagues in the hallways, they didn't say anything. Dougal gave her a quizzical look; the others simply ignored her.

'What about Mayumi?' Dinah asked Yasuko when Yasuko first invited her.

'What about her?'

'She hates me. Haven't you noticed?'

'Oh, Mayumi doesn't like anyone. She has boyfriend troubles. Leave it with me, I will sort it out. There is nothing that a box of butter cookies cannot fix.'

And it seemed that Yasuko was right, because since then Mayumi had left her alone.

Yasuko's colleagues seemed to accept Dinah's presence within their group without comment.

She was happy to be included. The Japanese lecturers were much nicer than her old colleagues. Machiko was pretty and sweet-natured and very pregnant. She would shortly be leaving, but in the meantime was a wonderful, benign presence.

Chiaki was friendly also, though with a sort of madcap air. She broke her silences with sudden bursts of speech, leaning forward with her whole body, her eyes clamouring. Chiaki had a German boyfriend called Dieter whom she had met on exchange in Wales. He was a source of hope and bitter disappointment. He often forgot their weekly Skype calls and he was probably going to forget Chiaki's birthday. She was poised on the brink of tragedy. Remained poised, always, on the brink.

Okinawa very rarely spoke at all. Okinawa was not his real name; that was some kind of joke which Dinah did not understand. However, even Okinawa's silence gave off a grudging aura of good will and amusement.

And then of course there was Yasuko. Dinah felt herself pulled toward her, riveted. She seemed to float, shorn of social markers. Her face with its piquant, elfin chin and rounded apple cheeks. Her one tooth just slightly crooked in the front so that it added a perfect charm to her smile. She wore eye shadow with a faint purple glimmer similar to that worn by the eighteen-year-old students. She seemed to carry a different Louis Vuitton bag each day. She possessed the best of everything, like a joke she was playing on the world. Her gloves were Dents of London and her scarves were Hermès. Her phone case was shaped to look like a kitten. She wore fishnet stockings the same colour as tanned skin.

Teaching was still unpleasant. But every morning, she and Yasuko caught the train together.

The best part of the day, however, was when all of the teachers, except for Okinawa, took the teachers' bus back to the station. They milled at the far end of the platform, as far from the students as possible. The sun shone and Dinah selected a can of fruit drink from the vending machine and it clanked down into the hole. All leisurely now, with the evening stretching ahead. Then the station lights flashed, and Chiaki and Machiko walked to stand at the head of the queue at one door bay, and she and Yasuko at the other. There was a tango studio up above the station, beyond the platform roof and from that angle you could see the couples silently whisking past.

Dinah and Yasuko stood side by side, waiting for the train.

Then the train came, and it was cool and silent and almost empty. Yasuko and Dinah sat next to each other, Chiaki and Machiko halfway down the carriage. They sat holding their paperbacks, their totes on their knees.

Farmland flew past.

The train's speed freed them from the world outside, and that was when they talked.

It had to be noted that the lie still lay between them, but a fine layer of skin had grown across it.

Dinah touched the lie lightly. Something was growing underneath.

'Tell me about your brother,' said Yasuko. 'Are you very close?'

'Oh yes,' said Dinah. 'Sometimes I think we have two halves of the same brain.'

Yasuko watched her with great attention.

'We speak the same language, I guess,' she said.

Yasuko nodded. She understood. She understood everything.

Dinah thought of lying in bed next to Michael, side by side in the dark. She hadn't let herself think of it for a long time, but it did not hurt her. It was a thing that she had noticed since her shift into the new teachers' room, the new routines. Something in Yasuko's presence like a necklace of protection. Her grief resting lighter when they were together; the outside world moving past without a whisper.

'Actually it has nothing to do with speaking,' she said.

Yasuko looked up at that. 'Yes,' she said. 'What a wonderful thing.'

She and Michael were lying facing each other. Something lay between them that lived outside of language. It rendered language unnecessary. The street light was shining through their patchwork curtains. The beds were close enough that she could see every part of his face, and he could see hers. They were mirror images of each other.

It was the relief of it. That was it.

Somebody who saw you, but who was not you. The relief. They used to lie staring at each other like that for hours. It had felt like hours. Dinah would raise an eyebrow; Michael would stretch his mouth. Sometimes this would make them laugh. What passed between them wasn't speech. It was understanding. She felt it deep inside her, the memory of it, the calm of it. It was like swinging from something high up. Like a current that passed between them. Like a glass of clear water. When you moved, even if your thoughts moved, you could see the

129

vibrations. They were trapped, rendered visible.

Yasuko nodded.

'I know exactly,' she said. 'You understood one other completely. You didn't need words. That is how it is with my son.'

As she walked across campus, at lunchtime, Dinah was struck by a feeling that was almost happiness. She walked lightly across the latticed concrete between her classes. She had begun queuing with the students in the cafeteria. This was a new discovery of hers and a good way to avoid the other native English teachers. For a few hundred yen she was given a tray of curry and rice, a bright-pink pickle, green salad. Students greeted her in line. 'Hello, Sensei!' they called. 'Hello, Sensei!'

A holiday. A reprieve. She smiled almost without thinking. 'Hello!' she called. And yet something was coming. It couldn't be a holiday forever.

'Thank you, that looks delicious,' she said to the white-clad woman behind the counter. Her Japanese was improving.

Today Okinawa-san was a few steps ahead in the queue. He saw her also and nodded in a collegial manner. Then, to her surprise, he dropped his place and came back to stand next to her.

The queue inched forward. Neither of them spoke. It was an easy sort of silence. Something Dinah had noticed about Okinawa was that he cultivated a very deliberate, very careful rebelliousness. His hair, for example. It was always neat and cut into a blameless George Harrison–esque bowl cut. However, it was just that one centimetre longer than was truly acceptable for the workplace. Today he was expressing his rebellion via footwear. He had on a pair of plastic slippers of the sort in which old men scuffed to the local bathhouse. The slippers were down at heel and had been conspicuously repaired several times with Sellotape. He was wearing socks too, mismatched.

She glanced down at his feet. Okinawa looked quietly gratified.

'How are you finding the job?' he asked.

Dinah was taken aback. It was almost certainly the first time she had heard him speak straight to her, and definitely the first time she had ever heard him ask a question.

'I like it,' said Dinah. 'It's good. Thank you.'

They shuffled forward. Then he confounded her again by asking a second question.

'Tell me,' he said. 'How are you enjoying working with Yasuko-sensei?'

Of course she could have said something bland and noncommittal. But she felt that Okinawa would see through this, so instead she told the truth.

'I think that she's remarkable.'

Okinawa nodded thoughtfully. 'Yes. Yes.' He seemed pleased with her response. 'I think so too.'

They stood in the queue for another few minutes. Moving forward slowly. She felt a sort of comfort that she was not the only one to be transfixed by Yasuko, not the only one to see something worthy of note about her.

'What do you find remarkable about her?' she asked. She felt quite comfortable, speaking to him. He frowned.

'I have been working here for ten years,' said Okinawa. 'And I have been waiting to see what she would do all that time.'

Dinah turned toward him, giving him the space to speak.

'What do you mean?'

'Just that. Whenever I think about quitting this place, it holds me back. You don't meet someone like her every day.'

'No,' Dinah agreed.

'It's a bit like living with a tiger, isn't it?' Okinawa said.

Dinah smiled. She shook her head to convey that she wasn't sure what Okinawa meant.

'I'm not quite sure what you mean,' she said.

'Aren't you?' He looked at her, over his crooked glasses. 'Well, a tiger is very beautiful, very majestic. But also,' he gestured. 'I'm not sure of the right word in English. You know,' he gestured again, a nondescript sort of swooping movement in the air. 'Very strong.'

Dinah nodded, as if she were following.

'Does one ever really know how long it will last?' asked Okinawa.

'How long it will *last?*' Dinah paused in the queue.

'Yes,' said Okinawa, nodding. 'Exactly.'

She must have looked confused. Okinawa smiled at her kindly.

'Maybe the tiger is not tame at all. Maybe it is merely tolerating us. One day it will return to its natural state and eat us all up.'

Then it was his turn to hold out his plate for curry, and she had no time to ask him to explain.

'Seven-Eleven. Lawson. FamilyMart,' Chiaki was counting them off on her fingers.

'Sunkus,' offered Machiko.

'Oh, yes. Sunkus. That wasn't so bad.'

'Circle K,' said Dinah. 'You forgot Circle K.'

'Oh yes. Their pudding was very forgettable.' She smiled at Dinah.

They were continuing their current lunchtime project, which was ranking the pumpkin puddings that you could buy at the different convenience stores in Tokyo. Everyone spoke in English during the lunch hours. Occasionally the young women returned to speaking Japanese, but then, by some consensus, they would switch back again. Yasuko had not joined them in the half-circle of seats for lunch today. Dinah tried to catch Yasuko's eye; she was reading something at her desk.

'Well?' Machiko asked Chiaki.

Chiaki held the small punnet up higher so that they could all get a good look. It was an important part of proceedings.

'Daily Yamazaki,' she said.

Machiko nodded: serious, focused. They all watched.

Chiaki's spoon hovered above the punnet. They all waited without speaking. The spoon plunged. A mouthful was consumed. Silence as Chiaki tasted, contemplated.

It was Dinah who broke the silence. 'Well?'

'Hmm,' said Chiaki. She took another spoonful.

'Yes?'

'It's ... good.'

'Just good?'

'Actually, *quite* good. It has a nice texture. Not too grainy. It actually tastes like pumpkin.' This was not something to be taken for granted.

Chiaki took another bite. The others waited. Her face soured. 'Oh no,' she said.

Dinah saw the disappointment on Chiaki's face like a blow. How could anybody disappoint Chiaki?

'What is it?' asked Machiko keenly, her voice vibrating in sympathy.

'The caramel.' Chiaki held the punnet up again and indicated the subterranean layer of brown sauce. 'It's *very* bad. Like something died inside it.'

Dinah smiled across at her then turned back to her other colleagues. Chiaki drew her arm back and threw the half-eaten punnet of pudding into the bin. It made an elegant arc, but fell a few centimetres shy of the rim. Chiaki sighed dramatically as if this were her lot in life and went to fetch a cloth to clean the spattered caramel.

Machiko folded her hands across her belly and twinkled.

Chiaki got down on her hands and knees by the bin, wiping up the splatter, but she wasn't silenced. 'Guess where I went this weekend?' she said.

'Shopping for a new sweater?' said Yasuko innocently. Dinah glanced up at her.

Chiaki turned her whole attention to Dinah. 'I went to Beard Papa in Shibuya,' she said, triumphant.

'Oh,' said Dinah. She didn't know what that was.

'No!' said Machiko. 'It has reopened?'

Chiaki nodded. 'Yes! The grand opening was Saturday. You wouldn't believe the queue. All the way past East Exit, down Dogenzaka. As far as the crossing.'

'My word,' said Yasuko. 'And you waited there all that time, just like little dog Hachiko?'

This time Dinah caught Yasuko's eye. A smile passed between them.

'I waited for an hour,' said Chiaki, with great dignity in her hectic eyes and frazzled fringe.

'Was it worth it?' Machiko asked.

Chiaki's forehead was taut with energy and disappointment.

'It was *completely* worth it,' she said. 'Oh my god, you guys. The cheesecake: you have no idea.' Her eyes rolled back and for a brief second her face became an ecstatic mask. 'I almost came.'

Then Yasuko relented. She laughed: dignified, munificent. And they all joined in. Chiaki blossomed in the laughter, like a flower drinking in water.

But the laughter was for Dinah. Dinah primarily.

Dinah sat back in the glow of it. At her desk Yasuko turned her head with a sudden movement, and Dinah thought of Michael, pacing at the back of his primary school classroom. Something moving through the undergrowth: shadowy, beautiful, an unthinking flash of power. 'Maybe the tiger is not tame after all,' Okinawa had said.

But perhaps it was wildness that Dinah missed the most. Entering the classroom alone, the flash moving between them. The sense of election, of standing between the two worlds.

Something was coming, she thought. Something that would change it all.

5

Another way, a third way. It was certainly possible. Yasuko had thought about it and found herself increasingly certain. It had something to do with the girl.

Yasuko was watching the girl. At SDU. On the train. But also, in her mind's eye. This gift had been given back also. When she sat in her empty apartment, she closed her eyes and was able to see, as clear and vital as ordinary sight. She saw the girl sitting in the dusty park next to her apartment. She watched her prowl through the neighbourhood down to the river. Yasuko was surprised to find that she was sympathetic to the girl's plight, even in spite of the bloody-mindedness and blindness of her self-punishment.

The world had offered itself to the girl, as it does to everyone. Here is tempura, it had said; here is silk. Here are tree geckos and fireworks and paper fans. Here is Juyondai sake. Here are the Bach cello suits. Here is Alexander McQueen. Here is the Icelandic language. Here is Tadao Ando and Antoni Gaudí. Offered this richness, the girl had chosen instead a small room in an empty apartment block in a foreign city. She had chosen a six-pack of aloe yoghurt, a bowl of instant ramen, and a chuhai tallboy. She had chosen sleeplessness in the park, and grief.

Yasuko was sitting in the train. Opposite her was the young boy in the cram-school uniform that she had noticed last week. He was seated next to the same office lady — clearly his mother. Mother and son, she thought. The woman looked tired, tolerant. She touched the back of the boy's head with a casualness, almost an indifference. It cut Yasuko to

135

the core. But he will betray you, she thought. He will betray you.

She turned away, back to her thoughts.

The girl's stubbornness and refusal reminded her of something. When Jun was angry with her he used to turn away. Even as a baby. Turning away. Simply refusing to look, to answer. As a toddler once, banging his own head on the wooden frame of the door. When? What had it meant? She thought of a bowl of white rice with a red plum in its centre. A child has no control over anything. No choices. No power to wound except by punishing the self. No means for revenge except by withholding. The ability to turn its head away.

'We are sending you a girl.' But what for? She still didn't know the girl's purpose.

Was Dinah's company meant to offer some sort of compensation for the loss of her son? She had set about befriending her, in any case. It was not difficult to do so. Before they had met, the girl had never visited the market floor at the bottom of Seibu. She had never been to Shinjuku Isetan. She had never eaten ikura, had never had a martini at the top of the Shinjuku Park Hyatt. It was an easy pleasure to introduce her to these things. To teach her to crush the salmon eggs with one's tongue until they released the sweet salt oil that was intoxicating in its recollection of the origins of life itself. Yasuko took delight in dazzling her with the boundlessness of Tokyo's consumer choices. You want a pair of sandals? Here are the floors and floors of sandals. You want a strap for your phone? A new lipstick? A coffee brewed as they do in Tibet? Follow me.

She had asked the beetle. 'What am I meant to do with her?' She had bought four more beetles and the answer still wasn't clear.

She waited now, listening to the currents of the city.

What did it mean?

Impatience and fear rising in her. Mother and son.

The pair were directly opposite her, the boy's head shining. She caught his eye and he ducked down, bashfully. At this age Jun had been watchful also, but bold. He had held her hand firmly and stared the world down. That had been his age of nightmares. He woke and told her things that made no sense, and she had feared he had been given her gift. He was a gentle soul; what would he do with such affliction? 'I was sinking into the ground. My eyes were covered over.' She held him and felt a wave of relief and gratitude that she had rescued him from her father.

She watched the boy opposite. He had sensed her looking, and looked up, then away. She held her gaze, and when he looked up the next time, he did not duck, but caught her eye, and she smiled. With a quiet, happy calm the boy leaned his head back against his mother's arm, watching her. Yasuko offered him a wave. Just a small motion, and a smile that was genuine. Then with a flash of inspiration, she pulled a square of notepaper from her tote. She placed her Vuitton flat across her knee, the paper on top. She folded swiftly. Under her hands a little bird took shape. She cupped it, blew the breath of life inside so that it took flight and fluttered across the carriage.

Paper wings, feathered wings. The boy held out his hands. Caught it in the cage of his fingers.

What alerted his mother was the small noise of delight he made, the pleasure of a secret and clever trick. When she looked down her son was holding a small origami bird, and she nodded a confused but polite thank you to the woman seated opposite with her gleaming hair and eyes.

In that moment Yasuko understood. It was very simple.

At the height of her powers, her son would find her hideous, repulsive. But Dinah would see her and understand. The girl would be the bridge, the pathway. She would be the one to draw them back together.

Yasuko settled back into her seat and did not look back up again until she heard the reluctant double hiss of the internal carriage door opening.

As usual the odour was what alerted her first. So thick as to be almost a bodily presence. There was a familiar shift in the carriage toward a slightly altered silence. A retraction as the women — and they were almost all women — drew subtly inward. Yasuko caught the boy's eyes and widened her own. The boy transferred his earnest gaze to her as if for safekeeping. Then his mother's hand came from behind and tapped his head down and he bowed again.

The homeless man took his usual path down the carriage, swinging along the handles. Everyone was seated. There was no impediment to his progress. He dragged his feet behind him, his toenails clacking. He chuckled at something invisible. He stopped in the same place as he had previously, directly in front of the boy and his mother.

'You again!' he said. 'Little larvae!'

The boy raised his eyes to look.

'Little squirmer. Little blind one,' he crowed. He put his face right down to the boy's clear eyes. 'Why don't you break free, little one! Break free! They're trying to put you in a cage. They'll lock you up and throw away the key.' Yasuko could only imagine the smell of his breath in such close quarters. The boy sat calm and polite and looked down with respect.

The mother did not flinch, but she did raise her head slightly, to politely acknowledge the man.

'I'm telling you the truth. Look what I have! Look how I know!'

Then the man lifted his blue tunic. He revealed a weathered stomach, concave and muscled. On the field of flesh was a large ancient scar, neat and white. It was the shape of an L on its side.

'This is how I know,' he said. 'Because I am already *dead*. I am a ghost. None of these others will tell you.'

The boy stared up at him, his lips serious, struggling to understand, and for a long while after there was a moment in which nothing happened. Then the man reached out and began to stroke the boy's dark, shining hair. One might argue that the man could not be blamed for this impulse. The boy's hair was very beautiful. It was as black as water and it shone like polished wood. The man reached the edge of the boy's hair where it met his neck and raised a hand to stroke again.

She did not have to put up with this anymore. She did not need to be demure, to sit and bow her head.

Yasuko sat forward in her seat.

'Leave the boy alone. You don't know anything, Grandpa. Not a single thing.'

The man paused and turned. Something old woke up in his face, and he sneered with delight and leaned forward toward Yasuko. He pushed his chin out and inclined his body toward her.

'You,' he said. 'You!' Then he stood taller like a defiant child and raised his voice. 'I see you, lady. Nice clothes, and nice breeding. But you're just the same as me, lady. You're dead too. You're a ghost just like me.'

The train was travelling past an immense low-rise white factory complex, rice paddies, a conurbation of dormitory apartments each painted a different shade: pale orange, pale pink, pale green, duck-egg blue.

Something changed in the carriage. It was a thing that was happening to Yasuko. A rippling and a shivering like a quake that began beneath the water. A fluid toppling that started in her feet and rose up, peerless and unchecked, through the long bones of her legs and out to each part, irradiating them.

It was anger. So intense that it was like joy. It built and built, and expanded inside her until it found her edges, and tested them — almost as one tests the pressure of a car tyre. She was no longer a woman but simply anger in a woman's shape. How much of her must have been extraneous before.

When Yasuko spoke her voice was clear and cutting. 'What tipped you over the edge, old man? Did the wife catch you diddling your daughter? Did the boss catch you with your hand in the till?' She stood up. 'What makes you think you can stink up this train carriage with your craziness? What makes you think you can touch this boy?'

The man released the vinyl strap and looked at Yasuko.

'The people here don't want to see your stinking stomach. You should be ashamed of yourself. And that scar. Put it away. It's just another thing you failed at, isn't it?'

The train was slowing; the tannoy sang a little tune. They were nearing the final stop before Ikebukuro. The man mumbled and stepped backwards. He pulled his shirt closed over the old suicide scar and hunched his shoulders. The train slowed before you could see the

139

station, and suddenly there it was — an arc of concrete around them, a yellow line running parallel, and brakes braking. He had pulled into himself and stood now like a parody of good citizenship, queueing in the correct spot as he waited for the doors to push themselves open.

Yasuko watched. She reached into her wallet and removed some change. 'Don't you want your money?' she said.

The door pushed itself open with a reluctant sigh, and the man turned back and stared at her. Several emotions were battling it out. Fear, envy, a vestige of pride. He extended his palm toward the woman.

'Here's 2,000 yen,' said Yasuko. 'Go home and do it properly this time.' She stood, and with an underarm tossed a handful of change onto the concrete of the platform.

The tannoy voice chimed again, and the homeless man scowled and hunched as if acknowledging the justice of his punishment. Then he ducked again and made his run for it onto the platform, chasing after the coins, tramping them down to arrest their roll, falling to his knees and stretching his arms out to retrieve them from the new homes they had found for themselves beneath the vending machines.

Yasuko sat back calmly on her seat. She smoothed her silk skirt beneath her legs.

6

It was Machiko's farewell dinner. It seemed to them all that she had been pregnant forever, but time had been marching along all the while and she could not be pregnant for much longer. It was time for her to go away and leave them. Time for her to have her baby.

Here they were tonight, then, all the Japanese English programme staff to celebrate this important moment. They would send Machiko off to motherhood in style. Yasuko, Chiaki, and the new honorary team member, Dinah. Okinawa had demurred, of course. 'He is a socialist,' said Yasuko. 'But not really the socialising type.'

Things had changed between the four of them over the last few weeks. As Yasuko and Dinah became closer, a sense of the other two curving round them. Dinah could feel Chiaki's jealousy.

Other things changed also. She was still sleeping in the park, but it no longer disturbed her as it had done. Leaving Itabashi station at the end of the workday, walking back toward her apartment, the lightness followed her step by step. Still, she felt that there was a test coming. She didn't know what it would be.

Tonight they had together entered a kind of toppling hilarity. Clearly neither Chiaki nor Machiko had realised what had been apparent to her for some time now. How delightfully *rude* Yasuko could be. She had embarrassed them all in the train by speaking in loud whispers about the man who had started asking her out on dates. He was a Beatrix Potter scholar, she said. In his sixties.

'It is time I settled down and found a man to look after me. The older ones are reliable, at least. Or so I have found. And quite generous, you know. When it comes time for the Mr McGregor role-play, I'm sure he will provide the little blue jacket!'

They had all stifled giggles. She could see Machiko's eyes widen. Impossible to imagine. Yasuko with her twin set, her Chanel necklace, her wisdom.

The queue at Malabar Indian Restaurant doubled and tripled around itself in the atrium, so that people could wait in the air-conditioned cool. Behind the glass counter that divided the guests from the kitchen, a tall white-jacketed young man stretched tablets of dough with his finger-tips until they were shaped like tears. In spite of the fierce air-con, his handsome face was wet with sweat. Yasuko raised her eyes suggestively at Dinah.

They were seated. Machiko and Chiaki ordered mango lassi. Dinah and Yasuko ordered jockeys of Kingfisher beer. There was the sensation of being on a platform with invisible machinery moving an apparatus beneath her. She could not resist turning, turning toward the light that Yasuko gave out. Something was bound to happen, she knew. It was a special night.

'You don't mean to tell me you have never *noticed* the hidden meanings in Jeremy Fisher? His dear little rod and his bobbing red tackle?'

Yasuko gestured lewdly and Chiaki giggled, helpless.

Dinah felt the air crackling with danger. Something was coming, but what was it?

Above them was a painting. Dinah found herself examining it like a puzzle.

It was strangely one-dimensional, and yet several things were happening in it all at once.

In it was a hunting party, on horses and elephants and in boats. It was very detailed, and you could make out the differing facial expressions of each man: anguish, excitement, valour, fear. Across the breadth of the landscape there were three different tigers painted. From left to right, the first was walking, snarling, teeth bared. The next was leaping into the air above the guns cocked by the hunting party. The final tiger was in the river below, swimming toward a tongue of rock.

As a group they ordered, and after some time another young man appeared at their table. He was carrying an immense platter of grilled food, which he set down slowly on their table. His dark-grey polyester Nehru jacket was shiny with grease and improper ironing. He was certainly less well-favoured than the dashing chef.

The arrival of the food signalled a new mood — the deep, thoughtful acquisitiveness of hunger. The four of them arranged a fair distribution of the chicken pieces, the enormous prawns, the meat kebabs. When their plates were piled with orange meat, Yasuko took the closest prawn with her fingers. She raised it to her mouth as if she meant to kiss it or to use it as a microphone, then she decisively bit off its head.

They ate, in silence, for a while. Dinah could feel Yasuko's electric mood, the resonance of it drawing them all together. Something was coming. Something. She looked at Yasuko and at that exact moment the older woman drew herself taller and began to speak.

'Tell me,' she said to all of them. 'Who of you has Keisuke Kobayashi in their class?'

Chiaki looked round. She cast a brief glance at Dinah.

'Keisuke Kobayashi,' Chiaki said, as if pondering.

'He's quite good-looking — tallish and with the hair, you know,' Yasuko continued, gesturing to suggest the frosted, whipped coiffeur that was popular amongst the young men.

Dinah didn't know the student. 'Perhaps.' To be honest, she was still having difficulty with some of the students' names.

Yasuko leaned across the table. 'I think you'd know him if I pointed him out. His girlfriend too. Masumi. He's actually taking conversational English for the second time. He failed last year.'

Chiaki picked up her mango lassi and sipped. 'I have Masumi,' she said, 'in my grammar class. She is lovely. I don't know what she sees in him.'

'Well, I met Keisuke-san for a private tutorial yesterday. If he doesn't pass English this year, he will fail his degree and his father will disown him.'

Machiko laughed. 'You always inspire such confidences, Y-chan!'

'Heaven knows why,' said Yasuko. 'Perhaps they see my maternal side.' She batted her eyelashes. 'He wanted an extension on his assignment. Told me all about his family life. All about his mother. He confessed all of his problems with Masumi. He's very mixed up.'

'He doesn't deserve Masumi,' said Chiaki. Her voice was full of irritation.

Yasuko smiled at her. 'You are lucky you are able to avoid such pastoral care, Chiaki-san. It is very exhausting. However, Keisuke told me a funny story, to explain things. I thought you would all like to hear it.'

They all nodded and murmured sounds of agreement.

'Well, as Keisuke told me, his mother is very beautiful. In fact she used to be a well-known tarento.'

'Oh yes,' said Chiaki. 'I did know that. She was in a Lancôme commercial a few years ago.' She searched out her phone and began scrolling for images.

Yasuko tapped her nails on her glass.

'Yes, but that is not the point. What he told me is that his mother has a fatal flaw. Did you know this?'

Chiaki was intent on her phone. Dinah shook her head.

'She always falls in love with ugly men.' Yasuko chuckled. 'Ugly men. Isn't that funny? Something in her is drawn to the ones with deformities. A large nose. A club-foot. It's like a sickness — she can't fight it. This is what Keisuke told me. Just like a fairy tale.

'This is how it goes: Once upon a time, Keisuke's mother was a young woman and she fell in love with a man with one leg. It was not the leg that sparked her admiration, but his face — just the right sort of ugly for her. Large lips. Low brow. The type that looks like one of those big goldfish, if you know what I mean.

'They were deeply in love for several years, she and the one-legged man, and engaged to be married. Then one day, just after a lunch date, he up and disappeared. Not a word or a phone call. She thought he must have died, but a body was never discovered.

'Of course she was heartbroken, but she was also confused. She

144

didn't know whether to grieve him or curse him. After several long months she met Keisuke's father. He was the photographer on one of her shoots. He was pleasant-looking, and he had been in love with her for some time from a distance. She was so confused that after two dates she agreed to marry him. Some time afterward she fell pregnant with Keisuke, and her life settled into its current course.'

Chiaki looked up at Yasuko. She had put her phone down and was smiling, waiting for Yasuko's point.

'Anyway, finally we come to Keisuke's big excuse. His reason for not currently applying himself to his studies. Last week this old paramour just showed up at their door. Completely out of the blue. Keisuke answered the door, and the one-legged man was standing there, ugly as a slapped face, wearing a blue shell suit with the leg pinned up. "Is your mother home?" he says. Apparently he knew straightaway who Keisuke was, because he looked so much like his mother.'

Each of them was transfixed, listening. Machiko was chuckling under her breath softly.

'And then the mother comes along. She sees who it is at the door. And right in front of Keisuke she walks into the bedroom to get her purse, she gives Keisuke a kiss on the forehead, and then she leaves. Forever. She walks away from a marriage and two children: a teenaged son and a five-year-old daughter. Can you believe it?'

'I can't believe it,' said Machiko. 'What sort of mother ...'

'Well, exactly,' said Yasuko, smiling at them all. The moment lasted for a few seconds, but it seemed longer. It stretched.

Dinah cleared her throat and looked at her drink.

'Did you give it to him?' Chiaki said.

'Give what to him?' said Yasuko.

'The extension on his assignment?'

Yasuko was smiling now, solely at Chiaki, as if delighted by the question.

'Oh no,' she said. 'That would not have been fair to the others.'

Chiaki laughed with pleasure. Yasuko was just too subtle, too perfect. She paused, thinking.

'So what are his problems with Masumi?' she asked.

Yasuko was suddenly very serious. She shrugged.

'He has realised that he is not in love with her and they must break up. It turns out he has the same problem as his mother. He can only fall for ugly women.'

Dinah looked up at the painting again. There was the first tiger, she thought, with all of those teeth. There was the second tiger, leaping into the path of its bullet. There was the final tiger, swimming across the river, seeking land, but never arriving. Swimming, swimming, with a grimace of anger. She shook her head. Why had it taken her so long to understand? There were not three tigers, but only one. There was only one tiger.

It was important not to take this moment for granted, she thought. Something was coming and when it did it would change everything. When it happened, she would wish to remember everything, all of this detail. It would all at last be part of the tale.

'And there I was,' said Yasuko. '"Aha," I thought. "Here is my chance. He is finally single."' She delivered her line with relish and sat back, regarding them across the debris of the meal.

Chiaki's eyes flickered. It was clear she was searching for what she should say, for the right thing with which to respond. Dinah felt no guilt for interrupting.

'It would never work,' Dinah said.

'What wouldn't?' asked Yasuko.

'You and Keisuke.'

'Well, no. I was only joking. I am old enough to be his mother.'

Dinah saw Chiaki smile a little into her drink. But Dinah had all the time in the world, so she sat calmly, as if she held something in her palm and was turning it over in order to examine it. There was only one correct answer to Yasuko's story, and she had it, so she used her time to speak slowly, carefully.

'Not due to that,' she said. 'It would never work because you are far too beautiful for him.'

Yasuko looked up. Her furred eyelashes, her heart-shaped face,

146

her acne-scarred skin, and the rest of her luminous beauty. Her smile conferred a fine approval. She gave it to Dinah and in that instant the entire restaurant was lit.

7

They were walking, Dinah and Yasuko. They had left the restaurant together. It had not been discussed; Chiaki and Machiko had simply peeled away to go to the station, while she and Yasuko had continued on. Dinah saw nothing to her right or left as they walked. She focused on a spot just ahead of her face and allowed her peripheral vision to fall away. In this fashion it was possible to believe that the pair of them were floating. A bubble suspended. The world even more beautiful than she had imagined.

Whatever-it-was had happened, Dinah thought. It had happened, but it was still happening.

They walked through Harajuku. Yasuko stopped. They were right in the middle of the pavement and there was a shout of irritation from behind. A group of schoolgirls who had been following pushed roughly past them. One narrowly avoiding hitting Dinah.

'What is it?' asked Dinah.

'It is driving me crazy,' said Yasuko. Her voice had changed. There was a new richness to it, an urgency.

'What is?'

Yasuko swished her hands around her head as if a fly were buzzing there. She resumed walking. Dinah followed her, a little behind. They were nearing Yoyogi Park.

'I have been trying to distract myself with work,' said Yasuko. 'And men. There are men out there who want to spend time with me. But I cannot do it anymore. Do you know, I used to have hours to read, to listen to music. But all the time has gone, just evaporated. There is none left. I don't have time to do anything. And I am terrified. Terrified. When I sit down, I can hear my heart going.'

It was so exactly Dinah's own experience, so exactly how she felt — the emptiness and panic at once — that through a door in her chest came a breathlessness, a weightlessness, a feeling as if someone had pushed air into the space there. She didn't know if she could speak.

'Why do you think you feel like this?' She said it calmly, with utter familiarity. Any other tone would have been incorrect.

'I think he took it all with him. Time. He took it. Is that foolish?'

Dinah looked at Yasuko's face. It was remarkably the same. The agony was so much a part of the other balanced elements of her face. There was no surprise at all in this transition in their relationship, this move into a greater intimacy or revelation. She saw that they had been moving in this direction all along. It was part of a larger shape.

'Who has gone, Yasuko?'

'I have approached this in a back-to-front way,' Yasuko said, and paused. They waited at the pedestrian crossing. 'And I am so tired. Though that is probably just age.'

Dinah reached out and touched the yellow pole. A gentle feeling of blur around the periphery of her vision.

'No. I feel that too. I think it is grief.' Dinah looked back across the flow of foot traffic. 'Grief is very tiring.' The words left her, found their way to Yasuko.

'Indeed? That is curious. Why do you think that is?'

'I think because when you lose someone, you have to relearn everything. You have to learn the whole world all over again. But the world without that person in it. That takes a lot of energy, and a very long time.'

Yasuko was watching her.

Dinah kept talking. 'That's what I think. But I never trust any of it, you know. Before I walk across the street or get off a train, I think: what if that's not concrete? It might as well be sand. Or jelly. Is there any reason for it to be concrete more than sand? I have forgotten the reason, if there is. Whatever held things together. Whatever that was.'

'Yes,' said Yasuko. She didn't look surprised at Dinah's words. The crossing signal had stopped flashing, and they were still standing there on the same traffic island.

Yasuko turned to face Dinah. 'And how about you? Do you get angry?'

'Yes,' said Dinah. 'Oh yes.'

'I find myself so full of anger!' said Yasuko. 'I have great surges of it. It comes up from nowhere. It's almost a relief when it comes. But afterward I think that I am even more tired than before.' She laughed without mirth.

Dinah nodded. The mood hung between them like a spider's web. If she put out her hand or spoke too loudly, she might disturb it. A sound came from her throat that was like a sob, but it was not one.

'Who have you lost, Yasuko?' she asked. The unnamed emotion approached like a rising tide. She knew the answer already.

'I talk about Jun as if he were just sitting at home, waiting for me.'

Dinah nodded.

Yasuko turned to her. 'Why shouldn't I? Maybe he is there after all. Sitting in his room, reading his novel. Perhaps when I get home tonight, I'll call out and he'll come out into the kitchen and we will chat, just like we always do.'

'Yes,' Dinah said. She felt the burden of love and sympathy along her cheekbones and shoulders.

'When I am with you I feel this could be true. I feel that it is true in some way. I don't know why this is.'

'Yes,' Dinah said.

Yasuko turned to look at her. 'Maybe in the same way you feel it is true about your brother.'

Here was the secret then. Dinah had been nursing it, hiding it, like a shameful wound that could not be exposed to the air. And yet she should not have worried. Yasuko had known of it and seen it from the beginning. Everything had already been understood. Understood and forgiven. She and Yasuko were joined in the fluid warm air of understanding that was the same temperature as blood or skin and offered no resistance or pain.

The rest of the street had disappeared. Yasuko looked at her. She extended her hand.

'Come. If I hold your arm we can cross. If it is not concrete but sand, then we will drown together.'

They crossed. The ground held them up and was warm. They entered the park.

In Yoyogi the blossom had disappeared and the trees were in full green leaf. Yasuko stopped at a vendor's stand at the threshold gates and bought a paper carton of takoyaki.

A group of men were standing in a circle just inside the gates. Their hair was curved into tall, hard quiffs and they wore pegged jeans, plaid shirts, crepe-soled shoes. They were listening to rock and roll, and dancing. One by one they entered the circle and performed their dance. It was a bending, contorted dance, with movements that seemed full of symbolic meaning. There was a rocking back, a retreating, a leaping up.

One of the dancers in the circle was much older than the others, as if he had been there for lifetimes, dancing in some form of private expiation. His face was crooked, an asymmetry that was hard to place. He fixed them with a long, hard look as they approached. It was a look that had intimidation in it, and as they drew nearer Dinah saw the crooked place was in fact a scar, an old disfigurement along the seam of his jaw. She turned quickly from his gaze and they walked on.

They came to the foot of a tree. Yasuko reached inside her bag and removed two of the magazines one could pick up for free at HMV and Kinokuniya. She passed one to Dinah and laid the other down for herself.

It was as if Dinah knew the story, knew the landscape they were moving through. It was all very familiar to her. There were reeds and rushes and mist. But there was something new. Something that flexed inside her and put out a new bone structure. Go slow. Move slowly on the plank that is extended. One step, then another.

'Tell me how you lost your brother,' said Yasuko.

Dinah looked at the grass.

'He was studying performance piano. In Auckland. It was the last year of his degree.'

'I see.'

'He was meant to be going to the Royal College in London for postgraduate study. Everything was fine. Then he stopped playing.'

'Why? Why did he stop?'

'It was going wrong for a long time, but then it went properly wrong.'

'Poor boy,' said Yasuko. 'How awful.'

'I thought he would get better. He went home for a while. Then he moved back out. He was on medication. I had all that time when I could have helped him. That is what I find hardest, I think. That whole time, when I was losing him, I could have done something different.'

Yasuko sat very still. 'I am sorry,' she said. 'I am very sorry.'

'When it actually happened it was like being in a train carriage that comes off the rails,' said Dinah.

By 'happened' she meant the phone call in which she had been told of his death. Even with Yasuko she was still a long way from being able to use such words.

'I remember the feeling of flying through the air and knowing it was too much to survive. That I would never recover from it.'

In her mind she saw the train's vertebrae, its nervature. She saw the carriage that had housed her and Michael moving impossibly through the air, away from all the old links and couplings.

'But, you know, I don't remember the crash. I just remember waking up afterward. And how it was so strange that the world was all still there.'

'Yes,' said Yasuko.

'I was wrong about that, though,' said Dinah.

'What do you mean, wrong?'

'It wasn't really the world. It was a new place. It was completely different.'

152

'How so? How was it different?'

'It wasn't the world anymore, it was just the field where the train wreck had happened.'

Yasuko nodded.

'There was grass growing under the carriages. That is what surprised me the most. It was still growing. Everything was continuing on under the wreckage. Insects moving, going about their lives. Birds. Each going about their insect life, their bird life. I thought, "That's what the world is now." I knew I could never get back to the other place, where I was on a journey, going somewhere. I couldn't get back even if I tried. So …' She shrugged. 'That's where you have to live. In that other world. The one that belongs to the grass and the birds and the insects.'

Dinah thought she felt tears on her cheeks, but it was just sweat, rolling down. She didn't try to wipe it off.

'It is a very good description,' said Yasuko, 'of survival.'

'It doesn't feel like survival.'

'No.' They sat next to each other.

'What made him stop playing the piano? I am curious about that.'

Dinah thought about how best to explain. 'He was injured.'

'His fingers? His hands?'

Dinah saw him as she had in the car window, cradling his hand. But that had not been Michael. That had been her own reflection.

'No. Something inside his brain.' She didn't want to explain. She didn't want to use the right words, the words of diagnosis and explanation.

'Do you know that science experiment, where you put a straw in water? You look at it one way, it's straight. The other way, it's broken.'

'Yes, of course. My father was a scientist. *Refraction.*'

'Yes, we did that experiment at school. That was Michael. I thought it at the time, and it's still true. He could make two things real at once. He made whatever was inside his head real. He made it true. When we were young, everyone was worried about it. Then when he was good at music, they all said, "Ah, well, that's the reason."'

Yasuko was nodding and nodding.

'I see.'

Good at music. His gift taking off at speed. She was standing behind, watching. Left behind in the world without Michael's magic. It had been so thin at first, so terrifyingly thin and lonely.

'But it wasn't enough,' she said. 'In the end. Music.'

'Yes.'

'And then it got worse.'

'Yes.'

'But do you know the real reason he died?'

'No. Will you tell me?'

Dinah paused. It was a shock to feel that the reprieve of the last few weeks had come to an end. She had had a holiday from her memories and her guilt, but that couldn't last. She might as well get the worst of it over.

She tried to breathe through this emotion and she looked through it, at Yasuko.

'He died because I betrayed him.'

Yasuko laughed.

At first Dinah did not understand. She thought Yasuko was coughing, but no, it was definitely laughter. Then Yasuko shook her head.

'Of course you betrayed him,' she said. 'That's how it is with people you love. It was the same with Jun and me. That doesn't make it your fault that he died.' She shook her head again.

It was remarkable that Dinah felt better. Yasuko had not known Michael, or anything about their relationship, but still she felt something drift away. She put her hand out on the threadbare grass. She wanted another beer.

'I'm sorry,' she said.

'What for?' There seemed a warning in her voice, but Dinah ignored it.

'For lying. For letting you think Michael was alive.'

Yasuko shook her head. 'There is no need for apology between us.'

Dinah sat silently. She didn't know if she should ask the next question, but she drew on a reserve in herself. She closed her eyes. She thought of the train and its awful violent rupture.

'When did Jun die?' she asked.

She closed her eyes and waited, but there was no sound. It did not come, the jolt. Yasuko reached out a hand to hers.

'Oh, darling. He isn't dead.'

Dinah's body flooded with such relief that she could not see for a few seconds. The canopy of light and air remained intact. They were floating together.

'Your son isn't dead? He's still alive?'

Yasuko nodded. 'Yes. I am sorry. He is alive. It's a much smaller matter.'

Dinah blinked. 'Where is he, then?'

Yasuko shook her head. She was smiling, but it was a rueful smile.

'To be honest, I couldn't tell you. That is the problem. Of course he was always entitled to leave home. It's hardly unusual to do so. He is twenty-one. An adult. But, well, if you knew Jun …' She smiled and shook her head ruefully. 'He has made it some sort of grand statement. To punish me. All or nothing.'

Dinah nodded.

'And. Well, I am worried about him. We are very close. We have always been close — and he is very trusting. But he is not as wise as he thinks he is. So that is the world I am in. It is not the same kind of loss as yours.'

'Haven't you seen him since he left?'

Yasuko shook her head.

'Oh no. He is not even speaking to me at present. He does answer my text messages. I should be grateful for that. But he writes like a robot. He won't even say what I have done wrong. I understand, as a parent, that I should ignore him. I should let him get it out of his system. But it is harder than I thought. I am quite a weak person. I have become so used to having him with me. It is like having a part of oneself amputated. Do you know what I mean?'

Dinah blinked. It struck her. She nodded.

'Would you like to see a photo of my awful son?'

'Of course,' said Dinah.

Yasuko awoke her phone. She scrolled and selected a photograph and held it out to Dinah.

Dinah took the phone and held the photograph up so that it caught the light. The eyes of the young man on the screen met hers and seemed to look away also. It was a startlingly clear image, caught in autumn light. He was standing under a ginkgo tree that was almost too perfect: its leaves clear, unblemished yellow.

She saw that his face had a pleasing symmetry and that there was something guarded in his eyes. His mouth was slightly open, his hand slightly raised, as if he were speaking to the photographer, asking for a reprieve of some sort. His eyes were green, and his hair was a lighter brown than Yasuko's. It was a beautiful, diffident face.

She nodded.

Dinah tapped the photograph on Yasuko's phone to undim it. She looked again at the face. Yasuko was watching her. As if she had given her a piece of work and was waiting for her.

'Do you have his phone number?'

Yasuko looked up at her. Her lips slightly turned down at the corners. She didn't speak.

'Yes,' she said. 'Why?'

'Perhaps I could speak to him.'

'Really? You would do that for me?'

'Of course, if you think it might help.'

'I'm not sure, to be honest. Probably he won't even answer.' She paused, thinking. 'You know, he has asked for space. I should let him have it.'

Dinah felt an unexpected disappointment. She passed the phone back to Yasuko. The yellow ember of the image kindled in her memory and then faded.

'Of course,' said Dinah. 'But if I can do anything, please let me know. Let me know if you change your mind.'

They walked to the station. It was still quite early. They boarded the Yamanote in the direction of Shinjuku.

'Where do you live, Yasuko?' asked Dinah, when they had arrived and disembarked on the platform in Shinjuku.

'Oh, not far from here.'

Yasuko looked up at the train boards. 'You need to get the Saikyo,' she said. 'But I don't think you should. I don't think you should do that. Come with me.'

Dinah followed Yasuko through the complex maze of Shinjuku station. It was still just as much a mystery to her as ever, the tides of people. She knew where she was and yet didn't. Yasuko pointed to their left and they took a corridor and then an exit she did not recognise and had in fact never once used. They emerged on a street, and there were concrete planters nearby and Yasuko gestured for her to sit on the low wall they formed.

'Now, please. Wait here,' she said.

Dinah waited. There were taxis at the rank opposite the bench, squat and silent. A few minutes later Yasuko returned, carrying a large white carrier bag with black handles. She took Dinah's arm gently then and they crossed the road, their elbows linked together, like an old-fashioned courting couple. Next she leaned into one of the cabs and spoke to the driver and passed some money through the window. Dinah saw what she was doing and protested. 'No,' she said. 'I can pay.'

Yasuko shook her head. She held Dinah by the wrists and stood back to regard her. Then she escorted her around to the other side of the curb and the taxi door.

'I have a secret for you, my friend,' she said. 'But you must not blame me. I almost don't wish to tell you, in case it worries you. But it is part of our shared story.'

'Tell me,' said Dinah. She was intrigued and leaned in toward her friend. Yasuko leaned forward also so that she was speaking close to Dinah's ear. Her voice came, low and sweet.

'Michael will come back. He will come back.'

Dinah almost stumbled, but Yasuko's arm bore her up. She wished to ask Yasuko what she meant, but could not bring herself to do so.

The sky was a fuzzy pink, particulate, like static. It had the appearance of something too full, almost pregnant with its own substance.

Dinah shook her head. Yasuko fixed her with her speaking eyes.

'Michael will return,' she said again.

Dinah shook her head, and the blur returned. The world for a moment lifted and changed.

'Really?' Dinah asked. Something came to her that she thought might be happiness. It was unfamiliar and welcome. She rendered herself up to it. Just for a second.

'Of course. I am right,' said Yasuko. 'I always am. Which means you have no choice but to trust me.'

Dinah was inside the taxi now, the door still open.

'I do,' she said.

By some miracle it seemed that she was speaking the truth.

'Good,' said Yasuko. 'And this is for you.' She placed the carrier bag on Dinah's knee. 'But don't open it until you are at home.'

Yasuko spoke to the driver. The door swung shut by some invisible force, and the taxi pulled out and away down Meiji-dori. Dinah looked back, but her friend was looking away already, up toward the sky of Ikebukuro.

8

Yasuko walked up Meiji-dori. She would taxi also, she thought. But not yet. Not yet. The sky opened up to her and the city spoke and she was walking to Aoyama. The path had opened up ahead, and she was flying.

9

Dinah placed the carrier bag on the table. She cleared the pile of advertising circulars, the plate from this morning's breakfast, the new letter that had been misdirected, sent to a different prefecture, finally redirected to the correct address.

She looked at the carrier bag on the cleared table and reached inside. It held a box made of thick, quality cardboard, white as snow, white as bed linen, folded along pre-scored lines. Inside the box she felt something shift, an object both heavy and unevenly weighted. It slid.

She put the box down in order to delay the moment of opening. She went to the bathroom, studied her face in the mirror. Her heart was beating. She washed her hands and face, removed her make-up. She drew the curtains so she could see the light outside.

Then she walked back to the table and opened the lid.

Inside was a pie. It was the pie from Shinjuku, the one that she had not bought. She sat down.

Had anything before ever been so beautiful? It was unlikely. The pastry was crisp and fragile like a bank of fine, sunny, buttery sand. The apples and sweet potato were so thinly sliced they were transparent. Glimpses of the apples' perfect pink skin shone through the caramel glaze, like flowers caught under ice. It was a fairy tale of a pie, a platonic vision of a pie. It was a pie you might find cooling on a windowsill with a red gingham cloth beneath. She folded the lid to prop up the interior, so that the box sat on the table like an expensive display case. Then she took a knife from the drawer and cut herself a thin slice. She took a clean plate from the cupboard and returned to the table and placed the thin slice of pie on the middle of the plate. She sat down.

Outside it had started to rain lightly, and the sky was a vessel slowly filling with dark resonance. There must be a hole in it somewhere, something leaking in. She thought about that bit of lore — was it true? — that if you were in a car accident and the car was submerged, you had to wait until the vehicle filled up with water, until the pressure of inside and outside equalised. Then and only then, you pushed the door open and swum out. What strange beauty there must be in that darkness, she thought. The car's headlights illuminating the silt-world of the water. You would not need to surface then. You would be able to swim forever.

She looked at the piece of pie on the plate, then she took a fork and ate the first mouthful. She placed her head in her hands.

His voice was there. It was just the same.

'Are you crying?' he said.

'Don't be stupid,' she said.

'You *are* crying.'

Of course she was crying. She couldn't stop it. Warm tears ran down her cheeks. She couldn't stop them. She didn't want to stop them. There was so much pleasure in the warm flow and in the opening and release inside her, like a valve. The more she chewed the pie, the flavour of caramel like the answer to a supplication or prayer for forgiveness, the quicker and more wonderful was the flow of tears.

'Why in god's name are you crying because of a pie, Dinah?'

She didn't have to answer or explain. She didn't have to do anything. But relief made her generous. She sat up; she looked up.

'Because it's so beautiful,' she said. 'And because somebody gave it to me. It was a gift.'

The voice was so familiar that it lulled her. She continued. 'And I'm crying because I forgot,' she said. 'I can't believe that I'd forgotten.'

'What did you forget?'

It was Michael's voice. Of course it was. It had never gone away. But something — this relief, this flood, the warmth and the beauty of it — had made sufficient space for it.

'Hello?' the voice asked. 'I'm still here. Forgot what?'

He was right here. Here in the room with the other shadows. The shape of her futon, half-made. Darkness of shadow. Darkness of a substance that was not shadow.

She stood slowly and walked into the room. She did so without looking directly at the shape in the corner.

'Is that you?'

'Of course,' said Michael. 'Who else?'

The outline of Michael's arms, folded. His profile. The side of his cheek. Was it? She looked at what might be the side of his cheek then looked away. She looked back. She looked at his jaw, the familiar set of it. She saw the flickering of the pulse at his neck.

'Forgot about what?' he asked again. 'Not about me?'

'Forgot about beauty,' Dinah said. Said it to herself, really. 'I forgot that beauty could exist simply for its own sake,' she said, 'because it didn't apply to me anymore.'

'That was very solipsistic of you,' Michael said.

Dinah didn't say anything. She sat in the half-light of the apartment. There was a glow in the sky from the street lights and from a moon that had risen very low in the sky. She didn't want to move or say anything, because she didn't want to disturb the room or find that it was empty after all.

'I'm still here,' said Michael. 'Still watching you weeping over baked goods. I'm not sure you cried that much at my funeral. Must be a very good pie.'

'Well, just look,' said Dinah. 'I mean: look at it. It's the most beautiful pie I've ever seen.'

'You can ask me questions if you like,' he said, as if he were being very generous. 'Do you have any questions?'

The sheer ridiculousness of this was so Michael that her breath caught. But she was not going to be angry. She would never be angry again. She let out her breath in a sigh.

'Okay,' she said. 'What are you doing here?'

162

'I don't know, actually,' said Michael. 'I find that I don't know. But here I am, after all. With or without any say-so on my part. Here with you. It's very quiet.'

Dinah nodded. 'Yes, it is.'

'Is it always this quiet?'

'I think so.'

'You should buy some speakers,' said Michael. 'Put them by the window over here.'

'I don't listen to music anymore,' said Dinah.

Michael didn't answer. He kept looking out of the kitchen window instead. She wanted to tell him that there was nothing out there. That it was all just waste. She didn't know what to say.

'Come with me,' Michael said, then. She stood up, out of habit. She walked beside him, and pushed the door open. She was the first to walk out into the night-time world. Michael came after. His footsteps followed hers. They walked down the street. They moved through the stretching shadows. When she stopped he stopped. She listened. The echo of their footsteps continued for a moment and then there was only silence.

'Are you there?' she asked, not ready yet to look.

'I'm right here,' said Michael. From the corner of her eye she saw his chest and his legs in the overalls' paint-spotted blue drill. His profile nearly identical to her own, but different. 'I'm not going away.'

'Okay,' she said. 'Where are we going?'

'Down there,' he said.

'Where?'

'To my park.'

'That's my park,' she said, and laughed. He was just the same.

When they reached the swinging chain she reached out and picked her customary leaves from the trees by the entrance. She walked onto the fine gravel and stopped. He stood beside her. The feeling of standing like this, the two of them side by side, was so deep in her memory that she thought she could go through layer and layer, unpick everything, and would never be able to find a part of her that did not contain it or call out for it. It was just how it was.

Inside the entrance of the park, ahead of where they stood, there was a sea of cats. There were too many of them. Far too many, their number an affront to sense. Together they stretched and curled and walked. All neatly outfitted in pale orange or grey, with trims of dun or white. They stood and stalked and stretched and reclined. No fear in the slightest. The cats, it struck Dinah, were siblings too. It was their consanguinity that was the source of their fearlessness.

She stood still for a while. They both stood, without moving. Were they waiting for something? Yes, it seemed they were. The cat that was closest to her, the orange tabby, stretched lazily and rose to its feet. It turned, walked to the side. One by one the adjacent cats followed him. Each of them moved a little, and a clear space opened up in their midst, a parting.

She heard Michael mutter something. She was not sure exactly what. She opened her own mouth and loosed the air that had been contained inside her lungs. It moved up past her like a bubble in the dim, submarine light. She took Michael's hand and led him through the path that had opened in the mass of cats. She walked to the bench. They sat. His hand was reassuringly warm and dry. If she squinted she could see the quilted, padded substance of his body.

They sat there together. Substance. Shadow. The light in between.

It was the easiest thing she had ever done, to just sit there in the park, her cheeks wet with tears the same exact temperature now as the outside air, and listen — in out, in out — to the breathing of her dead brother.

10

When Dinah opened her eyes the light was warm and golden and came through the curtains in angled rays, falling on the tatami. Dust floated inside the rays. Each speck moved slowly, turned, and glinted.

Something was different. It was unmistakable. There was a slow but steady ticking. A pulse moving along beneath everything. Time had started back up again. It had started again as if it had never been gone.

Futon. Kitchen sink. Muji convection oven. Fridge. Rice cooker on top of the fridge. Windows. Trees outside the windows. Nothing had been left out. The world had been given back its dimensions.

It was all very simple: the texture of the sheet and the firmness of the futon. Her muscles aching a little from the long walk last night. The mild pain of the pleasant ache, a reminder of her body.

This was how it was for most people. You didn't even think about breathing. And things stayed still, they didn't move around, they didn't trip you up. Shower, clothes, food. You performed each task because you wanted to. Because it didn't even matter. And it was so easy as to be laughable. Dinah raised her hand and swept it through the air in an arc. She pushed the covers off her body and jumped up. All of the things she could do.

She would not test it at first. To call out or speak directly would be gauche, too obvious, fated to fail.

She showered in the yellow-tiled bathroom. A rush of fondness for the sickly buttercup colour of the tiles. A rush of fondness for the smell of the water, peppery from chemicals. Her eyes pricked with this access of affection and gratitude. And then a quick jolt of fear. She could not worry about etiquette.

She turned off the shower and left the bathroom without even drying herself properly and the light was far too bright all of a sudden, stark and awful.

'Michael?' she called into the apartment. Her heart began to quicken. She thought of answers. Could she return to the park? Had she somehow left him behind there?

She dressed and left the apartment.

'Please,' she said. 'Can you say something, please?'

She was walking. Not knowing where at first, but then clearly in the direction of the station. Footsteps echoed behind her. A wave of dread and sadness rose up, but she did not accept it as her own. She was hungry, she thought defiantly. She would eat. Not a boiled egg or a CalorieMate from the convenience store. She would eat. She would eat. She would eat at the ridiculous diner above the station. That was all she allowed herself to think. The only thing she allowed in her head was a picture of this diner. She had passed it hundreds of times. It had never seemed to apply to her, so she had ignored it. But now she would go there because she was a different person. A person who ate at the ridiculous diner above the station. She walked up the stairs. Footsteps on the wood and bitumen steps ahead. A woman and two children walked down toward her. She passed them.

'Michael,' she said. Hissed it, rather.

The diner had a view over the whole funny little neighbourhood. There were people in here. It wasn't empty. She was the one who was empty, she thought. But it was too obvious to be any comfort. She ordered at the counter. She went to a table and sat. She put her phone out on the table. Her heart was beating too fast. Her breath was rising inside her.

'Just piss off, then,' said Dinah under her breath. 'I don't need you.' Eyes turned from the family at the table next to hers.

Her pancakes arrived. A neat stack of them on a white plate with a pat of butter on the top. She poured the syrup over. The butter melted and spread into the syrup so that for one second it exactly resembled the picture in the menu, then she destroyed this with her knife and fork. The pancakes tasted like clay and dust.

Dinah picked up her phone. She entered her code.

There was a message on the screen from Yasuko. It had arrived very early that morning. There was no text, simply the photo of Jun that Dinah had seen last night.

She opened the image. He was handsome, she decided. Not just symmetrical. The cast of his eyes, their slight downturn at the corners, the air of sadness. They were objectively attractive. Yet he looked at the photographer with such blankness, a blankness that was almost aggressive, she thought.

She could not stay here. She put her knife and fork down. She did not yet know where she would go, but she picked up her bag and called thank you to the server behind the counter and went back down the stairs, the wood creaking.

She took the tunnel beneath the tracks. Walked blindly.

'I don't need you,' she shouted into the darkness of the tunnel. A schoolboy in uniform looked up, startled, entering from the other end. The whites of his eyes were very bright in the gloom. 'Sorry,' she said. 'I'm sorry.'

Out of the tunnel, down a street parallel to the train tracks. Down another street. Then in front of her, a rusted wire fence. She stopped walking. It was as far as she could actually go. She recognised the house, because she passed it every day on the train. From the train window it was a brief flash, and it was strange to be viewing it from the street with all the time in the world. A sort of collision. Like when you were small and bumped into your teacher in the supermarket.

Through the fence the yard of the house was stacked with old appliances. This was why it was so memorable, a landmark for her from the train. Toaster ovens, wall ovens, air-conditioning units. An entire car chassis up on blocks, bundles of rebar, old office chairs and tables, microwaves, televisions. Further in, bundles of newspapers and magazines and advertising circulars in neat stacks, all tied with twine.

She stared so hard at the hoarder's house that finally she saw it all clearly. It was not rubbish at all. If the waters rose, this would be where they all gathered. It might take a long time to piece them back together, the world's fragments, but it would be possible. There would be plenty of time in those long, still twilights. Perhaps she was crying.

She took her phone out and illuminated the bright screen. She selected Yasuko's number and pushed call and held it up to her ear. 'Hello?'

'Hello, my dear. How nice to hear from you.'

She turned and leaned against the fence.

'What are you doing?'

'Nothing much,' Yasuko said. 'Sleeping. Cleaning my apartment. And you?'

'I am going for a walk.'

Dinah pushed herself off the fence a little. The sound of wire protesting. A squeak of metal in a musical note. A shift in the shadows that suggested she had disturbed something hiding there. A ticking like an insect or a watch. She looked to her right and saw nothing. She looked to her left and saw nothing. But then: something. Standing a little way off, next to the bamboo fence that continued past the hoarder's rusted wire. He was standing between a poster for the local election campaign, and another, about a lost dog.

Dinah didn't move.

'I wanted to thank you for last night.'

'What for?'

'For listening to me talk. And for the pie.'

'Oh, of course. Those are my favourite. I had a feeling you would like them too.'

Dinah stood up straighter and walked toward the figure.

'Will you let me try to talk to your son?' Dinah asked.

There was no answer.

'Yasuko?' said Dinah.

She was looking ahead now, directly. Straight ahead. No more pussyfooting around. Michael was wearing the blue overalls and heavy cap-toed boots that he'd worn in the maintenance job. He looked exactly as he had the last time she saw him alive. Only the name badge was missing. That made a sort of sense, as she herself had the name tag in her possession. It was inside one of the pockets of her own suitcase. She had stolen it from her mother's dresser before her flight.

Her look was full of poison and she wanted to push him or give some other sign of her hurt and indignation. But she was too tired. She turned away, but so she could still see him in her peripheral vision.

'I will message your son,' she said. 'Sometimes it's easier to talk to someone who is removed. I won't put any pressure on him. I will just check in.'

'Really?'

'Of course.'

'That would mean a great deal to me.'

'Will you send me his phone number?'

'Yes.'

'Is there anything else I should know?'

In television shows a detective walks around in the snow with a photograph of the missing person. *Have you seen this man? Have you seen this man?* What could she know about Jun? What did she even know about Yasuko, really? The city's vastness stretched out and out and she was tiny within it, like an insect. But maybe she could do something. The thought of doing something, helping her friend, made the city suddenly cohere around her. It came into focus, into shape.

The line was crackling, as if Yasuko was walking in a great wind. 'He is very … impressionable, my son. I wonder. Would he have left by himself? Perhaps someone is influencing him.'

At least that's what it sounded as though Yasuko was saying. The line was crackling louder.

'Okay,' said Dinah, and she felt full of a strange confidence, a determination to protect Yasuko. 'I will find out.'

She looked at Michael. She beckoned to tell him to follow her. She was too angry to do more but walked down the street toward the station.

Dinah took the Saikyo to Ikebukuro and at Ikebukuro boarded the Yamanote line.

Dinah looked out the window. What a pleasure it was to be moving, the overwhelming surplus turned simply into a backdrop. *Ikebukuro, Otsuka, Sugamo, Komagome.* It was all happening. The city's buildings being pulled down. New ones erupting into the gaps like teeth.

In Asakusa, Dinah walked down Sukeroku Yumedori and then down to the dock and the gangway. There was a queue to enter, but it was already clearing. Two men in uniform turned to the dock to untie a rope. A boat horn sounded, and she began to run. She passed a ticket to the uniformed pair, and she was on board. Almost immediately the ferry began to pull away from the dock.

'Can I?' she asked in English, breathing air in ragged gulps and pointing to the outside area where there were wooden bench seats and a roped area. All the other tourists and day-trippers were inside in the air-conditioned cool.

The guard nodded gravely. 'Dozo,' he said and stepped back.

She stepped through. The boat pulled further out and away into the dirty grey ribbon of the river, and she raised her head.

Dinah stood on the ferry and looked across and saw it all. The river stretched out between the city's two sides, the empty void of it. Some effort had been made to contain it, certainly, between these concrete banks. But the river refused. It continued to flow — blank, dirty, impossible. How did the people in those towers full of windows cope, staring down at it all day?

It was too late to step back off the ferry. She was in the void of the river, moving toward the flowing centre of its blankness. It was hot, but there was a breeze from the ferry's speed that stirred her hair. She gripped the side. She tried to breathe.

Downriver a rubbish barge idled and turned in the ferry's wake. She could see the captain, an elderly gentleman, sitting out the back. It was one of the rare bright days when the pollution had burned off and the sky was blaring out a reminder of its true colour to all who might have forgotten.

She turned to Michael.

'Where did you go?' she said. It didn't sound as angry as she meant it to.

'I don't know.'

'You can't do that again.'

'Okay.' The mild interrogative of his voice.

'No,' she said. 'You don't understand. You can't go and not come back. You can't come and then disappear. You can't do it.'

They stood together for a long while and she began to breathe again.

'It was ridiculous to mourn so much,' Michael said.

'Yeah,' said Dinah. 'I know.'

'You can't keep it up, you know, that kind of grief.'

'Thanks,' said Dinah. It didn't sound as sarcastic as she meant it to.

She looked around to see if there was anybody watching. The guard was standing impassively by the polythene flaps that divided the interior and exterior of the boat.

'Nobody really cares if you talk to yourself in public,' said Michael. 'It actually takes quite a bit of effort to get people to pay attention to you. Especially in a big city like this.'

'Is that so?' said Dinah. 'I'll keep it in mind.' This time the sarcasm was much clearer.

She took her wallet and walked down to the vending machine. She didn't look back. She chose a chuhai even though it wasn't yet midday. The can dropped with a crash and she bent to get it, and before standing she looked back over her shoulder.

He was still there, as solid as anything else on the boat. Solid as the windows and the chairs. His hair was blowing in the wind, and his arms were braced to absorb the movement of the flat-bottomed ferry on the water. She walked back.

'Are you okay?' he asked.

'No. You can't do that ever again.'

Michael shrugged. 'I'm sorry. I don't know what happened.'

'Perhaps you shouldn't have come back at all,' she said. The can was very cold, beading with condensation. It made a rude rush of noise when she pulled the tab. The grapefruit flavour was winter and Michael biting into his fruit and eating through the thick skin.

'Please don't be so sad,' he said. He put his hand on her shoulder.

'You don't get to choose how I am.'

'Okay.' Michael looked out over the water. 'Look, I don't know what the rules are. I don't know what makes me leave or come back. But what I think it means is that we should make the most of being together now. That's what I think. Today.'

The most sensible thing would have been to resist the current of happiness that was lifting her, but it didn't seem possible.

'Well, I know there are some gardens. Further down the river. I don't remember the name.'

Michael nodded.

'Okay?'

'Of course.'

The sky was blue. There were birds flying in it, sketched fingernail crescents like the pictures of birds you draw as a child. Sunlight reflecting on the ripples of the grey water, glinting off the mirror glass of the buildings they passed. Shadows of the buildings, then sun. Shadow then sun, as if nothing had changed. Dinah, breathing shallow in case she might blow her brother away, heart splitting with happiness, felt herself thickening, solidifying: cornflour stirred into the soup; seventh week in the mother's womb, when life says yes to the weight of the future, becomes permanent.

She looked at him. His nose was the same. The bump at the ridge where it had been broken.

'Thank you,' she said.

'For what?'

'For coming back.'

He nodded again, very serious. Perfectly serious.

'I have to go inside and get a map,' she said, 'so that we know where to get off. Stay here?'

'Of course.'

She stood without moving, just looking at him. A hard stare, with the corners of her mouth turned down as if to guard against further pain.

'Go,' he said again and made a shooing gesture with his hands. 'I'll be here.'

'You act as though I should trust you,' she said.

He made a face of mock hurt and pretended to stick a dagger into himself. It was one of their mother's trademark expressions. She stood and waited to see if he would come up with anything better.

Michael shook his head. 'I'll be here,' he said again.

She turned quickly and walked to the door. Her mouth was filled with far too much saliva, and she leaned over the side and spat into the water. Her hands were shaking. She turned back to check on him. She couldn't help it. If he was gone again, it should be like ripping off a Band-Aid, over in a second. But he was still there, standing looking over the side.

The rubbish barge had accelerated. It was passing beside them as their boat pulled into its first stop. The barge was really only a floating platform with tyres strung around it. There were two small cranes and a small hut, and at the back the elderly gentleman sitting on his white moulded plastic chair. The chair had been bolted onto the deck. The man had his feet up and a can in his hand. He raised his can to her, and she raised hers also. Then she pushed through the door, and it closed behind her.

They lay on their backs. They were in the gardens. Past the manicured lawns the grass grew tall, like a meadow. A meadow in the middle of the city. There were wildflowers growing everywhere, and when you lay down, as they were doing, you could forget where you were. Only the very tops of the towers of buildings were visible, detached and shining. Down below, the river flowed on and on.

She reached out and slid her phone from the pocket. It was difficult to see the screen against the sun's glare, but she found the number Yasuko had given her and typed a message.

'Who are you messaging?'

'Nobody.' She pressed send.

Lying with their arms over their eyes, Dinah slept a little, in and out of dream.

In the dream she was floating, flying over a huge river. The water was shadowy and dark and in it were sharp rocks sticking up like needles. There were cliffs scored away on either side, sheer cliffs all covered over in dark-green bush. Unclimbable. And in the sky were immense dark-grey clouds, their undersides lit now and then with flashes of lightning. They were beautiful, the clouds, like huge space stations, like battleships. Like whole cities, complex and underlit.

When she woke she opened her eyes and the sky was warm and pale and feathery. She didn't know where the dream had come from, where she had been. The chasm and bush were like a landscape in New Zealand, but she had never been to that exact place, she was sure.

She rolled over onto her side and told Michael. His eyes were open also, and he was looking up into the thin, pale sky. She told him about the dream.

'Where do you think it was?' she asked. They were lying on their sides facing each other. The thing between them that exceeded words. She could hardly bear it, and sat up.

'Do you know where that is?' she said.

'Of course I know it,' said Michael. 'That was my dream that you dreamed just now. I was dreaming it too, and I shared it with you.'

It was so Michael that she had no choice to do anything else but laugh.

11

The anticipation was almost too much. Yasuko resisted the urge to call the girl. The apartment was very quiet. She had placed the small glass terrarium on the credenza. The beetles were doing very well in their new dwelling place. On the floor of the terrarium there was a fine substrate. There was a small dish filled with the bran meal, and next to that she had placed some of the small jelly capsules that Seito had sold her. She had clipped an incandescent bulb to the top of one of the terrarium's glass sides.

She peered through the glass. The pair sat on the fine bark surface, resolute. Wise. She felt the pattern of their attention on her. They were the same breed, a pair, the male slightly bigger. Their black carapaces were shiny, segmented. Their legs were both delicate and forbidding, sensitive and preternaturally strong.

She had read that Tylenol eased heartache and thought she would go out for some more shortly.

Was what she had told the girl true? she wondered.

She thought it must be, and she shivered. Almost as if by speaking the fear out loud, she had allowed the ice to enter. Jun would not have left by himself. He could not have done so. Even his mother must admit that he had neither the strength or resolution for it. Not to mention a lack of cash. She thought of her PO Box, the plain manila envelopes.

They had been safe for a long time, ever since she had lifted Jun out of his warm bed and carried him on her back. If she had not done that? If the lights in the soles of his shoes had flashed into the night and someone had happened to look out of the window?

When they arrived at Tomakomai, the morning had been cool and salty damp — the mist filtering up from the sea. Jun had been too tired to walk, by then. There had been nothing open. They looked for a ryokan or hostel where they could pass the day and night before the next ferry sailing.

The threat of her father sat on her skin, and she couldn't warm up. She remembered that they had passed a Catholic church with a gravelled courtyard and cacti and camellias lining the fence. The nuns had all been out in that very early morning, walking in an orderly line in the frigid air, taking their exercise. At first she could think of nothing worse than being seen by these women in their ugly dun dresses. They watched her with such awful rectitude. What else could she be doing but running away? And at that hour who could she be running away from but a man?

But when they finally found a ryokan, the proprietor was even worse than the nuns. She had beady eyes and a stained apron and made them pay for a double room, though Yasuko had hoped to save money with a single. She had given them ugly plastic slippers and threadbare towels and a laminated information sheet about the bath. That in itself was an insult, as the information was clearly meant for foreigners.

The tatami in the room smelt of cigarettes, and the fan heater sent out a hard column of hot air like a hairdryer. There were cheap, thick polar-fleece blankets with satin edges. It was all awful. In the darkness of the night Yasuko had heard the nuns singing.

She had been very afraid. At least on the ferry they were moving. People did not notice a single mother and her young son, or her look of desperation either. The sea was rough, which meant that you constantly needed to brace and flex your legs in order to stay upright. It brought an odd feeling of holiday. The world was moving up and down, but it was a mutual affliction, not something Yasuko had to suffer alone.

Jun's height gave him the advantage of a low centre of gravity, and he was able to run ahead confidently. She encountered another young mother moving down the corridor. Her daughter too was running ahead. Yasuko crept past the young woman, holding the handrail, looking green. They exchanged rueful glances.

'Rough, huh?'

The sea calmed a little in the early evening. Standing amidships, looking over and down, they saw waves in a cold grey impasto. Covering and destroying and being destroyed forever. Yasuko's hands gripped Jun's small shoulders until he whimpered.

'Is this the ocean, Mama?'

'Yes.'

'Are there fish down there?'

'Of course.'

'Will I see them?'

'I don't know.'

She felt rather than saw a glimpse of a fish, an old fish, turning and turning. Rising up to touch the meniscus. Bubbles that opened into the air. She wished to lean over, lean closer. She wished to call out. Why have you forsaken me?

Jun would not stop talking.

'Are we going on a holiday?'

'No. We are setting out on an adventure.'

'Will granddad come on the adventure too?'

Her breath caught with the injustice.

'Perhaps,' she said.

In the sleeping cabin, with a vinyl-covered foam brick each for a pillow, she positioned Jun next to the wall, placed her coat over him, and lay down alongside, making a wall with her body. More questions.

'Will they turn the light out, Mama?'

'I don't know, darling.'

'Mama, what is that thing on that man's face?'

'Ssshh.'

The middle-aged man next to them caught her eye and smiled. She knew how to return the smile. Not sufficiently warm to encourage; not so cold as to alienate. The man's face was dull and safe, but it paid to be careful.

'You have your hands full there,' he said. 'Off on holiday?'

Yasuko smiled and nodded.

'We are leaving forever. We are going on an adventure!' Jun announced.

'How exciting,' the man said, and leaned forward. 'I have just been on an adventure myself.'

'We left my granddad at home,' said Jun. Yasuko placed her hand on his arm and gently laid him down again.

The man smiled in a knowing way and winked at Yasuko.

'Granddads just aren't very adventurous sometimes.'

They disembarked in Oarai, and he helped her carry her bag down the ramp then presented her with his card. An academic at one of the lower-tier universities. A lecturer in mycology with a port-wine stain on his cheek. She took his card politely, as she had done everything then. She had carried Jun on her back to the station, as if this somehow disguised their lack of luggage. They had boarded the next train to Tokyo, where they would, for the next fourteen years, manage to lose themselves entirely.

She forced herself to think about the early years. How slow it had been, peddling her way across that flat, flat world. Without vision, without powers. Everything was agonisingly slow. She had found the job, found the apartment, found the preschool, and then the school. She had moved through it all, every minute and hour. She had carried them both.

But no. Not every minute. Not every hour. There had, of course, been the times of weakness, of which she did not like to think. And whenever they passed, those days or weeks of extreme hope and panic mixed together, there came the period when she had to close her eyes and turn her own face to the wall. She would know, usually, a day or two beforehand, because she would feel the cold creeping up on her, the ice coming down.

When Jun was younger she felt certain that he understood none of what was happening. Perhaps he did not even notice her mania and then her absence. Children are selfish after all. Or rather, focused on the self.

And she had never left him. She had simply stayed in her room. A room with no door. The sound of scratching in the wall cavity, following her always. A snivelling sound like a dog crying. 'Go away,' she had shouted. 'Go away. I can't understand you anymore.'

Her father was gone forever, but then whose was that narrow unwashed face at the door? Too scared to come in. Too scared to see her transformation. She thought of it and could not stand the shame. How old? Five? Six? His face with its gnawing look, and the shadow against it.

'Please?'

She felt the panic rising up thinking about it. Must not think about it.

Jun had saved her life. What a miracle to have the chance to start again. A child's forgiveness.

And hadn't she always come through? Always she had pulled herself up. She had broken the ice again. She had warmed him, their bodies both together in the bath, soaping and slicking his hair off the rounded brow. Kissing his temples, the narrow bird bones of his back.

She bundled him into his favourite clothing, a grey marle tracksuit from Gap. It was his favourite, he never wanted to take it off, but today, somehow, it was too small. As if in a single day he had grown an inch, perhaps two.

'Did you grow, Jun-chan? But never mind, we will go shopping. You need ten sets of brand-new clothes.'

Drying his hair and her own hair with the towels. The regret as thick and strong as the love. Stronger by far than any old grief. Its own intoxicant and heady brew remaking her. I will never give in again.

'I am sorry, darling. I am sorry. It is over now.'

Pulling the bike out of the storage cage, her muscles weak from lack of use. Pumping the front tyre. The crows flapping in the garbage. The whole raw assault of a world that had, in a single day, shifted from summer to autumn.

She moved off, down Meiji-dori. A steady barque. Her heart bursting in her chest as she looked at the miracle of her son, her cargo.

'Can we go to Mister Donut for breakfast?'

'Of course.'

She sat for a while and watched the beetles in their terrariums. There were still not enough. She would go to Ikebukuro today to buy some more.

12

Michael's voice was different now that he was dead. It was lighter, less substantial. It came from the centre of his chest and had a light buzz as if he were blowing through a tube.

He was there when she woke. Often he spoke to her as she ate.

'Fuck's sake, Dinah, there's no nutritional value in that bread whatsoever,' he would say. 'It's like a mattress. Like a life raft. When you push it down it reconstitutes itself. I don't think you should eat that.'

Dinah did not draw attention to Michael's hypocrisy at such moments. She did not mention the concerted project he had undertaken in order to alter his final human body. She didn't remind him of the loaves of Tip Top bread and cartons of ice cream they had found in the freezer of his flat.

'*I* like it,' she said, spreading a second layer of Bonne Maman jam on her toast. That, it seemed, was that. Had she ever been able to do that before? Shut Michael up?

Dinah texted Jun for the second time, and then the third.

In the evenings they went out. Dinah was able to visit all of the places she had travelled past or been unable to enter alone.

They found a restaurant that appeared to have been uplifted directly from 1950s America. It had black and white chequerboard linoleum, a chrome-edged bar with swivelling stools, and booths in red leatherette. She ordered a hamburger and fries and a malted shake. The flavours of the food were so bright and intense that she thought she might be sick. The feeling passed. Dinah nudged Michael's elbow with her own to point out the girl sitting next to them who wore a perfect ponytail, a tiny cropped sweater, a circle skirt with a poodle appliqué. He nodded in approval.

They went into shops she would not have dared enter. One that sold squares of brightly coloured cloth, printed with fish, birds, spinning tops. A sock emporium. Stationery. In the bookshop, flicking magazines backwards, Michael hummed under his breath. They bought deep-fried oysters and cans of beer and ate them standing in the street.

The days stretched on and on, but when the dark came, it happened without warning. Slow, slow, and then very fast, as if the light was gathering up its belongings, running for the last train.

On a Saturday night Shinjuku was giddy with contained, jostling human emotion. Like somebody had shaken a hive. Dinah and Michael moved through the crowd. Dinah watched the moving, smiling, laughing, urgent people. She watched the couples, the groups of friends, the businessmen out on their weekend jaunt, the tired mothers holding the hands of children who were up late, very late, too late. Surely they should be in bed at this hour, those children. But why indeed when all around was a wonderful air of safety, of kindness? She exited at the South-East Exit. It was so warm. The city's concrete was still radiating the sun's energy, like breath.

She took Michael's dry, solid hand in hers. She navigated the foot traffic, agile against the flow of people.

'Where are we going?'

'Need beer,' she said.

'Follow me,' said Michael. They walked away from the station and into a narrow street, and he pointed at the sign. Through the door was an establishment that appeared to be a replica of an English pub, as imagined by someone who had never been to England, and never set foot in a pub. There were dark beams overhead, artificially aged. The whole place was lit with miniature gas lanterns. There were carefully weathered tin signs on the walls advertising cold cream and cough tincture.

'This is crazy,' said Dinah. She went up to the counter and ordered two beers. She stood at the counter and took her phone out. She looked at the photograph of Jun. The gaze, just off centre, not quite at the photographer. She sent another message, with her left hand, tapping at the screen.

The bartender brought back the beer in two metal tankards; he looked at her so straight-faced that she cracked up. When she reached the table she was laughing so hard she sloshed one of the tankards over and had to request napkins to wipe it up.

'It reminds me of that tea shop in Mount Eden,' she said. 'The one that looked like the inside of a cuckoo clock.'

'Did I take you there?'

'Yes. Don't you remember?'

'No.'

'You were rehearsing the Beethoven and the Brahms violin sonatas. The violinist lived around the corner.'

'Oh yes. You know, I've been listening to the Brahms sonatas again recently. They're very good.'

This made her laugh.

'Oh, really? Very good?'

'His parents made him play at dance halls and pubs frequented by prostitutes. Brahms. Did you know that?'

'Frequented?' She laughed at him. She had drunk her beer too quickly and felt giddy.

'They used to make him play the piano, and the women would lift him onto the tables to dance. Poor Brahms. His childhood gave him a very poor foundation for future relationships.'

She imagined a tiny, eight-year-old Brahms with a full beard doing a sad jig on one of the tables of a low-ceilinged room. The air was heavy and filled with a sad malty light.

'Poor Brahms,' she said. She checked her phone. Still nothing. She texted again, using the same message. She didn't see what changing it would do.

'It's all there in his music — beer and prostitutes. That pale green that comes creeping over everything in Germany when it's nearly spring.'

'Yes.' She didn't know what he was talking about, but it was easiest to acquiesce with Michael. She had learned this from many years of practice.

'In one of his letters he wrote about walking for miles and miles — he'd set out and just go for it. Just walk. Like this.' Michael demonstrated Brahms' strolling style, with his hands clasped behind his back.

'On this one particular day he came across a small lake, and it was surrounded with baby frogs.'

'Frogs?' Dinah felt she was missing things. She needed to be more alert.

'Yes. Frogs like jewels. They were waiting there, as if just for him. When he arrived at the lake, one frog jumped into the water and then, as if to imitate it, all of the others followed. He wrote that each time one plopped in, it sounded a perfect descending minor third.'

Without wanting to, she could see it. The lake lay beneath a blue sky, all of it glowing an unearthly pale green. A meadow alive with tiny frogs.

Michael was looking back at her. She didn't say anything. Then he blinked.

'But tell me about your friend,' he said.

The shift was very sudden. She felt a sort of vertigo, again, things were moving beneath her feet.

'Yasuko?'

He nodded.

'What do you want to know?'

He shrugged.

'What are you doing?'

'I'm helping her.'

'Do you think that's a good idea?'

184

'What do you mean?'

'Helping people is difficult. More difficult than it seems. Most of the time people don't actually want to be helped.'

Dinah looked down. 'You didn't. Is that what you mean?'

He didn't say anything. His face was in shadow, but he looked sad. She didn't want to make him sad.

'Show me his picture?'

She passed her phone.

'Oh,' he said. 'Well then.'

'What?' Dinah was blushing. 'What's that supposed to mean?'

'Nothing. I didn't say anything.'

Michael turned and looked at the queasy brown walls. He scratched at something lightly on the wall next to him and pulled. A thin strip of gluey brown came off. He passed it to her thoughtfully. 'Essence of London filth. Distilled from the sweat of Dickensian orphans.'

She nodded.

Michael sat looking at the bar. There were old West End theatre tickets stuck inside the lacquer, many layers down so it looked like they were floating. Michael had gone somewhere she couldn't reach him.

She held her breath, as if this might bring him back.

'You know,' he said, 'the first piano concerto was incredibly unpopular when it came out. Brahms wrote to a friend after the premiere. Probably Joachim, I don't remember. He wrote about how the audience refused to clap at the end of the concerto. They booed instead. And then somebody in the audience actually started to hiss. Then just like that, they all started hissing.'

'Like the frogs,' Dinah said. 'One started and then all the others went.'

'Yes,' said Michael. 'He was so hurt by it. He explained just what happened. They all started hissing. "Surely they didn't need to *hiss*."'

She nodded.

'Isn't there something heartbreaking about that? "They didn't need to *hiss*." But it's not the saddest thing. Do you know what the saddest thing is?'

How was it, she wondered, that they had arrived at this discussion of the saddest thing?

'In Brahms, I mean. It's the second movement of the first violin sonata. The bit where the melody comes back on the violin. It's like the violin's bridge is going to break with the weight of it. Relentless. It just keeps on going.'

He stopped talking. A dark room and the shape of his back in silhouette, awkward and dead like a stuffed horse.

'He wrote it after his godson died.' he said. She looked sharply at him. His face was the same as ever, but she didn't know him. She didn't know him at all.

'He never married, you know. Never had kids. Consorting with prostitutes at a young age really did for him in that department. He was in love with Clara Schumann all his adult life. Her son was the one that died.'

Dinah looked at her hands, still holding the beer tankard, which didn't seem funny anymore.

'I think that might be why it's so sad. It's not really his grief to feel — it's hers. But he wants to take it for her. He's coming up beneath it, trying to hold it. As if he could take some of the weight.'

'That's not what I'm doing,' said Dinah. 'If that's what you're trying to say.'

Michael sat silent for a bit. He shook his head. 'I didn't say it was.'

13

There when she woke. There while she was packing her tote to leave the house.

There when she came home from work.

By the time she reached the end of the under-bridge that ran from beneath the station, where the bicycle repair man slept under his blue tarpaulin, Michael was walking beside her.

There were certain topics they did not touch on. Neither of them mentioned their mother, for example.

Back in her bed at night she lay in the dark, and he sat in the chair or on the balcony, looking out to the park. Occasionally in the darkness she caught the gleam of his eyes, the odd intimacy of knowing exactly what his face was doing, knowing exactly what it looked like.

They put the garden of their childhood home back together as if it were an intricate machine. When all the parts were assembled in the correct order, it might spark back into life again.

'Do you remember the grapefruit tree?'

'Of course.'

'And the mosquitoes.'

'Yes. And the way the punga hair used to get down our necks, and itch, and you couldn't ever brush it out.'

'Snails.'

'Baby's tears.'

'The horseshoe we found under the deck.'

'The little people.'

Dinah sat and waited. The night air so warm and humid that she could barely breathe. There when she went to sleep at night. Miracle that kept her breath shallow. Happiness that returned the world to flesh.

She held her phone under the canopy of the sheet, and cupped its sallow glow so that it did not disturb her twin brother, if he was there.

My name is Dinah. You don't know me ...

In Shinjuku there was a konbini on the bottom floor where she picked up their Sapporo tallboys. The attendant returned them to her in a thin plastic bag, and she slung the bag over her arm and led them through the crowd.

The night was warm. The sudden expanse of sky above the huge, un-healing scar of the tracks. A valley carved by the trains, and the buildings rising up all around. The vast crystal palace of Takashimaya department store, the Gotham clocktower of the Docomo building.

She walked to the end of the boulevard and crossed the bridge across the tracks and stood there briefly, in the civic flow, in the consensus of people and commerce and leisure and warmth.

She turned from the tracks to watch the people instead, coming toward her in a steady stream, flowing past and down toward the East Exit. Individuals looked back at her occasionally; some people smiled back.

They found their seats, their customary spot. Wooden slatted benches with a view of the tracks.

She cracked open a beer and passed the other to Michael.

There was a wonderful ease in sitting here, watching. As if she had been in a desert and the rain had come. Such pleasure simply to look at people, their haphazard, hopeful faces and how they leaned in toward each other to speak.

She watched them emerge into the city in an endless stream, disembarking from the station and meeting friends. They had phones that moved in patches of glowing light. It was beautiful to watch them. Mothers and sons. Lovers. Brothers and sisters. If she stayed for long enough she would certainly see a young man amongst them with dark-brown hair and a pale oval face and green eyes like her own, that were still and watchful and did not flinch.

She smiled and tilted her head at Michael to say that she loved him and that it was all okay. She was entirely replete in the warmth, his presence, the beer. She had acceded to all of it, and she sat there, smiling at the crowds.

She took out her phone.

There was a message.

'Dinah?'

She sat there, unable to speak for a second. It was surprising how it struck her like a blow. A closed door.

Hi Dinah. Thank you for getting in touch. I appreciate your concern, but I am afraid I don't have time to meet. I hope you have a nice day.

They sat in silence for a while, sipping their beer. She looked out over the tracks; people streamed past her on their own tides.

Michael half-turned to her. A commiseration. 'Sometimes people just don't want to be found.'

'Like you didn't?' she asked.

'You're angry.'

'Of course I'm fucking angry. Of course I am.'

She felt the ripple of something old passing through her. Why should it all be so easy for him now? Why should she be the one still grappling with human problems, like failure? Disappointment?

'I'm angry,' she said. 'I thought it was my fault.'

'It wasn't.'

'Of course it wasn't. You were the one who left.'

She had a sudden memory of standing in the garden, listening to Michael practising. Scales. Always scales. Perhaps he would come out. Perhaps he would come back out and the game would start again. The snails making their tracks across the brick, the leaves curling up

189

to protect their secrets. Time slowing to a crawl, and the tick of their twinned pulses slowing to match.

She looked again at the message on the home screen. It was so short she didn't need to open it. She could delete it and the entire problem would disappear. She opened the message and pressed the call button.

The sound of her call ringing. She held on. No reply. She hung up and sat for a second, then called again and waited. She listened to the answer service, or what she assumed to be an answer service as the voice spoke in rapid Japanese. She heard the low pip that presumably signalled the invitation to record.

'Hello?' she said, into the recording. 'Hello? Is this Jun?'

The name had taken on the blankness of a code. It was opaque, flat, just like the face in the photograph. Yet she thought that if she said it in the right tone or at the right speed, it would make sense. It would open. The phone's silence expanded around her like a balloon. She heard the sound of a sob.

'My name is Dinah,' she said. 'Dinah Glover. You don't know me. I'm a friend of your mother's.' She let another pause enter and wondered how long before she was cut off. 'Your mother,' she started, and then stopped. 'Is my friend.'

'I don't understand,' said Dinah. 'I have been thinking about this a lot. I don't know why you found it necessary to leave.' She hunched over. She held the phone closer and began to speak more quickly, urgently.

'Do you know what it's like when you're the person who's left behind? Do you know? It is like a light shining down. The brightest light you can imagine. An awful fluorescent light. It's everywhere. There's no relief from it. There is no escape.'

Her hand was sweaty. She was looking at the woven fibres of her own coat. 'Did you know this? You couldn't possibly have known it. You couldn't possibly have known.'

There was a beep from the phone to signal the end of the recording. She took it from her ear and looked at it like a strange sort of artefact. The screen had returned to blackness, which made her think perhaps she had been speaking to nobody. The glass was fogged and humid from the warmth of her hand and breath.

She felt exhausted, and thought that she would go home. She would go back to her apartment. Tomorrow she would go to Bic Camera and get a new SIM. Perhaps even a new phone. Tomorrow she would change her number.

Michael seemed to have disappeared, faded into the crowd. Surprisingly, she didn't even care. She sat on their customary bench for a long time. The number of people milling around thinned out further. She needed to get a train before they stopped running, but somehow she couldn't move. She didn't want to go home.

Then inside her coat pocket her phone vibrated. It would be her mother. She had not called her once this week. She felt guilty, but it was too hard. Talking to her mother was like spanning a huge chasm, her whole body stretched and aching from the strain.

The phone rang on and on. It stopped and then it started again. She realised that it could not be her mother. It would be too late in New Zealand, the middle of the night. It couldn't be a middle-of-the-night call from her mother because there were no emergencies left; they had all already happened. She reached into her pocket. She didn't recognise the number on the screen.

'I have to answer,' she said to no one. 'It could be important.'

She answered the phone.

'Hello?'

Nobody spoke.

'Hello? Who *is* this?' she asked.

'You called me,' the voice said.

'No you called me,' she said.

'I'm returning your call,' said the voice. Weary but patient.

'Jun?' she asked, into the warm night.

JUN

1

Yasuko knew that the next act was beginning long before she saw the phone light up.

Thus when she heard the girl's voice on the other end of the line, she was able to answer with equanimity and composure.

'Oh, I knew that you would do it,' she said to the girl. 'I had no doubt in you at all. Where are you meeting him?'

A pause as the girl explained, and she listened. Then Yasuko spoke again and silenced any unnecessary discussion with a single question. 'No, no. There is a far more important thing to consider. What are you going to wear?'

Yasuko had not doubted the prediction, but the relief was immense nevertheless.

She looked around with clear eyes. Without Jun the apartment had become untidy. She shook her head, put on gloves, and cleaned the kitchen. She scrubbed the benchtop, mopped the floor until it was sparkling. Then she ground the whole coffee beans that she had bought at Yamaya and put the moka pot on to boil.

Happiness percolated through her bloodstream. She drank her coffee down and went into the tatami room. The light was dim. She opened the good antique tansu where she kept the many terrariums and removed the one that contained her favourite. She placed the terrarium on the floor by the wall and stood and bowed.

There was a clicking noise in the gloom, a rapid wave of Morse-like spots of sound. Yasuko took a slim piece of chalk from her pocket and drew straight onto the tatami. She paced, thought, then drew more lines. She assessed, and was satisfied at last with the markings. She removed the lid from the small terrarium and took the largest of the two handsome iridescent beetles on her hand. She returned to her knees and laid her hand carefully in the centre of the diagram chalked there. The beetle obediently trotted onto the concrete field, like a knight entering the lists.

'Tell me, please,' said Yasuko. 'Will the girl be successful in bringing my son back?'

Yasuko drew back, then, and sat on her heels, her knees clear of the floor. She balanced on the balls of her feet, like a boy in a park, her hands clasped on the nubby tweed of her skirt. She sat and waited as the beetle performed its task, surveying the tatami, the white chalked runes, planning the line of its journey in a way that would do honour to the day's magnetic lines of fate, to the season's shifts and cruelties, and to the unpredictable vagaries of human will.

From the human perspective the floor was flat. From the beetle's it was a domain of hills. The distance was invested with energies and perils that she did not understand. Yasuko sat and watched the beetle traverse.

'Do not doubt,' it said. In the movement of its antennae, the fine code of clicks and bleats, the shine of its carapace, the shape of its journey. 'They will meet. We said that we would assist. We have sent a girl to you.'

'That is not what I asked,' said Yasuko.

Beetles spoke like old ladies. They were pedantic and circuitous. Inexact; living in the past. She sighed. It was no good.

'Thank you,' she said with great formality. 'Thank you. I do not deserve what you have done for me.'

But it appeared the beetle's journey was not complete.

It continued on walking across the tatami, moving from one pole of her marking to the other.

'There is something else,' said the beetle. But really she was almost bored and made a move to signal that she had no further need of counsel. She crouched forward, ready to make a ledge of her hand.

'What is it?'

'There is an impediment coming,' the beetle said. 'A man. Somebody you know very well.'

Yasuko felt a shiver go through her. A surge of anger came along with it also. She felt her chest constrict; she heard the sound of scratching, but it was just the beetle, making its way back toward her.

She allowed it to walk onto her hand. Beetles were next to useless. It was silent now, in any case. An elegant ovoid with bullet-like intent, its wings tucked discreetly back into itself like an expensive convertible car.

She transported the tired creature back to its terrarium and placed that back on the shelf. She bowed once more as she shut the door and noiselessly turned the key in the lock.

She felt a sickness stirring inside her. She thought of the only man she had known well.

'The key to happiness,' her father had said, 'is to choose a job in which you continue learning.'

Yasuko walked out and into her bedroom. She turned to the shelf and looked and selected a book. It was a pale blue, the one she chose. It had its title written down its thin spine in a childish mixture of hiragana and katakana. She carried it with her into the tatami room. She lit a candle and opened the cover. It had been a long time since she had looked inside. Her father had chosen the endpapers of the book with such care. They employed a black and white photo of snow falling, slightly blurry, like a still from a 1940s movie. One could imagine Cary Grant and Loretta Young ice-skating just out of shot beneath such snow. The kind of snow that falls from the sky in a child's picture, next to a sun with a face on it and down to the earth's straight, estranged horizon. It was a ruse, a deception.

Inside the book's cover was the author photograph. She looked at her father and the way his eyes hid behind his glasses. She sat still and felt the associations shuffle around her, paper thin, like a membrane, like an extension of her own body. She turned the pages. It was a primer, a children's book. He had written it for her. Though of course he never did anything that was not for himself. When her teachers asked the class to explain their father's job, she had shifted uncertainly in her seat. He is a scientist of crystals, she had said.

The book was meant to explain it. Inside there were carefully rendered X-ray images, the snow crystals each different, crisp and exclusive as cyanotypes on their blue ground. The atomic fractal structure of each revealed in infinite care. She kept turning, knowing what was coming and dreading it even as she turned. There she was.

In the picture she looked straight at her daddy behind the camera. She was wearing her red Snowpro padded snowsuit and yellow galoshes and a knit hat. In the next photo, peering into a microscope, and in the next, hunched over her trusty magnifying glass, scrutinising fragments of snow that lay like scattered diamonds on a black velvet jeweller's tray. There she was at eight, petite in her red tracksuit, still with the shoulders-back, belly-out stance of early childhood, eyes not yet hiding. She left the book open on the table as a reminder.

There were so many mistakes that you could make. So many that it was almost beautiful, the variety and richness of them. And yet the issue was all the same — a flat and unremitting weariness.

Her father was not someone who was available to forgive. He would never forgive her.

When she had emerged from her room, slid her pleated gym skirt back on over thinned hips, it had been too late already. She was no longer Waseda or Keio material. Her high school had allowed her to complete her final year by correspondence. She had achieved a good result in her exit exams. But that was where it ended. She took night classes in English and a certificate in teaching from her local community college. She lived in her room, much as she had done during the year of their first estrangement. The door was open now. She could come and go as she pleased. Sometime in those years her father remarried.

Her stepmother was a quiet woman, had been the administrator of a university department. She had a large mole on her right cheek.

What was Yasuko to do with herself in a world without any powers? She lived quietly in the house with her father and her new mother. Occasionally she learned that so-and-so from school had married, or so-and-so had left the prefecture. Mei, her best friend, had completed her journalism training. Mei had given birth to her first child. Her stepmother stopped her in the hall and told her these things. For herself, she did not know what would happen next. She no longer gave herself licence to enquire about such matters.

One day she had arrived home from an English lesson to find the kitchen in disarray and her stepmother distraught. Her father was bringing someone home from his lab, a graduate student. Such a thing had never happened. In her panic the stepmother had gone to the most expensive supermarket in the city and bought the most expensive items she could find. There were plates of soba, an immense softshell crab, chawanmushi.

The graduate student was American. He was of solid, dense build. His brow was heavy, but he had a sharp, cultivated mouth. Yasuko sat at the table dutifully and did not speak. When she looked up she saw her stepmother swaying as she crossed the floor with the chawanmushi in their porcelain pots on a tray, clinking together.

'And you, Yasuko-san?' said the graduate student. His name was Scott. They were speaking of their favourite novels. He spoke Japanese like a child, so that she cringed in embarrassment. At the bottom of the egg custard, there was a river prawn curled up like a drowned child. Yasuko stared at it and remembered a time when she would have seen a sign in such a thing.

Toward the end of the meal, her father handed her a taper and asked her to light the lanterns. The foreigner invited himself along. Neither of them spoke as they entered the garden. He walked beside her, very large — one of his hands could easily have encircled her upper arm — yet moving lightly, barely making a sound. He trod as if noise caused him a sort of pain. This was interesting, she thought. Here was a person of considerable physical power, who had taken great pains to cultivate his own restraint. To what end? she wondered.

When her taper blew out, he handed her a silver Zippo lighter, warm from the inside of his breast pocket. Yasuko nodded. She slid the lighter open and flicked the wheel until it bit. Then she relit her taper and passed the lighter back to him. Instead of putting it back into his pocket, she noticed, he took it from her precisely between his thumb and forefinger, so that his fingers were touching the spot that she had held. They walked and he watched. The taper burned quickly, as if the night itself were burning. It burned right down to the bottom while she held it and he watched. At last the fire licked at her fingers and the man, Scott, continued watching, waiting for her to blow it out. She found that she was quite unable to do so. She saw in that moment what this man had to offer, and that it was violence. The flame made a door in the night. If she held on long enough to burn also, she might be able to walk through it.

It was no longer possible to bring to mind anything of the year of their marriage. What she did remember was his smell. He always smelled pleasant, even after drinking, even after a packet of cigarettes. Some men wore aftershave that stung the eyes, as if its purpose was to intimidate or excoriate. His was a gentle warm balsam, almost sweet. It was mellow and kind and without any rough edges.

He hit her the first time during their honeymoon. She stayed with him for another eleven months after that. It was a lesson she had some trouble learning: you cannot heal loss with further suffering. By the time she returned to her father's, she was already seven months pregnant with Jun.

When something new occurs it appears to emerge from nothing. Things happen slowly; they stop until they almost do not move. And then things happen very quickly. The story begins, it rushes forward. A young mother takes her son upon her back one night and they leave, silently, over water. They meticulously manage to lose themselves in a different city.

She stood up, decisive.

The beetles were next to useless. When she got home tonight she would take the cage and empty it in the park. But the doubt had been raised. She needed a clearer reading, a proper answer.

The trip to Ikebukuro was easy now. She did it almost without thinking. The taxi pulled up as she reached the street outside her apartment. The crowds thinned as it drove up Meiji-dori. The heavens themselves opened as she passed, and shone a single ray of sun through the clouds. Her path was correct.

'Seito,' she called, when she had passed the plastic threshold. She called in a wry, humorous voice, because Seito of all people would understand that this was how she signalled a true and urgent need.

'I am sorry to tell you that I'm back again, my friend. And this time I shall need a bird.'

2

Dinah was in a bar in Ebisu, waiting.

'I'm going out,' she had said to Michael. He was standing on the balcony and had raised his hand to her through the glass of the sliding door. She had stood for a little longer than was truly necessary after he turned back. It was okay. Things were okay. The shape of the back of his head and his ears, the familiar hunch of his shoulders. But the urge to stay with him was very strong. Why was she leaving? She was doing it for her friend. Michael would still be there when she returned. She had turned, checked her reflection briefly in the dark mirror of the window, left. The door clanged behind her.

Yasuko had printed the map and annotated it with directions in English. Ebisu was a bland, moneyed sort of suburb. Dinah had walked down a shopping street, into an arcade, up a flight of stairs and had emerged in a room with a long, elegant stretch of windows and a floor that stepped down toward them. The space was like an extended, cantilevered balcony. She thought that perhaps eventually, down below on the street, a grand performance would begin to unfold.

Dinah waited. She tried not to look around. A waiter approached her table but she picked up a book from her bag and he gave her a berth.

She spotted Jun before he saw her. How strange it was. How peculiar. Like seeing a character in a book made flesh. She felt a sort of swaying in her blood, as though none of this were quite real. As in his photograph, Jun was very pale. At first glimpse he was almost plain: a sort of asceticism to his appearance. He was wearing dark green chinos and a blue wool blazer. Beneath this a faded grey tee-shirt with text on it. His hair was short; his skin was perfect. He was carrying two glasses, which he placed down on the smoked-glass table.

'I made a guess,' he said. 'Gin.'

He retrieved two white dimple-edged coasters from his blazer pocket and put them down carefully, then he transferred the glasses onto the coasters. His movements were polite and precise.

Then he sat. He did not take the chair opposite, as she had expected, but sat next to her at the back of the table, so they were side by side, each with a view of the window. It was a strange choice — overly intimate. Yet at least it saved them from the discomfort of eye contact.

'Thank you,' Dinah said. 'Gin's fine.'

She did not know where to start. Adrenaline had driven her all day, a sort of hectic buzz. She was becoming, she thought, almost used to it. But Jun's manner seemed calculated to absorb electricity. He had a careful, polished politeness of bearing.

'Did you have far to come?' he asked.

She really didn't want to make small talk. For some reason she felt reluctant to give Jun any additional information about herself. Every piece of ground should be fought for. She tried to put a finger on his manner. He had, she thought, an air of humouring the world, of extending courtesy. It rankled. She began to feel an urgency, a mild tremor. She had felt this way at university sometimes, when listening to someone who was palpably wrong about something. A sense of affront that made her tremble, rendered her unable to speak. It registered in her hands first. She thought maybe the impulse concealed a different person, one who relished the chance to debate, to hold forth. Who were they to each other, she and that other person? Complete strangers. 'I came straight from work,' she said, giving nothing away. 'I arrived in Shibuya early. So I walked.'

'I hope you didn't get caught in the rain?'

His English was as perfect as Yasuko's, and Dinah remembered the American father, though this did not seem to explain anything. Dinah pointed to the furled umbrella beneath the table.

Jun nodded. He scanned the room then and raised his chin and eyebrows at somebody. Out of habit she looked at his hands. They were broad across the knuckles. His nails had been bitten down and the cuticles were ragged. Jun saw her observing him, but didn't move or withdraw. If anything, he stilled further. He took a sip from his drink as if he were submitting to a normal process, one with which he was familiar.

He folded his hands, waited for her to speak.

His cheekbones were broad and high like Yasuko's, and his chin similarly narrow. For a second Dinah saw Yasuko's face in the dark screen of the windows. However, when she turned, she saw it also in the polished glass of the bar behind her, the bottles of whisky, the pinkish plane trees with their percussive leaves in the night. That was what love did, she thought.

She immediately knew that Jun would say nothing of any use, would reveal nothing about himself. His patience and self-protection were very deep. He would wait and wait for her to show her hand.

She leaned back a little in her chair. Doing so, she thought of Dougal's insouciance and what she might learn from it.

'When I came out of Shibuya station,' she said, 'I saw a crowd of office ladies. They were all wearing the same thing: a pencil skirt, a blouse, and a cotton cardigan.'

Jun looked at her, bemused.

'And as well as that they were each wearing a trench coat in a different pastel colour. I was waiting in the overhang of the station entrance, and they were coming down the concourse. That was when the rain started. They all began to run, shoes tapping. And then they all stopped at the same moment, just like a chorus line, and put up their umbrellas: Pop, Pop, Pop, Pop, Pop! — just like that.' She mimed the gesture. 'It was like being in a musical.'

What did she hope to achieve with this speech? She gripped her drink and took a long sip. The gin was too sweet and too warm. She heard the rippling notes of a pianist start up in the corner, but she did not turn to look. Perhaps if she ignored it, there would be no consequences. Jun's expression did not change.

'I suppose that is the sort of thing a foreigner does notice,' he said. 'It is the sort of thing my mother enjoys also. She likes it when people notice things. I can see why she likes you.'

She almost laughed out loud. He was so rude. She had not anticipated this similarity.

'Was that also your role with Yasuko?' she asked. 'To notice things? To point them out?'

Jun looked back out the window, sipped his drink dismissively. 'Oh no,' he said. 'That was never my role.'

He placed his drink carefully back on its coaster and with infinite patience stretched his legs. He turned back to her, as if returning to a task.

'How long have you been in Tokyo?' he asked.

Dinah shook her head. 'Four months?'

'Ah.' A pause as if he was thinking, running through an internal checklist. 'And how did you meet my mother?'

She thought about refusing to answer, but there was no way to do so.

'We work together.'

Jun nodded. Each action was slow and articulated. She noticed that each of his physical movements had a separate set of smaller movements, a courteous suite of genuflections. It was a little like watching a ballet dancer — anticipation, execution, recovery. Even his glance moved in a slow polite sweep as if to allow her time to adjust to its choreographed arrival.

'Why do you ask?' Dinah said.

'I am trying to understand your relationship to my mother, that is all. Why you are involved in this situation.'

'I am her friend,' she said blandly. 'I am just trying to help.'

Jun shrugged. 'How does this help? I doubt you understand anything about her. Perhaps you are the kind of person who is drawn to other people's pain,' he said.

Dinah shook her head no. 'No,' she said. What else could she say? She could never explain by saying that she loved Yasuko. That wouldn't do. It wouldn't adequately cover it. She felt the same anger again, and the pressure of knowing she could not express it. She pinched the web of skin between her thumb and forefinger.

'Maybe nothing difficult has ever happened to you, and this has left a bit of a gap,' said Jun. 'You are on the search for something to fill it.'

'No, that is not it either,' she said.

'Well, what is it? I know my mother, and she doesn't tend to make friends.'

'We *are* friends.'

'I see. What do you talk about? Do you talk about me?'

He seemed to think this was impossible.

'Your mother misses you. She wants to understand why you left. She wants to talk to you.'

'I see,' he said. His voice was very calm. 'She misses me, and has sent you to find me and bring me home. But what I want to know is why she chose *you* to do this job. Is it something you have experience in? Is there someone in your life whom you've misplaced?'

The private, voiceless anger that had been kindling in her stomach gained a clear force and filled Dinah in a sweep. It was exhilarating, like downing a single glass of strong alcohol. Everything became very clear. Dinah felt herself get to her feet.

She had lost so many things, in fact. She thought incongruously of the lost property the teachers used to spread out for collection on the concrete steps at school. The kids pacing along diligently studying the objects: a shapeless sweatshirt; a pair of socks; the twisted bathing costumes.

'Shut the fuck up,' she said quietly.

Her own things had probably been there too, laid out on the concrete. But she had never recognised them. Possessions had seemed to fall off her as a kid. Things did not adhere, did not know how to stick. It was always the same. Ownership on one side, and on the other, absence. Who could locate the moment when something dropped away? Just that airy blankness in between. Breathlessness, the haze of something dissolving. Losing Michael was exactly the same feeling: blankness. And the dreadful, awful blamelessness of that.

He was watching her again. She did not want him to. Did not want to return his look, did not want to give him anything.

'Sit down,' he said.

She didn't move.

'Sit down,' he said again, more gently.

Finally she sat down. Not in order to obey him, but because people were looking.

Dinah shook her head.

'I'm sorry,' he said. 'I don't know what I'm saying. I'm on the defensive when it comes to my mother.'

He might have been laughing at her, but she saw he wasn't. His face was grave. He sat looking at the table.

'You are a serious person. I see that now. I am sorry.' Each word articulated carefully.

Dinah sat still. Her hands were still shaking. She felt a shame at this ongoing betrayal by her body, its lack of faith in her.

She saw Yasuko's face, the bravado and humour. She saw the pathos and discipline of her eyelashes and cheeks, the steel of her shoulders. She tried to take strength from that.

'Tell me, then. As you are friends. How is my mother?' he said. 'How does she seem? Is she doing okay at work?'

Dinah blinked.

She thought that she would refuse to tell him anything. She had not planned on doing so. But she was disarmed by his clear concern. She felt a small surge of intimacy.

'I think so. I mean, she is a very strong person,' said Dinah. Then the dissonance returned, his intolerable calm. 'She is grieving. She misses you. She would never let anyone know.'

'Nobody except you.'

'She is distraught.'

Jun nodded, as if he were agreeing. Dinah's anger rose up again.

'Why are you doing this to her?'

'What do you mean?'

'Just that. Why did you cut yourself off?'

'Isn't it a normal thing to do? To leave home? Surely you're not still living with your parents?'

'That's not the same.'

'How is it different?'

'Because my mother knew I was leaving.' She heard her own hypocrisy but was too angry to pause.

He shook his head. 'I don't need to explain myself to you, but I can tell you this. If I had told her I was leaving, I would never have done it.'

Dinah looked at him. She looked at his handsome, symmetrical face that was like a dulled mirror reflection. Pale like moulded clay. Something had shifted in the air. All at once everything had too much detail, so that Jun became strange, almost ugly. She saw every pore of his face. She saw the blocked, inflamed hair follicle at the edge of his left eyebrow. She was hot all over.

As if in response the room itself shifted. A brief rumble and a flickering of light. The skin of the building made a gentle alert twitch, like an animal flicking an insect from its back. She met Jun's eyes, to see if this event was solely happening to her. But no. She saw his simultaneous pause and his air of listening. She saw the people in the room grip their tabletops, hold their drinks. She saw them one after the other look up with an air of enquiry.

A gentle pantomime tinkle of crystal and glass from the bar. Shaking. A shaking that continued until it seemed it could not go on in the same fashion but must choose whether to diminish or accelerate. Inside her, somewhere, there was a licking hunger. She reached without thinking toward Jun to steady herself. His arm was hard, surprising. He returned her grip, holding her forearm. They stayed like that as the room shook, and she realised that she was hungry for the quake's acceleration. For its inevitable triumph. Slowly, however, imperceptibly, it stopped.

'That was a long one,' Jun said, his eyes still on hers. He released his breath. 'Were you scared?'

When he released her arm Dinah noticed that his hands were trembling. She was surprised by an impulse to reach out and take hold of him again. Jun turned aside quickly. He placed his hand on his chair seat and looked back toward the bar. The barman was wiping the bench, joking with one of the customers at the counter. She noticed that Jun had a double crown — two whorls.

'No,' she said. 'I wasn't scared.' It was true. She had not been scared at all. Was it a new revelation? She would not be touched by such things.

'Perhaps you are one of those people who wants to burn everything down. Are you? I'm not like that,' he said. 'I have always been afraid. Yasuko never forgave me for it.'

'What do you mean?'

'I can never go back to her.'

'Why?'

He didn't answer for a while.

'You know,' he said finally. 'One thing has been bothering me, though. In your phone message.'

Dinah blushed. She had hoped he would not mention the message.

'It was deranged, by the way. Partly that is why I agreed to meet. I wanted to make sure you were alright. But you had it all the wrong way.'

Dinah breathed through her anger. 'What do you mean?' she asked.

'You said that I was the one who left. But that is not true. It was the other way around. Yasuko was the one who was always leaving me.'

'I don't believe you.'

'Why would I lie?'

She shrugged. 'I don't know. I don't understand you. But why make such a complete break now? Why does it have to be all one thing or the other?'

He shrugged. 'Maybe sometimes it just has to be.'

'You will regret it.'

'I might.'

'No, you *will*. I know that you will.'

'Maybe I don't have a choice. This is what it came down to.'

'What do you mean she left you?' She saw Yasuko's face, the glamour and particularity of it.

'Nothing,' he said. 'Forget it. She always did her best.'

Dinah saw, with a radiant clarity, Yasuko sitting on a child's bed. She saw her refreshing a flannel in cool water, wringing it, holding it against the child's forehead, and then lifting and turning the flannel carefully over, to use the other side, which was still cool. Dinah felt the great and unplumbed resource of care in Yasuko, like a dark well. She saw Yasuko's strength and that she would easily endure many days and nights without sleeping, and emerge as if newly made. Dinah thought of a breastplate knotted with criss-crossed silken threads.

'She looked after you. She cared for you. She loved you.'

Jun looked at her. He was surprised but not upset.

'I didn't say she didn't look after me,' he said, 'or love me.' His voice with its forbearance. 'Of course she did.'

'Then what are you saying?' She felt a great hurt speaking inside her. It was somehow imperative that Jun admit that the memory was true, that Yasuko had stayed up with him night after night, that she had placed her own needs behind his.

'When you are a child you should have a chance to be a child. That is what I think. There are some kinds of love that are very hungry. It is probably very selfish of me, but I wanted a chance to live without getting eaten up.'

Dinah shook her head. She saw that she had failed comprehensively, and there was a rushing inside her head, a swooping upward.

'I think that's bullshit. First you say she left you, and then that she loved you too much. I think you know that that is bullshit.'

Jun looked at her steadily. She watched him blink, something come down over his face like a shop window closing. 'I don't think there's much more to be gained here, do you?' he said. 'I don't think we should see each other again.'

3

Dinah stayed inside her flat all the next day. It was Saturday. The minutes and hours were gluey. She ate very little. It was so hot she did not feel hungry.

Around six pm her phone lit up. It was her mother calling. She let it ring and go to voicemail.

'You can't blame yourself,' her mother had said. 'If someone is going to kill themselves, you can't keep them locked up, day after day. You can't police their brain, go in there and open up the doors and pull out the bad thoughts like rubbish. You can't follow them into their dreams.'

But that wasn't true. She and Michael had often shared their dreams. She could have.

She pulled on running tights and sneakers. She had not seen Michael all morning. Since the first few weeks of his return, the cord that had bound them had loosened slightly. Sometimes when she opened the door after a day of work, she almost found herself hoping that the apartment would be empty. Just for a few minutes; a breathing space between her worlds. But then if it was empty she was filled with concern until he came back and everything was once again healed over. He would be back soon, she thought. She must not worry. And it was much easier to leave the house when he was not here. She felt no guilt and none of the urgent hunger to stay and look at him or fill any silence with questions so that she could memorise the music of his voice.

The air was clear. Hot but almost without humidity. She blinked in the bright sun. She had been out every night that week, and teaching every day in air-conditioned rooms. The day was like a different country.

Really, she thought, she was very disappointed with Jun. Some part of her had been curious to discover what elements of Yasuko's charm he had inherited. If she were honest she would admit it wasn't entirely self-less, her impulse to reach out and draw him back to Yasuko. But he was ordinary. Utterly ordinary. Handsome, in a smooth, unobjectionable way. Without friction. Only his eyes offering any contradiction. She thought about his eyes and the fact that, even when he was defending his decision, they had been wary, protective. She had seen that look before, she thought. In her own face in the mirror. It bored her.

She was ordinary also. They had that in common. And people had no doubt felt her disappointing after meeting with her brother. But how hard was it, really, not to be a fucking traitor and a coward? It was the easy way out.

She had not taken it.

There were times, of course, when she hadn't wanted to leave her warm bed and follow Michael. She thought about the shape of him, standing up, blocking the street light that glowed through their patch-work curtains. But she had never turned over. She had never shut her eyes and locked him out. She had never left him behind.

She had been the one who was left behind. For the whole first two years of university. But that had not been her choice. Michael had chosen Auckland and music. She had gone to Christchurch. And it had been miserable.

She thought about the hall of residence, the cold, damp campus with its bitter-bark mulch. Her inability to speak the same language as the other students, who flitted around and called to each other with carefree agreement. Oh how they used to move in groups, and from one thing to the next. She had not understood them.

She remembered the endless identical houses, the wide streets with their gravel, the watery blood smell from the butcher shop on every cor-ner, and those awful, ubiquitous bullying rhododendrons. Those first few months she had never risen above any of it. She had scraped along over the city's flat concrete belly every day and called home every night.

Perched on the window seat, holding the shared phone, trying to look past her reflection in the dark glass. Trying not to cry. She called her mother, but all she wanted to hear about was Michael. Her mother could never keep the note of apology out of her voice. 'He's doing well I think, love. He called earlier. He was just off to a movie with some people from his course. I'll tell him you called.' She could tell her mother was concerned about her, but there was an impatience too. Why was she still calling in this manner? Why was *she* not out, at a movie, or a concert? When would she come to terms with the loneliness that was the true initiation into adulthood? She tested it out on her, gently, that ordinary form of torture, like a mother bird pushing the fledgling out of her nest.

Yet it *had* become easier. She finally did have to admit to herself that the worst of it was past. She had begun to make friends. You just needed to learn it, like a language. It was a different language; not her native tongue, but in fact much simpler.

It had its own pleasures. She had to admit that also. She had befriended a girl on her floor who invited her home to Rangiora for a weekend. It was the first home-cooked meal she had eaten in months. She sat on a couch, and the parents both seemed delighted to have her there, as if this kind of ordinariness were something to be celebrated. The house was so warm she had fallen asleep right after dinner, sitting there on the couch. They had laughed about it later. That was what normal people did. They fell asleep and then they laughed.

But that was survival. It had not been her choice.

She walked and walked. She walked through her neighbourhood. Down to the river, which was lined in concrete. It was a glorious, sunny weekend day, and there was nobody out at all. Silk carp flags flapped on poles at the top of the bridge. She heard a dog barking. She stood there, looking out at the rush of water, the way it carried the blossom down. Sometimes the blossom was pushed down by the current, turning.

Her mother had been wrong anyway. Things had been taking off for Michael, sure. But he still needed her. He still wanted her company.

She knew this because, in the final year of her degree, she joined him in Auckland. She would complete her BA there. She took a room in a flat. On paper it hadn't looked too far from where Michael was living, on one of the main streets down from the university. In reality it took three-quarters of an hour and two different buses. But they were together, in the same city. It was the two of them again.

She remembered the rush of joy, the ebullience of that knowledge. The freedom of it. How could anyone else know that feeling? Time started like a wheel spinning, and everything fell into place, gloriously concentric and full of meaning. She began to read again. Music ceased to be a meaningless progression of notes and offered up its secrets. For a while they did everything together. He was flying, anyone could see that. The great propulsion of his talent pushing him up. But she was beside him. They met at the German coffee shop in Mount Eden. He was heading to rehearse for his final graduation concert.

'I'll wait here. I can't come with you.'

'Yes, you can.'

'Won't the violinist mind?'

'Trust me, she's an egotist. She loves to have an audience.'

There was the joy of dropping back into the rhythm of speech and silence and walking. They walked together in the shadow of the volcano, through the suburb with its large expensive wooden villas, their paint glossy like cake icing.

'Somewhere around here,' he said. And then he was knocking at a heavy wooden door with an elaborate brass mechanism, his chin up in its usual challenge, and she was standing in the shadow behind him, all of which was very familiar.

'My sister,' he introduced her. 'She's going to listen in.'

The violinist had long sleek blonde hair and wore expensive-looking jeans and sheepskin slippers. She cast a glance behind Michael to Dinah and gestured the direction ahead of them. She held her violin in one loose hand, her bow swinging casually as she strode down the thickly carpeted hall.

She pushed open the door to a room with the same lush cream carpet, a wide dormer window with tall, heavily swagged curtains that looked out onto a neat lawn with box hedges.

'Sorry about the piano,' she said.

It was a baby grand, and cream, to match the carpet. Michael laughed and sat at the stool, adjusted the height, and opened the lid. Then he struck a chord and grimaced.

'I know,' said the violinist. 'My parents are the worst. It's the only room in the whole house that gets sun and they put the piano in it. It needs tuning every few months.'

Michael shrugged and ran a rapid two-handed scale up and down, thundering into the low notes, listening. Then he shrugged again and turned to watch the violinist, who was rosining her bow. Dinah saw that even his surliness was charming. That was the power of talent. Even with her immaculate polish and confidence, the violinist was already half in love with him.

'No bother,' he said. 'As long as you're tuned to the piano, I'll put up with it for an hour.' He struck a solicitous A.

Dinah sat on the padded seat that was built into the dormer window. The sun fell on her back. After her own grimy, depressing flat in the damp gully of Richmond Road, it was astounding to be in a place where all the surfaces shone with care and money.

She listened.

The movement of the sonata they were rehearsing was like a stately joke. The violin ran ahead, and the piano followed, obedient and dependable. It was so unlike Michael to be obedient and dependable that she smiled in spite of herself. In contrast the violin was like a young animal, straying too far, almost tripping over itself in giddy enthusiasm.

The violinist was clearly enjoying this. She flicked back her long hair, and the bow danced with exaggerated precision. Then the piano returned to chastise her, and they resumed the melody in new partnership. The piano pulling backwards, backwards, like an ice dancer, and the violin following demurely behind.

Then a new movement that seemed entirely made of trills. The violin and piano caught in a sheer excitement that could only manifest in pizzicato, trills, still more trills. Theme and variations. Theme and variations. Each repeated into greater complexity and innovation, as if they were playing a game of Dare. Then chastened, balletic, again and gliding backwards over ice.

It was beautiful. She could see the violinist watching Michael, and for a second Dinah saw herself, her own habits, in that alertness, that readiness, that careful listening. When they rounded on the theme it was such a relief. Like they had solved it all.

Afterward, after they had both had a glass of water in the kitchen like servants, and she had felt the violinist sending her daggers and wishing her far away so that she could have Michael to herself, they were walking back to the village and the bus stop.

She hadn't heard Michael play in person for over a year. She tried to convey how impressed she was. She wanted to tell him that it was something quite different, watching him now. He had changed over the last few years. So much had been deftly folded into second nature. He commanded an entirely different vocabulary. But she found she couldn't speak yet, with the beauty of the music ringing inside her. She saw for a second that he was heading in an entirely different direction and toward an entirely different life. It was painful, but the memory of the music filled it with a glamour and beauty. This was what she wanted to express, to share.

'It sounded good,' she said, instead. Michael laughed dismissively.

'Yeah, well. The Kreutzer was her choice.' By her he meant the violinist. They were both being assessed; it was the final exam of their degree. 'I wanted to do two Brahms sonatas. Not impressive enough, apparently.'

'The Kreutzer *is* very impressive,' she agreed.

'Of course it is. Beethoven is like a children's birthday party.'

They kept walking. Though it hadn't been meant for her, was just a dart she had stumbled into, the insult still registered. She wondered if they had slept together, he and the violinist.

And she was unable, as ever, to avoid rising to his bait. 'How exactly,' she asked, 'is Beethoven like a children's birthday party?'

He smiled at her. They kept walking, almost at the bus stop. There was something careless about huge talent. Something almost obscene about it, perhaps. \

'Because there's always something happening. Streamers, a magician, the cake. It's exhausting.' He looked at her, a wry grin for her benefit. 'Everyone has a good time, though, and they all have a good cry at the end.'

She laughed. He laughed too, until they were standing just laughing at each other, and at the two of them laughing.

It was impossible to say who had stopped laughing first, but after a while they were silent, and Michael wiped his eyes and they sat on the bus all the way back into the city.

They were going along the ridge of Great North Road when he turned around. The sky stretched up from both sides of the ridge so that you seemed at the top of something. It was quite different from the town they had grown up in, and the city where she had studied, both of which were like being at the bottom of some deep well, with the stone of the sky over the top. Michael turned to her, and she saw that there was something different, something around his eyes. He held up his palms to his cheeks and she saw that his cuticles were ragged down to the flesh on both hands.

'I'm glad you're here, Dinah,' he said. 'I've missed you.'

'Me too. I'm glad too.'

'Shall we go, then?'

'Go? Where? I have to get back to my flat. It's my turn to cook.'

He had looked at her, genuinely befuddled.

'But you're here. We have to go. We have to go.'

'Where?' she had asked again. Something was wrong, but she hadn't wanted to say anything. If she had it might have broken the surface of the day and the magic of being united.

He gestured beyond the window. Pointing somewhere beyond. Somewhere she couldn't see.

'We have to go,' he said. 'Out there.'

*

Dinah turned from the river, and walked back up to the rail bridge and crossed it, and strolled back through the village. A fruiterer turned and pulled the roll-top awning of their shop down as she passed. A child held her mother's hand and hopped on one foot. Her hair was in pigtails and she wore a yellow rain jacket even in the heat and cloudless sky.

The day was breathlessly hot. In the apartment Dinah took off her shoes and ran a cold shower. Afterward she turned the air-con up so high that the water beaded on her goose-pimpled skin. She stood there with the towel around her.

'Michael?' she said into the room.

'Hmmm?'

'Why did you do it?'

'Do what?'

'Stop music. Leave everything behind.'

'I didn't want to. I don't think I wanted to.' Michael had become smaller, she thought. His presence in the room was suddenly compressed, nuggety.

'Was it my fault?' Dinah asked.

There was nothing. Silence in the room.

'It was that summer that it started, wasn't it? When I came up to Auckland.'

'Do we have to talk about it?'

Dinah shook her head.

'There's a woman in the park,' said Michael. 'Have you seen her before?'

'What kind of a woman?'

'A photographer. She has a backpack and she's walking round and around the play equipment. She has a tripod, a light diffuser, and a camera.'

'Oh yes. She comes once a week to photograph the play equipment.'

'What on earth for?' Michael said.

'I don't know. Maybe some kind of an art project.'

Michael moved, and the shadow moved with him.

'You know the piano, the one in the Grafton practice rooms?'

She did not want to think of that piano.

'It had a tiny little buzz. A hum. I was trying to fix it. You could hear it in the upper registers, especially playing softly. But the only way to fix it would have been to take the whole freaking thing apart.'

'Actually you're right. Perhaps we shouldn't talk about this,' said Dinah. For the first time since he had arrived, she felt an irritation. Not with Michael, but with herself. It was no different now to when they were kids. She had always ceded so readily to Michael's vision. As if there were a part of her that longed to just hand everything over. But what was she losing in that exchange?

'I think I was a bit like that,' continued Michael. 'Just something wrong somewhere down deep in the mechanism, you know.'

'Michael,' Dinah said warningly. 'I want to sleep. I need to sleep.'

'You can't blame yourself, Dinah.'

Dinah sat up.

'It was just how it was. Something down deep in the hammers and wires. Nothing you could do. You would have had to take the whole thing apart to fix it.'

But Dinah didn't reply because she knew of long habit that there was nothing to be gained. He had taken it all apart, hadn't he? And it hadn't fixed a single thing.

4

The bird was there to tell her about her father.

It was a paltry, small thing, the bird. She had gone to Seito for something large, something dirty and undomestic. What she needed was a creature with a raucous voice, pigeon or crow.

Seito must have been having a laugh at her expense. 'This is the only one, so if you want a bird you need to take it.' And then he had blamed his useless son — who spent his days giving away free packets of tissues to foreigners, and failing to catch pigeons in the park — for missing his delivery. 'Oh I have seen your son,' she said. Which made him sit up. But she had taken the canary. She felt a great distaste for it. It seemed to have given up its freedom without fuss. It was the wrong bird entirely.

She shook the cage a little to see what it would do. It barely flapped its wings, simply hopped from one rung of its enclosure to another. Then, gallingly, it began to sing. A twittering, tuneless, meaningless sound. She sat back on her heels in disgust, wanted nothing more than to replace the cover and shroud it back up again in an artificial night.

But she had travelled all the way to Ikebukuro and back.

She framed the question in her mind clearly. She framed the threat of her father. He was standing there, outside her door. She could feel the ice and hear his breathing. She placed her hand on the small ledge of the bamboo door and nudged it gently upward, so that the skewer rods slid up inside their holes and cleared enough space for her to place her hand inside the cage, up to the wrist.

When Jun was born, after the nightmare of her pregnancy, her father and stepmother had given up their room for her and the baby.

She thought of those early weeks. Those months like years. If an animal had tried to speak to her at that time, she probably would not have even noticed. She would barely have broken stride. There was no longer any space in the world. There was hardly sufficient space for her. Something enormous had taken place that filled the world entirely. Her ears were tuned entirely to the fragile, surprising creature in the pram.

Here then, she thought, was a gift that could never be taken away. She had been given her child.

Every day was full of tragedy and wonder. Every one of his movements was a sign of something. The whole world was waiting to be decoded. If he yawned three times, then she must feed him straightaway and rock him until he fell asleep. If he cried in just that way, he was not hungry; rather, his stomach hurt. His cry. That siren that woke her into every morning. She no longer looked for animals. He turned his dark wordless eyes on hers, and they lived together in the world.

Her father paled and moved to the side. She witnessed him go, like a chess piece. No longer somebody to fear or be chilled by. She had replaced him. There was no one else in the world apart from her and the child. But she had been wrong. Perhaps she was wrong again.

The bird flapped away from her hand. She brought it closer, until the whole small creature was encased in her hands. She felt its small life beating against her fingers.

The pattering of its heart moved her. It was a surprise, to be affected in this way. She felt a quick affection and an unexpected desire to protect and comfort the small animal, to keep it safe. She held her hands loose and firm. She cupped the bird inside her palm and withdrew it, and it sat on the platform of her hand, bright and trembling. She had not wanted a small bird, a trembling bird, but now that it was sitting there in front of her she saw that this was correct, that nothing else could have been quite right.

The bird was her own thing. Her very own. Feathered, clasped. She looked at its pitiful smallness, its tiny unconscionably bright eyes, the cock of its handsome, perfectly groomed head, sharp in silhouette against the dull curtain.

She held it safe and it held her, with its brightness. The yellow so bright in the darkened room. Her heart moved up in her mouth. Her throat filled with dreadful eloquence. The knot of the waiting speech was huge and immovable, like a birth.

'You are my very own thing,' she said to the bird. It turned its head from one side to the other. She felt the power in her hand, the weight of it pressing down upon her, tiny and fragile. They were joined. She felt a surge of triumph. Then the bird turned, and it spoke.

'I am *my* very own,' it said, contradicting her. Its voice was strange and immeasurable. 'Always, and always and forever.'

The creature was laughing at her. But she bowed her head.

'It is love,' she said. 'Love and service that has brought me to you. Am I not owed something at least for that?'

Its laughter was cryptic and merciless, but then gentle, as it seemed to relent.

'Yes,' it said. 'Of course. But what we get is often very different from what we expect. Are you sure that you are ready?'

She nodded, conceded.

'I can cope. I can endure anything. I have done it all already.'

This was entirely true. She had. Nobody had been asked to endure what she had endured.

The bird hopped a little on her hand. She felt its tiny claws, the pattern of movement.

'Your father is waiting for you. You didn't outwit him at all. You will have to be smarter than your father.'

She saw immediately that the bird was right. Of course. He had been watching her all along.

She had been given her child. If she had wanted to keep him, she should never have looked away from that gift. Her first grave error had taken place on an ordinary old week.

It had started with the observation that her son was not a baby anymore. She had been lifting him into the bath and had realised she no longer actually needed to do so. Jun could stand alone and use the stool to surmount the ledge without any danger. He no longer needed her to help him. That was the start.

The next morning she woke and he was not tucked beneath her arm and neck in the futon as usual. She sat up and called for him.

'Jun?'

He was not there. Then she heard his voice. He was chattering to somebody. A rapid patter of sound that she had somehow never heard before. They rarely spoke to each other, perhaps because they were so very much in tune. Who was he talking to?

She stood and opened the curtain. She looked down into the garden. There were two figures standing: her father and her son. Her father was stooping down toward the boy and there was an unbearable gentleness in his posture. He had passed his grandson his precious garden scissors and was instructing him on how to prune his favourite maple. Their heads were inclined inward. Jun held out a hand to his grandfather's knee to steady himself on the gravel.

She had shut the curtains and returned to bed. She had known, then, that she would no longer open the curtain. That behind them the sky would be blank and oblivious and unblinking. That day she had turned instead to face the wall.

How long had he waited before he sprang?

Not long. A week? It had barely seemed a day before she heard his footsteps.

He came as if he had been lying in wait just outside the door, and he entered her bedroom, the bedroom that was Jun's and hers, and he brought a threat so terrible she would never thereafter forgive him.

She heard once again his cold voice, his awful patience, the ice sliding across her sky.

'Yasuko-chan,' he said, standing by her bed. 'We cannot go through all of this nonsense again, you know. But. See. We will help you. We are going to look after Junichiro for you now.'

She had escaped, had no choice but to escape him. She had taken her son and carried him on her back.

But her father had returned. He had found her again and come for Jun.

She held the bird on her hand and walked to the window. The bird lifted itself up on the palm of her hand and spread out its wings. She saw that the primary flight feathers had been clipped so that its wing-span was rounded off.

'You are right,' she said to the bird. 'You have helped me more than I can say. Thank you. I will release you. But your feathers are damaged. Can you fly?'

The bird hopped on her palm. It lifted its mutilated wings and seemed to shrug. 'There's only one way to find out,' it said.

'That's correct,' said Yasuko.

She stood tall, taller. She felt her powers like a breastplate across her chest. She opened the window.

'Out you go,' she said, and emptied her hands into the sky.

5

When Dinah entered the general staff room, there were two teachers there only. She knew them vaguely; the older woman Asano, who had an MA from a US university and was tall and angular in a slightly masculine fashion. And the old gentleman Oe, very serious, who smelt of mothballs and whose earlobes were oddly distended.

Dinah was looking for Yasuko.

Though it was far nicer than their office — it had a coffee machine, padded seats, windows — the English teaching staff rarely used this space. While technically it was available for the use of all staff, there was a silent understanding that English lecturers were not staff in quite the same way that Engineering or Science lecturers were staff. Nevertheless, today Dinah was there, looking for Yasuko. Or in fact standing at the coffee machine, pressing the button for a caramel macchiato with extra creamer.

Briefly, unexpectedly, the ground took a rushing swoop. The space around her head grew warm and dark. After a few seconds things righted themselves. She looked up slowly. Yasuko was standing next to her. She grasped Dinah firmly by the forearm and tilted her backwards so that she yielded and sat into one of the padded seats. Then Yasuko removed the beverage from the machine and handed it to her. She sat down also.

'You don't look very well,' said Yasuko.

'I'm fine,' said Dinah. 'Really.' She was extraordinarily tired, but apart from that she *was* fine.

They sat for a while without talking, and Dinah sipped her coffee.

'I was hoping I would find you,' she said.

Yasuko nodded. 'Have you ever seen such long earlobes in your life?' She tilted her head toward Professor Oe.

Dinah looked up abruptly. Her body hunched forward in a form of social protection, as if by moving close to Yasuko she could retroactively reduce the volume of what she'd just said, its awful rudeness.

'Ssshhh,' she said under her breath, without thinking. She looked around the room for invisible assistance.

Yasuko had an amused expression on her face. 'He doesn't speak any English.'

But Asano did, and Dinah looked indirectly across the room to see if she were listening. She had not looked up from her exam scripts. And Professor Oe was right there in front of them. Talking about him in such proximity felt illicit, like going to the toilet in a public place.

'How do you suppose they got that way? Perhaps his mother put weights on them when he was a child?'

Yasuko was looking almost directly at the professor. Dinah's face was burning. She could not speak.

The man was folding his paper into neat, socially unobtrusive quarters as if he were on a train. She didn't say anything. Yasuko looked at her, as if daring her.

'He could use them to stir his tea,' said Yasuko. She winked.

Then Dinah knew what to say.

'I spoke with Jun.'

Yasuko became still. She turned her face to Dinah, her eyes wide and gleaming.

'You saw him?'

'Yes.' Dinah paused. She didn't know how to explain.

'Shall we catch the bus to the station? Do you have another class?'

'It's only four. I can't leave yet.'

'In that case tell me now,' she said.

Dinah turned, began to speak, but had not formed a single word when Yasuko interrupted.

'No, no,' she said. 'No. Not yet. Wait.'

She went to the coffee machine and pushed the buttons and returned with her own drink.

Seated next to her, she turned to Dinah. 'First. What was he wearing?'

'Green pants. A tee-shirt. A blue jacket.'

Yasuko closed her eyes. 'Ah, yes. The Brooks Brothers blazer. And tell me, did he look quite well? Healthy?'

Dinah wondered what the right answer was. 'Yes. Yes, he did.'

'And what did you talk about?'

'About you, of course.'

'Me?' Yasuko laughed, as if incredulous. Professor Asano looked up from her seat at the other end of the room and smiled.

'Of course,' said Dinah. 'Yasuko,' she said.

'No,' said Yasuko. 'I don't want to know. Not yet.'

She exhaled in a concerted, focused fashion, then she turned so that Dinah could see her face in full.

'I am ready.'

'I am sorry, Yasuko. I didn't get very far. But I will try again.'

Yasuko nodded. 'First, there is something I must say.' She spoke firmly but with a trace of humour. 'I want to let you know that I am so attached to you. You have become like a daughter to me.'

Dinah bowed her head a little. It was like being handed a carrier bag weighted down by a gift. One could not open it and look at it straightaway. Later, when she was by herself, she would look inside the bag and see its worth.

'But there is something else I need to tell you.'

Asano was leaning forward in her seat, then she stood and walked to the centre of the room to pick up a magazine from the coffee table.

'Of course,' said Dinah.

'Do you trust me?'

'Yes, of course I do.'

'Well, in that case, you are foolish, because I lied. I did not tell you the whole story.'

Dinah shook her head slowly. She did not understand. She cast a look at Asano, who had returned to her seat and diligently opened the magazine.

'There was something else I did not tell you. There is another personage.'

Dinah turned back to Yasuko.

'Personage?'

'Someone else in this story. Another character.' Yasuko was very patient. She was thinking. 'Did you read fairy tales growing up, Dinah-chan?'

Dinah nodded. There was one book she and Michael had been obsessed with. *A Book of Princes and Princesses*, illustrated by Robin Jacques. They had pored over it. She was almost embarrassed to admit how much it had shaped their play. She and Michael had visited the underworld. She had passed through endless trials. She had not spoken for a week. She had drunk from the paw print of a deer. Together they had tended a golden snake.

'Well, then,' said Yasuko. 'I will tell it like a story. It is easier that way. Jun, of course, is the prince. As for me. I do not wish to be vain, but for the sake of symmetry — I will be the queen.' She batted her eyelids demurely; their purple mica shimmered. 'So that is clear enough.'

Dinah nodded slowly. 'Yes,' she said. She did not understand, but it was familiar also. She surveyed the new landscape. 'But who am I?' she asked. 'In this story?'

Yasuko laughed again. 'Why, you know!' she said. 'Don't be coy. You are the princess, of course.'

Asano looked up again. She smiled as a teacher smiles at two precocious students, indulgently, but without comprehension.

Dinah gave her a half-smile back, then she turned to Yasuko.

'What is the story?'

'Well, it is very simple really.'

'The queen is living with the prince, and then the prince goes missing?'

'Yes, yes,' said Yasuko. 'But what happened before? That is what I missed out. I did not tell you what happened before. Do you mind if I tell you now?'

'Please,' said Dinah.

'Once upon a time, the queen was just a princess herself. She lived in a different kingdom, with her father, the king. She was very unhappy. She had been granted great powers. But almost as soon as they were offered, they were taken from her. She lived with her father because he had trapped her.

'Then one day she was given a son. The princess was struck by this. It was a gift she did not deserve, but she made it her goal to deserve it. What else could she do? But the king was jealous. He wished to take the only thing she loved. So instead of allowing this to happen, the princess took her son and escaped.' Yasuko paused. 'Do you understand so far?'

'Yes,' Dinah nodded.

'I knew that you would understand. I thought that you might know this story.'

Yasuko looked across the staff room. Dinah followed her gaze. Asano was looking right up, at them, her mouth open as if she wished to speak. What could she wish to say?

'And so at night she took her young son on her back. They left the kingdom. They travelled silently over water. And then they disguised themselves and disappeared into a neighbouring land.'

'Yes.'

Yasuko paused. 'But the king has not forgotten. He still wishes to keep the boy. So even after all this time, he has returned.'

It was not difficult to understand. In fact Dinah did feel she knew the story already. Wasn't it second nature to her, in fact, to follow and to stand looking up at the vaulted space carved out by her brother's imagination? She had already known Yasuko's great power. It was radiant, shining from her. The skin of her cheeks, the time embedded in them and worn like a fine armour. She nodded as she listened, and looking out the window of the staff room, saw the world through Yasuko's eyes: the sunlight haloing the trees, the animals speaking, the vast energy that rose up around her.

Yasuko sat up straight, and the reverie was broken. 'But let us forget my son,' she said. 'It's a beautiful evening. Let us get out of here and walk to the station.'

Dinah nodded. She looked up. Asano was walking toward them. She was walking with a fixed look on her face, a serious intent. It took her only three strides to cross the room, she was such a tall woman. She stopped a few feet from them and bowed slightly; there was a look on her dignified, dry face of amusement and anticipation. She took another step so that she was right in front of the coffee table between Dinah and Yasuko. Dinah leaned forward, waiting for Asano's announcement. It seemed of a piece with this afternoon of revelation.

'Here,' Asano said. 'I thought that you would like it.' She smiled. Her eye twitched. Dinah saw that she was still holding the magazine she had been reading, extended from her body. She extended it further. She had bent the page back and now placed it down between Dinah and Yasuko on the low table and stepped back. 'Isn't it good?' she asked. Her eyes lifted open, widened.

Dinah leaned forward and looked at the magazine. It was an old *New Yorker*. The page showed a cartoon. There were two dogs, speaking to each other. One was on the ground; the other was sitting at a computer, like a human. A caption beneath it.

Hi, I'd like to add you to my professional network on LinkedIn.

6

'What's wrong with you?'

Dinah was pacing. She couldn't settle to anything. She wanted to leave her apartment, but she no longer had a reason to sit in Shinjuku and watch the crowds of people flowing past.

'Nothing,' she said.

It was something she had noticed for a while. When Michael was absent she felt pulled with fear, but when he was here she was distracted. As if there were insufficient floor space for her own thoughts. Really it was not surprising. The apartment was barely big enough for one person. She heard Michael's breath, in and out. She heard the familiar catch when he was concentrating, as if even exhaling would be too much interruption. He was sitting on the floor with the sliding door open and his feet on the concrete of the balcony. She felt a sudden claustrophobia.

'Shut the door,' she said. 'I want to put the air-con on.'

Michael moved out onto the balcony; he slid the door shut. She watched him with a kind of dread, but also a relief. She saw him walking up and down out there, leaning over the rusted railing to call to the cats down in the park. She had to shut her eyes to counter the wave of nausea that met her.

She turned away. Picked up her phone. Put it back down again. Picked it up. She opened her photos and found it. She stared at him. The pale eyes looked back at her. They were not the eyes of a young prince, but somebody very ordinary. Somebody who had made himself as ordinary as possible, as if ordinariness were a great prize. Something to be cultivated, to be fought for.

She didn't know what to do.

The security guard's concrete bunker was exactly where he had said it would be. Dinah pushed a button and heard a microphone crackle and saw a small video screen. A man's face was illuminated in black and white, edged with static. She caught, impossibly, a whiff of boredom, duty, and nicotine. She spoke in English, asked for Jun Kinoshita, and was buzzed in.

Inside the building were carpeted, soundless, wide, *wide* halls. There were windows along the corridors, but they were covered in angled blinds. Sunlight was visible around the edges. In spite of the polar air conditioning, the ambient heat was still proximate. She travelled by lift up to another identical corridor and stood in front of the door with the number Jun had given her. She studied the tiny fish-eye aperture in the door, moved to take up her place in the centre of its concentric world, and knocked. There was an institutional, chemical scent that was strangely comforting.

Inside there was silence.

Then the door opened and Jun was there.

'Hello,' she said.

'Hello. Thank you for coming,' he said, as if he had forgotten her apology, her request, the grudging nature of his own concession.

She smiled. She could not have expressed it, but it was a relief to be away from the apartment, away from Michael. There was something stringent about Jun's presence. She felt compelled to speak and to move lightly, deftly, in imitation of his movements. She felt she must speak equally politely, and in as light and modulated a tone.

Jun smiled and gestured to usher her into the room. A gesture in the manner of a host.

The studio was large and cool. Large for Tokyo, in any case. There was a concertina-style plastic room divider that ran on a ceiling track between bed and workspace, but this had been pushed back so that the whole space stood open.

Along the glass windows the long louvred blinds were turned at a slight angle and through them was the pale desert of an internal light well. She craned her neck and could see pink marble-look tiles that covered the entire courtyard, and the rectangular water feature below. The air conditioning was turned up high, and in its breeze the long louvres of the blinds stirred and tapped against the glass.

The first thing that anyone would notice about the room was its impeccable tidiness. There was a narrow daybed against one wall, and on the opposite a large metal-legged worktable with an angled wooden writing slope. The daybed was made neatly, the sheets and cover tucked in tight as a drum. A throw rug had been folded and laid carefully over the back as if to communicate that it was a sofa now, and it would be polite to ignore its previous existence as a bed. There were a set of familiar eau-de-nil-spined Penguin paperbacks on a shelf. On the bottom shelf was a carafe of water and a single tumbler, turned upside down so as not to catch any dust. There was no dust.

Even the papers at the desk were stacked neatly, carefully. She knew that if she were to rise and look at the papers more closely, the writing would be neat also. Neat, steady, careful.

Jun had taken his seat at the wheeled desk chair. He gestured to the daybed sofa. Dinah felt almost a qualm at sitting and disturbing its careful order, but she sat.

Jun looked down, then straight at her, with a smile, then away again. He rolled a little in the chair, pushing at the ground with his feet. He continued to smile. It seemed a declaration that there were many things about which they might speak and he would allow her to select amongst them.

She looked around at his room again.

'What does it mean?' she asked.

'Mean?'

'Isn't this kind of tidiness a message of some sort?'

She was looking at him as she spoke. His smile flickered, he went behind his eyes for a second, then he returned.

'Not really,' he said smoothly. 'I've always been tidy. Yasuko used to tease me about it.'

She saw immediately that he had not meant to mention his mother and that he was unhappy to have done so. She nodded. She knew the answer already. The message was surely that he didn't need anybody. That he had made himself completely alone.

'Please,' said Dinah, 'Don't let me interrupt you. I can come back if you're on a deadline.'

'Oh, no. That's fine. I needed to take a break anyway.'

'What are you working on?' It was strange, this mode of politeness between them. She felt herself not always able to meet his gaze.

'Public-policy analysis,' he said.

'I thought you were at med school?'

'No. Would you like coffee?'

'Yes,' she said.

He rose and walked out of the room, back toward the narrow gallery kitchen off the hall. She sat and then after a second followed him to offer help.

When she entered he was standing in front of the sink and leaning forward with his eyes closed. On his face was a look of utter anguish.

She paused, but the expression had already gone, so that she could not be quite sure she had even seen it, or read it correctly. Jun moved smoothly from the sink and, facing away from her, fetched mugs. He took another plate from the fridge and poured the coffee.

'Milk?' he asked.

'Yes. Please.' He took it and swung the door of the fridge shut with his hip.

They carried the things back into the main room. On the plate were some small custard tarts, their tops burnished brown with sugar.

'Do you mind the floor?'

'Fine,' she said, and he took throw pillows from the single bed, and placed them on the ground. But it was not fine. Something different and unexpected was happening, some balance had shifted.

When they had spoken on the phone, and in the bar, she had been so certain, so angry. She had known without doubt that he was in the wrong and her only thought had been to reveal this to him. To illuminate this. At that time his calm and the slight chill of his presence had only served to reinforce her certainty. Now she was encountering a different emotion entirely. Regret, perhaps. Or even guilt. She looked at the care with which he tended this private space and felt as if through clumsiness and ignorance she had placed a heavy foot into some carefully constructed world.

'I should go,' she said. She got up. She felt ungainly, stupid. She felt, oddly, like crying.

'That would be a bit strange, seeing as how you've only just got here.'

'I really didn't mean to disturb you. I'm sorry.'

'Don't be sorry,' he said. 'Sit down.'

So she did. She was silent. She looked at the mugs. They were mismatched. The only thing in the room that was. He was watching her.

'Where are you from?' he asked.

'A small town,' she said. 'The kind with one main street.'

'That sounds peaceful.'

She shrugged. 'Sometimes. Also it drives you crazy.'

He was watching her. 'You don't strike me as crazy in the slightest.'

She shrugged. 'That's probably not what others would say.'

'What I *would* like to know is what makes you so very wary.'

Dinah laughed. 'Me? How about you? I've never met anyone so untrusting in my life.'

'Well, of course,' Jun said. 'Why do you think I recognised it?'

Dinah said nothing.

'But of course I am too polite to ask about that. Instead I would ask you why you came here, to this city.' He shifted a little on the carpet, finding one of the paper napkins.

Dinah looked around at the room again. 'There was no single reason.'

'I wondered if you were trying to punish yourself for something.'

Dinah looked up sharply and met his eyes. His head was cocked, and he looked so much like Yasuko at that moment that Dinah felt dizzy.

'That's hardly polite,' she said. 'What do you mean?'

'Nothing really. I didn't really mean anything.'

'Is that what you are doing?'

'No. I've stopped all that.' He was looking down at the pastry. He picked at the crust with nervous fingers. Then he stopped and looked back up at her. His smile was suddenly very warm and frank.

'What do you think it is about us,' he said, 'that makes us so untrusting?'

'Maybe it is a rational response,' she said slowly.

'To what?'

'To an experience of being overly trusting at an early age.'

He nodded, considering this.

'Tell me, Dinah. Who was it that you trusted so much?'

She studied the carpet, which was industrial nylon, blue, very similar to that in her own hall of residence in Canterbury.

'My brother.'

She leaned back against the padded wood of the daybed. There was something stuck to the outside face of the shelf next to the bed. It wasn't visible from most angles. In fact you would only see it while lying in bed.

It was the only thing in the room that could in any way be construed as out of place, or decorative, or personal. Like an inkblot on clean paper. She stood up and walked over to it.

It was a postcard. A photographic reproduction of a painting on a field of gold. She knelt and looked. It was a tiger, very tiny, but giving out a kind of energy she didn't understand. The creature was bent forward on its powerful forequarters to sip from a small, dark stream. The perspective splayed the beast so that its ribcage appeared almost to have been split in two. Its black markings were very fine and irregular, rippled like marble.

'What's this?'

Jun came a little closer, inclined his neck as if to remind himself what was affixed to the wall there. She was very aware of his proximity.

'It's a reproduction of a wall painting, at Nijo Castle. In Kyoto. My mother and I went there when I was quite young.'

She looked again, more closely. The tiger's eyes were wide and fierce as if irradiated with love. Legs that seemed to contain a preponderance of knuckle. A tail that twitched and stood in a perfect, taut 'S'.

There was a second figure in the painting, she saw. It was not obvious at first, being nuzzled into the tiger's side. It was half effaced. It was a small leopard. A cub? It was tucked in, as if suckling. One clawed paw rested in proprietorial fashion against the massive side. The curve of its muzzle was visible, as in a smile.

'It must be quite something to see it in person.'

'It is. You should try to go, before you leave Japan.' He looked at her. He had gone behind his eyes again, was somewhere else. 'The parquet flooring in the halls is laid in intricate patterns. They flex together under the weight of anyone walking. It's called the Nightingale Floor. It's very famous.'

She nodded. The room was very quiet. The tapping of the blinds against the window, stirred by the air conditioner.

'That sounds like a good memory,' she said.

Jun shrugged. His voice was clear and detached.

'Yes and no. I got very sick there, in the ryokan we were staying at. I fainted. I remember waking up on the futon, and my mother holding a cool flannel to my head. She must have lifted me, though god knows I would have been heavy. She sat up with me all night. I kept on vomiting.'

Dinah looked up. 'I feel like I have seen that.'

Jun shrugged. 'It's hardly unusual is it? Looking after a sick kid. Isn't it what mothers do?'

Dinah nodded. It was what her mother had done. She felt that she had ruined something, somehow, but not how she had done so. She knew that she had to ask, so she did so.

'Jun,' she said. 'Are you in touch with your grandfather?'

He looked at her. His eyes were cool, curious. 'What has my mother told you?' he asked.

'Nothing,' she said. 'Not really. Stories, I guess.'

'I don't remember my grandfather. I wouldn't know him if I passed him in the street.' He shrugged. 'I should really get back to it,' he said, standing up. 'But thank you, for the break.'

She felt herself standing too, picking up her bag. She felt a cool current of regret.

'Do you miss her?' she asked.

'What do you think?' He took the plates from her, and they were standing close to each other.

'I think you didn't deserve her.' She had meant to send it with anger, to see it land and for the sting to help her in some way. She understood that she didn't want to leave this room. Her words must have carried that out with them, instead of anger, some kind of admission. When Jun's eyes met hers she saw there was a fleck of green in one of them. He was not angry. His expression was odd and gentle.

'How about you, Dinah. Did you deserve your brother?'

She couldn't say anything. She shook her head.

He came then and stood beside her.

They had walked and were now sitting. It was just a Doutor Coffee, almost empty, but the sun was coming in and she was sitting next to him.

'Can we walk?' Jun had said. 'I think I need to get some fresh air.' And she had nodded and they had taken the lift down, walked through silent, carpeted halls.

There was no one else in the café. They sat on bar-stools by the window. He ordered an iced coffee with half-and-half and took a pile of corn-syrup pods from the self-dispensary area.

'We were always alone,' he said, as if the conversation had taken a brief pause and had simply resumed. 'Just the two of us. That was normal. We were always alone.'

Dinah nodded.

Jun looked up and met her eyes and she nodded again He looked back at the iced coffee and peeled the adhesive from the back of a corn-syrup pod and added it.

'We lived with my grandfather until I was four or five, I think. But I don't remember it. I never thought something was missing. I thought I was lucky. I used to lie in bed and worry that something would happen to her.'

Dinah nodded again. She wanted to reach out and touch his hand, but she held her own steady on the counter.

'I knew that it wasn't exactly normal, to be that close to a parent. My friends used to joke about their mothers and fathers, criticise them, swear about them. Something would come over me when I heard that. Like I was physically sick.'

Another corn-syrup, added thoughtfully. He had a small pile, and he was systematically working through it. 'Since I left I have wondered. Is it really lucky to be so close to somebody? I think it leaves a kind of scar. Maybe you never really get over it. What do you think?'

'What happened in Kyoto?' she asked.

'It was a last-minute trip. Yasuko got it in her head we would go, and she picked me up after school. She'd packed a bag. She wanted to go to Nijo Castle, so we went all the way there, straight from the station. It was far too late, of course. It was obvious. But when we got to the gates it was shut, and she was so upset. But after a while we had to turn back and find a ryokan. We hadn't booked anything. We ended up finding this crazy old place run by two old sisters. Super expensive, but kind of dirty, like they'd fallen on hard times. They did the food themselves, very elaborate, kaiseki-style.

'When I woke up in the morning, Yasuko was gone.'

Dinah looked up. 'How old were you?'

'Ten? Eleven? I can't remember. Not that old.' He shrugged. 'It had happened before, so I was not very worried. Anyway, I waited for an hour or so, thinking she had gone to buy something. The sisters brought in the kaiseki breakfast and I had to pretend she was still asleep. I ate both of the meals because I was too embarrassed to return the food. Then I started to panic. I was old enough to mostly take care of myself, but I started to become worried about her. After a while I thought: she's probably gone to the castle. So I took the tram there.'

Dinah watched. He took another pod and peeled it, added it. She watched the syrup spooling down into the ice-cold coffee, eddying through the milky liquid.

'As soon as I got inside, it was obvious I would never find her. I mean the grounds are enormous, tourists everywhere. But I looked around anyway. What else could I do?'

Dinah watched in fascination as he continued to add syrup.

'It's a dark place, you know. It's been burned down twice. It's stark, kind of bleak, eerie. I pretended I was just there on a school trip or something. Looking for her, not too obvious. I went through the galleries. I saw the famous paintings, and this awful feeling came over me.' Jun leaned down over his drink and took an experimental sip. He shivered.

'How much corn syrup is in there?'

'Not enough,' he said. He paused. 'That's where the tiger painting is.'

Dinah nodded.

'And then I went straight out and I found her.'

'Where?'

'In the open grass by the ramparts.'

'What was she doing?'

'She was running after the birds.'

Dinah looked at him. 'What do you mean?'

He met her gaze, steady, wary. Testing. 'Just that. She was running after the birds. She was trying to catch one of them. They were crows, I think.'

Dinah sat quietly, looking at her hands. 'Why was she trying to catch them?'

Jun sat back and let his breath out. 'Dinah,' he said. 'Do you really want to know?'

'Jun. Please,' she said.

'She was trying to catch one so that she could speak to it. And if it didn't speak, then something else would happen.'

'What? What would happen?'

He sighed again. 'It was something that happened throughout my childhood. Right through it. Not all the time. I don't know how many times.'

'She left you?'

'No. No, she didn't leave. She went to her room. She disappeared inside herself. She didn't eat or talk.'

'What did you do?'

Jun shrugged. 'I didn't know what to do. I looked after myself. I tried to help her.'

'How long?'

'What do you mean?'

'How long would it last?'

He looked up, sipped his coffee. 'It depends. Sometimes just a week. When I was younger, sometimes for much longer. I was okay.'

'What about in Kyoto? What happened then?'

'Nothing. She didn't catch the bird. I caught her. She came back to the ryokan with me. I knew it was going to happen and I was terrified. We had never been away from home. I didn't know what to do. Later that night I fainted. I told you about that.'

'And after that?'

'I actually don't remember. I was sick for quite a while. Or it felt like ages. We actually had to move to a different ryokan because our booking ran out and there was no way I could travel. Then I got better and we went back home. Things were fine for a while after that.'

'Jun. I'm so sorry.'

He shrugged. 'Why be sorry? I loved her. I still love her. You know what she is like. She has such charm, such wickedness. She made the whole world come alive. And there were the times when her powers came back. That would last a week, maybe two, before she got depressed. When I was young those times were magic. She would take me out of school like it was a holiday. The animals spoke to us.'

Dinah looked at him.

'She made them speak. She did the voices. She made it up, like a game. But it was real. For me. It was real too.'

He paused. They sat there in the quiet.

'But you can't live like that, can you?' he asked.

Neither of them answered the question.

7

When Dinah arrived home Michael was not in the apartment. She felt relief. She sat in the dark and did not open the curtains to see down to the balcony, or to the park.

She thought about betrayal.

She thought about visiting Michael in his flat in that final year when she had joined him in Auckland. They had sat on the balcony, which had two or three threadbare couches and a scattering of beer cans. From the couch they could see out across the branches of an ancient magnolia grandiflora tree. There were tall buildings on each side. They smoked some of Michael's patchy weed and watched the sunset.

The sun went down across the hill; they sat next to each other and talked about nothing on the old springless couch. They put their feet up on the wall and they watched the evening light move slowly across the city.

When had she first betrayed him? Long before his first breakdown. She had betrayed him as she watched him tapping the silent keyboard of his knee, the rigid familiarity of his body next to hers, his demand on the world and the heavy cost. She had betrayed him knowing that she would return to her own flat and the negotiations over shared food and cleaning.

She had known it then. But she had sat next to him anyway. And when it was their turn for the sunlight, she had turned her face right to it and felt it shining directly and clearly and solely on the balcony for about two minutes as if were just for them, before it was gone.

'Michael,' she called out. There was no response.

'Michael!' She was full of anger.

Her phone buzzed.

Michael had been practising around the clock for this graduation concert.

It was not her imagination, the collective tightening of interest amongst the audience in the small auditorium as Michael entered. In particular she had felt it, or heard it, amongst the cluster of other students who were sitting in the elegant cerise-pink flip-up chairs at the very bottom of the theatre, essentially on the parquet stage itself. They lounged, in the relief of having performed, having discharged their adrenaline. But when Michael came through the double doors and sat down in front of the piano, they all sat up. A sharpness in the air.

The whole audience seemed to be lifting from their seats in excitement and revelation.

When he had finished, the applause was shockingly loud.

After, after. He had disappeared, like a magic trick. Out of the auditorium, out of the music school. It was almost funny. People were walking around with their hands in the air, looking behind pot plants as if he might have curled up there to take a nap. He had won a prize; they wished to give it to him.

She had walked to his flat. Some instinct for it. The floral smell of shampoo still lingered in the foyer, like an artificial garden. Usually she had to push the buzzer and wait a few minutes. She pushed the front door gently. It swung open a few centimetres then knocked against something hard. Dinah reached gingerly around the door and felt for the object that was lodged behind it. She touched wood. A chair. Then nail heads, frayed wool. A piano stool. She levered it up and pushed the door fully open.

'Hello,' she called as she walked in, past piles of clothing, books, pizza boxes, a clothes-horse. The usual mess. Nothing out of the ordinary. She walked through the communal kitchen. There was a track of dried leaves along the chess-square linoleum.

It was hardly cause for alarm, but it made her take her phone out. She began to type a message to her mother. It started, *I think Michael is.* She didn't write anything else, because she didn't know what the end of the sentence was. She no longer knew what Michael was.

The flat was empty. She called out. Michael's room was the worst room in the flat. It had been an internal office. It was big enough for a double bed and not much else. There were narrow safety-glass windows at the very top, and a large plain-glass window out to the kitchen. They were all covered in black cardboard for privacy's sake. The door was ajar, so she pushed it open.

There was an overwhelming smell of rot and shit. Michael was there, in the corner of the room. He had his back to her, hunched in one corner. There was a coat draped over his back. And then the leaves. Leaves all over the floor and every surface. There were pieces of paper too — bus tickets, advertisements, sodden wads of tissue. There were books, piles of them. Old clothing. Black and white photos had been stuck to the wall with something. She stood without moving in Michael's ruined room and stared at the walls. She did not see the pictures, did not take them in. But afterward an image returned to her. A photo of a group of children in shorts and knee socks, lying on the ground with their arms out and eyes closed, arranged by someone into a circle.

She pushed send on her phone without finishing the sentence.

I think Michael is. I think Michael is. And so he was.

'Michael?'

She knew he could hear her. When he turned she saw he was not wearing a shirt and his chest was smeared with something dark. Where had he gone? How had he achieved this transformation in such a short space of time. He stared at her as if he did not know her. Then he did, and he was so happy to see her.

'Dinah,' he said. 'I am so glad that you are here.'

She walked toward him, afraid.

'Dinah,' he said. 'Now you're here we can go. We can go. It's only us now.'

So sudden. As if the light had been off, and then it was on. Light flooded everything. She saw into the corners. She saw the outlines and shadows and edges just briefly enough to know how blind she had been. Relief filled her.

Then something else. Something not unlike disgust. Something not unlike shame.

Imagine you had survived an amputation. To get through you would pretend everything was just fine. The wound heals over. Perhaps you never had a second arm. Perhaps you learn to live without it. You could do most of the things that any able-bodied individual could do.

Then someone approaches you out of the blue. Here they come, walking toward you. Something is tucked behind their back. A surprise. A treat. And they are holding it out and there it is at last, outstretched in their hands. Your old arm. Just exactly as it was, that part of you.

'Dinah?' Michael's hands were open.

She had stood looking at him, her brother, and he was entirely separate. He was as somebody remote. She saw him as if he were a stranger.

She had not wanted that part of herself back. She had recoiled from it, its familiarity, the flesh that was mottled around the old ragged amputation scar.

And Michael had understood.

He looked at her. When he smiled it was slow and full of charm. Slow, as if his delight were a substance that could only reveal itself in stages or risk blinding them both. Then he grabbed her and held her around the neck.

It seemed like an embrace at first. Then perhaps like a game, like a continuation of games they had played when they were younger. She went slack and put her own hands up to reach him, his arms, or when that failed, his face.

'Michael, stop it. You're hurting me.'

He was very strong. The leaves were everywhere, all over the floor, and she couldn't get a grip. She was sliding in the mud and chaos. She managed to get an arm partly free and drew her elbow forward then back as hard as she could, into his ribs, his solar plexus.

Then they were apart. He was on the other side of her, by the door. She was not able to escape. She stood in the wreck of his room. She couldn't breathe. A deep ache in her windpipe as if she had swallowed something and it was stuck. She could hear him behind her. Slowly she found her hands and brought them up to her face. They were wet with blood.

'What have you done?'

There wasn't any pain.

'Michael?' He was hunched over, and she didn't know what to do. He was sobbing. 'What are you doing?'

'Can't you hear it?' His voice was calm, ordinary, very low. She could not understand him at first, but he repeated his question, louder. He raised his head. His look held something familiar. Perhaps a kind of hope. 'Can you hear it?'

She did not say anything. She listened, in spite of herself. 'What?' she said. 'What?"

'That,' he said. 'That!'

She knelt down. 'What?'

'Something is jammed. In the mechanism,' he said. 'You must hear it. There's a hum. Something stuck. I have to fix it. I tried,' he said.

'No,' said Dinah. 'There's nothing wrong. There's nothing wrong. I promise.'

His eyes shifted again. They moved around the room. He was standing in front of the internal window, the one that looked out to the kitchenette. He took hold of the cardboard and pulled it off its sticky backing.

'You're lying,' he said. 'You're lying. I thought I could trust you, but you're nothing.'

Dinah took a step toward him. The current was held between them, the clear water of their attention. But she did not recognise him. He saw her too clearly. He saw everything too clearly. The hatred in his face was like a scalpel cutting, and he looked at her as though she was part of the world to be dissected. She thought she was going to be sick, the wave of nausea was so intense. She saw and knew that he was right.

Then his face changed. It became almost entirely calm. He was holding a secret: A private source of satisfaction.

'Do you know how much has been broken?' He pointed to the window.

She didn't know what else to say. She shook her head.

'You can fix it.' He turned to her, and she knew what she needed to say, and she didn't say it. It was a choice, and she made it. It was her fault.

Then he punched through the window with both of his hands.

The sound of the glass breaking on the black and white tiles. Everything slow, impossibly slow. The look on his face was so familiar as he turned back to her, with his wrists encircled in their bracelets of broken glass, as if he had shocked himself back into his child self again, just for a second.

'Stand still,' she said. 'Stand still.'

8

Dinah waited on the platform for the Tobu Tojo line on Monday morning. She waited for Yasuko for the 7.05 train, but she did not arrive. She
had not yet arrived at 7.35, so Dinah boarded the limited express. She
caught the student bus from Kita-Sakado and was ten minutes late to
her first class of the day.

Dinah left her lecture and opened the door to the Japanese lecturers'
office and thought perhaps Yasuko would have arrived, but she was not
there. Chiaki only sat on one of the chairs by the bookcases, eating her
salad bento, leafing through the pages of an old travel magazine. Dinah
didn't say anything. She left the room and went to the student's cafeteria
and ate there. She could not go back to the native English lecturers'
office.

On Tuesday there was no Yasuko. Not at the station; not at SDU. At
lunchtime Dinah took her lunchbox and sat down across from Chiaki.

'How are you, Dinah-san?' Chiaki pursed her lips as she spoke.

'I'm okay,' she said. Fear made her swallow her pride. 'Have you
heard from Yasuko? Do you know why she isn't at work? I have been
messaging her.'

Chiaki's eyes widened. Okinawa looked up from his desk. He sat
up straight and leaned around so that he was visible past the protective
barrier of his computer screen. Chiaki made eye contact with him. Then
he looked steadily at Dinah, glanced quickly at Chiaki, then back.

'What?' Dinah asked. 'Where is she?'

Okinawa stood up and walked out past his desk. He leaned with his back to a table and picked up a workbook casually and looked at Chiaki.

Then the door opened.

'Ah, good,' a voice said. 'Dinah-sensei, I have a bone to pick with you.'

Mayumi had entered. She brought with her a palpable sense of anticipation, even pleasure.

'Yes?' said Dinah. She attempted a smile.

'A bone,' said Mayumi again. She looked up at the other two lecturers, who were standing immobilised in their positions. Dinah wondered if she had rehearsed this.

'It's an odd saying, isn't it?' she continued. 'It sounds as though I wish to share some food. But in fact I have a grievance. The bone is something that has come between us. Is it a saying you are familiar with?'

'Um,' said Dinah. 'Yes, though it's not one I use often.'

'Oh,' said Mayumi thoughtfully. 'Then there's an alternative? A phrase you'd say instead?'

'No,' said Dinah, pretending to think. 'No. None that I can think of.'

'I see,' said Mayumi. 'Well, in that case, it will just have to do. I have a bone to pick with you, Dinah-sensei, as well as our friend Kinoshita-san.' She leaned her head back a little. 'You have learned, I suppose, that she has left us?'

Dinah looked up sharply at Chiaki. She saw Chiaki quickly look at Okinawa.

'There have been problems in the past and I have been lenient. But recently there have been late starts, missed classes.'

Dinah tried to speak, but found she could not.

Mayumi looked at her wryly. 'I hear that you have been influenced by this. Leaving early. Missing classes.'

'I'm sorry,' said Dinah. 'It won't happen again.'

Mayumi placed a hand on the back of the chair opposite Dinah's; it was Yasuko's chair at Yasuko's desk. She smiled.

'No,' she said. 'It will not happen again. I will tell you why. Kinoshita-san might be able to afford the risk. Perhaps she has nothing to lose. But for you it would not be so pleasant, I think. If you lose your job you will lose your visa, of course, and you will need to leave Japan. In any case,' she said, breezily, 'I can see that you will be working hard to remedy the situation.'

She telegraphed a smile to the office, nodded gravely to Chiaki, then bowed goodbye to them all.

Dinah sat on the park bench and looked at her phone and dialled.

'What?' said Jun. 'What? Hello? Who is this?'

Dinah didn't say hello, but sat looking at the concrete dome.

'Dinah?' he said.

'Yes,' said Dinah. 'It's Dinah.'

'Has something happened? Do you know what time it is?'

Dinah looked at her watch. It was one in the morning.

'I'm worried about Yasuko,' she said. 'I'm worried about what she might do.'

'Okay,' he said. 'Okay. I am going to call someone. I'll get some advice. It's going to be alright. She'll be alright.'

'I'm sorry.'

He exhaled. 'You need to stop beating yourself up. The world is doing a great job of that without your help.'

9

Yasuko knew — how could she not? — that a different kind of reckoning was coming. She had not been able to travel to work. It was impossible. She could not brook the girl's bright and brittle disappointment. It was worse, perhaps, than her hope.

Seito had known all along and had tried to warn her. She herself had known back when she was a child. That was her father's lesson all along, wasn't it, when he withdrew his love? You cannot move between the worlds. And to reward her hubris, her belief that there might be a third way, a path between them, her punishment was definitively here.

She woke every morning into her childhood room. She smelt the mildewed, bodily smell of her unaired futon. She blinked in the half-light that was the light of that captivity. And then, as before, she tuned her ears to listen. And now, as before, there was silence.

She stood up, back in her own apartment. She listened and heard the silence. It could not be true, but it was. It was true, but she did not believe. She could not believe, because she had paid too high a price. She took the lift down to the basement floor. She stood in the courtyard where the gentleman had used to walk his dog, and she waited and listened.

There was nothing.

Yasuko did not allow herself to panic. She returned inside, avoiding the glances of the elderly couple who cast a look askance at her state of dishabille. What of it? It was her building. Didn't she pay her rates and taxes? She held her head high.

Inside her apartment again she dressed with infinite care. Her hands were shaking. She messaged Dinah. She messaged Jun. Perhaps they were together. Perhaps they had found each other and would never return to her. But she could not see anything. She could not see either of them, or hear them. The connections were blank, broken. She could not feel. She could barely breathe. The whole world was silent, blank. She felt her skin crawl in rebellion against the blankness.

It was her father's doing. It was her father's doing again. She knew it was not rational, but the disappointment, the bitterness, was rising inside her like bile.

She would go to Seito.

The Yamanote to Ikebukuro was mercilessly slow. She kept her eyes down, pressed her knees tight together. She did not wish to listen, lest her fears be confirmed. She pressed her hands tight to her ears. People were looking at her. She was dressed for winter, as if the layers would afford her protection. Eyes everywhere. She could not bear it. Through Seibu, from the ground floor up. Past the tea sellers, the taiyaki machine, the trays of eel bento to the lift bay. Up, up to Seito.

Perhaps the air had cleared a little. In any case she felt calmer, just being out on that concrete plane of the roof, the sun burning down, the sight of the shack in the distance, and the gathered shelving with the endless fish in their buckets and bins. She breathed in. She could not move and hold her ears at the same time, but she tried not to listen. She muttered under her breath, just in case. Everything would be fine. She simply needed to speak to Seito. Another beetle. Perhaps another bird.

She crossed the concrete field. It took forever. Had it always taken this long? The sound of her heels clattering and echoing, ricocheting off each concrete surface. She arrived at the polythene shroud of his airlock and pushed through the flaps to alert the sensor for the sliding doors.

Her hand met glass.

It was a strange feeling, meeting resistance where before she could pass through unimpeded. As if the air itself had crystallised. She stood for a second, then she peeled back the flaps and waved her hand directly beneath the sensor. She moved her whole body back and forth, but the doors did not open. She had to accept what was impossible to ignore. The doors were locked.

Yasuko stood back. She inhaled deeply to calm her quickly beating heart. She must not panic. Really, at her age, she should not give in to such panic. She rested her head slowly against the glass. In the dim gloom of the office, she thought she could make out the shape of Seito-san's stately partner's desk. She thought she could see the chair at which she had perched so many times. It was lying on its side.

She drew back. What did such disorder mean in Seito's world? Was it a sign of some kind of struggle?

She stood, about a foot from the door, wondering what to do and where to go. The sun was burning down. She removed her jacket.

How little one became used to the thick darkness of this. As if one's organs were shutting their doors on life. She could not even muster a feeling of sympathy for Seito. Perhaps, as for her, his past had finally come back to fetch him? And what could she be expected to do about it, if so? He was resourceful; he would find his way.

As for her. She considered the truth that there was nowhere left for her to go. Nothing left for her to do. She moved off, across the concrete to the side of the roof. She leaned against the concrete and looked down.

The city spread out before her, beautiful and useless.

She was standing in this position when she heard it. Nothing remarkable at all, really. A quiet hum. Gentle, like a cat purring. But she recognised it. It was a gentle chastisement. And she understood that it had been there all along. She had pushed her panic into it. The thousand things: fear, desire, panic. She had drowned it out. Relief came to Yasuko. But not like before, not all at once. It came quietly, steadily. There was no sense of desperation or fear. There was no grand delight nor rush of blood. It was something simple and steady. She turned and looked up at the sky with a stronger sense of gravity altogether.

Her gift was not an ignis fatuus. It would not go away and leave her.

It was in her and indivisible from her being, as she was part of the day, part of the sky itself.

The hum came from the sky. Her powers speaking. And a darkening, as if before a storm.

She stood and watched. The hum transformed. It became a flapping, a great and wild disturbance of the city's frequencies.

Then there were birds. Wings in the sky. She saw them: pigeons, crows, sparrows, magpies, thrushes, shrikes. City birds and those from parks and further afield. Wings up like sails. She felt her heart move in her chest, with gratitude. They came in waves and landed on the concrete, layers of them, a black and grey and moving carpet. In the pet shop down the concrete path, she could hear the tame pets shrieking. They were pacing, pressing against the glass. The lapdogs barking, the kittens scratching, the rabbits slamming at the boards with their paws as if they could dig themselves free. She stood in the middle of the concrete, and the birds of the air came to her.

Some perched on her body, some on her hair. Their claws grasped tight as if to say: you will never be alone. We are your children too.

10

Dinah wrote a message to Yasuko and deleted it. She composed another one. Deleted again.

Finally she wrote, 'Where are you?' and sent it. She sent it again from the teacher's bus on the way home the following day. Chiaki was not on the bus or the train platform. At home Dinah sent messages to both of Yasuko's email addresses. The addresses looked suddenly very provisional. It seemed almost impossible that such random strings of letters and numbers might lead to wherever Yasuko was. She lay on the futon couch and closed her eyes.

'Where are you?' she said to the ceiling, to the wall. 'Please?' She had not seen him since Yasuko's disappearance.

The light gradually ebbed. In the shadow, Dinah saw Michael's bulk. He sat on the faux-wood shelf that she employed as desk, bookshelf, and storage unit. He sat very close to her open laptop. She did not know if he was heavy, by what arrangement he managed his physical manifestation.

'Please don't break my laptop,' she said.

'I wouldn't *dream* of breaking your laptop,' Michael said, so that he won because he emphasised the word as if it were the most ridiculous thing in the world. He began to laugh. 'That's really the worst thing you can think of?'

'Of course it isn't. The worst thing has already happened.'

She thought she had silenced him, but it was only temporary.

'Do you know when I got really sick?'

'I don't want to talk about it,' Dinah said.

'When the worst time came I couldn't play the piano anymore. At my third-year exam I thought my thumb was jammed. I thought my arms were coming apart. There was a buzzing noise. I knew that it was coming from somewhere. I knew that I had to get to the bottom of it and that was my only hope of being able to unjam things. To start to play again.'

She nodded, trying to silence him. Her hair rustled on the couch cover. It sounded very loud in the noiseless apartment.

'How about when I saw you, the year after that?' She was there, again, in the car park. She saw with alarm and shock how he had made himself a new body, how it was clumsy and large in its newness.

'Oh, that was much later. After I started taking my meds again. I got fat.'

'How did that happen?'

'I ate. I was so angry with the chemicals in my brain, that I ate.'

She nodded again, as if she had been there and remembered.

'It was like a project. I remember. When I got up in the morning, I said, "Today I am going to eat," and I did. I bought loaves of bread and sunflower oil and peanut butter. Those big value tubs of ice cream that schools buy for camp. It cost a lot. Also, time. It takes a lot of time to eat that much.'

'Why are you telling me?'

'Because it didn't work. None of it. It's a mistake to think that you can punish yourself. The world can always go one better.'

'Maybe,' said Dinah. 'Maybe some people deserve it.'

He looked at her. It was very dark, as if the street lights had failed. His presence was nothing but a darker area of shadow, a blur in the black of the room. She saw the light of her laptop surge gently, then fade, then surge again, like a stooping pulse.

Dinah was asleep. Half-asleep. Wasn't she? The manifestation of her brother was her imagination, the thing she wished for and feared allowed out into the half-light. She felt his anger in the dark and waited for it to abate. He was never angry with her for long.

'You know,' he said, 'after I leave here I fly around. I fly over to that tall apartment building.' His voice was dreamy. 'From the top you can see all the aerials sticking up. They look like the antennae of some huge creature living under the city's skin. You can see the smog flowing in from the suburbs, making the sunsets all pink. It's beautiful.'

'That sounds nice,' Dinah said. She was nearly asleep. She was between two places. She was both at home in bed as a child next to Michael, hearing his breathing, and also here in this small apartment that was covered in flickering shadow and was cold in the air conditioning.

'I came here to tell you something. Quickly, before you sleep.'

She did not answer.

'Dinah? I've been thinking, Dinah.'

His voice was fading. Small sounds from the corridor; a cat mewling. The 'danchi kodan' was the name of the building he meant, the tall one. Public housing. She liked the sound of the syllables run together.

'That creature that lives under the city?' His voice low, making non-sense sound serious, as always. 'It is built in segments, like a caterpillar, like some sort of invertebrate. It is very old. Older than the concrete. It's asleep now, you know, and everyone is safe. But I've been thinking perhaps you shouldn't be here, Dinah, when the creature wakes up.'

Dinah was asleep and so could not answer. The last thing she heard before she surrendered to the blackness was the crash of her laptop as Michael pushed it off the shelf and onto the floor.

She woke with the knocking. Something was battering at her, she thought. She was inside a box or cage deep underground. She was encased and bound, and there was someone working far above her, working against the dark, levering it up, plank by plank.

It was painful but she felt herself rising.

She unwrapped herself from the sheets in which she was entangled, found her robe, stumbled over her laptop cord, and made it to the door.

Through the spyglass she saw nothing. There was a smear that she tried to wipe, but the blur was on the other side of the glass. She combed her fingers through her hair, unbarred the chain, and creaked the door open.

Yasuko was there. The light was so bright that Dinah blinked. She was perfect. Her teeth white, her clothing also. Dinah stumbled a little, backwards. She didn't say anything clear. She shook her head.

'Oh dear, Dinah-chan. Are you alright? Are you sick? May I come in?'

Dinah shook her head and stepped back, distraught. She pulled her robe closer around her. It was hopeless. It was too late.

'I've been calling you and calling you,' said Yasuko.

11

Yasuko removed her shoes and walked into the girl's apartment. She looked at the futon, the drawn curtains, and saw how things had deteriorated. She coughed and walked to the source of the smell, which was the white cardboard box on the counter. She opened it and saw the remains of the pie.

'My dear, you were meant to eat it. Why didn't you eat it?'

The girl drew the back of her hand across her eyes. If she guessed at the sudden heightening of Yasuko's powers, she did not reveal it.

'It was too beautiful to eat.'

Yasuko nodded. She felt at once great sympathy for and impatience with the girl. All that she had been given. She hoped that she would not squander it. She found a clean rubbish sack beneath the sink and whipped it open with a flourish. The sound shot out violently into the apartment. With one arm she swept the pie box, the empty bottles, the ramen bowls from the counter and into the bag. She frowned efficiently and looked at the neat stack of letters that were sitting on the ledge.

'These are all from your mother,' she said. 'You should really open them. You should know how mothers worry.' She shook her head. Then she picked up the phone that was sitting on the small table.

'Out of battery,' she said. 'That explains that.' She drew out a chair and sat, and the girl took the chair across from her and sat also.

She placed her hands over the girl's hands and stroked the back of her wrists gently.

'It is alright, my friend. Everything will be alright. You will see.'

'Where did you go?'

Yasuko shook her head and stood up. 'You must get dressed. Shower. It's already late in the afternoon. We are going out.'

'Where?'

She would not, she told herself, become impatient. She picked up Dinah's phone and plugged it into the charger at the wall.

'Shopping, of course.'

Yasuko escorted Dinah to the station. She held her arm as if she were an invalid. She guided her courteously through the gates, into the train. They changed trains at Ikebukuro and emerged in Shinjuku. Neither of them spoke. They walked along together. Their paces were perfectly matched. Neither needed to speed or slow.

'Well, then,' said Yasuko. And guided them down the street. She stopped in front of her favourite department store. It was of a different style to the other buildings. Older, darker. A brown-brick, tapering to a fine height, as if it had been made diligently by a colony of insects.

Yasuko took the girl's forearm again and they walked into the main entrance. Then they turned left and went into the shop. She saw the girl register the opulence of the shop, the famous logo with its interlinked Cs.

'Oh, no,' she said.

Yasuko laughed. The girl's resistance — she was almost having to push her inside — gave her life.

'Be patient,' she said. The air crisped as they entered. The interior of the concession, fitted out in cream marble, black glass, was a kind of balm. The air was scented from a machine in the corner that diffused a microscopic spray of the house's most famous scent.

A measurable instant's pause as the shop staff recalibrated. Yasuko saw Dinah's reflection in one of the tall mirrors, the girl's troubled face, the hair that was awry in the humidity. It would, Yasuko thought, be up to her to effect the transformation. It was clear that the staff, who knew her own presence well, were seeking to understand why she was here with this dishevelled young foreign woman. They took no more than an instant to overcome their disdain, however, and then gathered around, bowing deep so that they almost brushed the thick cream pile of the carpet. That famous colour — a pure white that had been sullied with a very specific measure of darkness.

'Can we help, honoured Madam?' asked the most senior of the staff, a beautiful woman, sleek and sinewed and elegant.

'Why, yes indeed,' said Yasuko, as if grateful for the reminder of her own presence in the store. 'I would like to purchase something out of the ordinary for my young friend.' She gestured carelessly to Dinah as if they had just met that morning. Had bumped into each other in the street, perhaps, as the sun was coming up. Dinah laughed then, and the note rang out incongruously amidst the marble and heavy glass.

'I see, Madam. Of course we can help you. Might I humbly guide your attention to this counter?' The woman was pointing to a display cabinet full of bag tassels, cell-phone covers, dog collars.

Yasuko smiled and bowed her head, a slight inclination that was not quite polite.

'No, that won't do at all. I'm afraid that is not the sort of thing I had in mind.'

She looked at Dinah, who was standing as if stricken in front of a mannequin wearing a frayed tweed miniskirt and a leather quilted bomber jacket. She shook her head and took her arm gently and walked through to the back of the shop.

They passed the sumptuous wall of handbags. Opposite there were racks of garments that looked old-fashioned in comparison. Yasuko's fingers played over the padded hangers like a musician at a keyboard, paddling the air above each. Feeling for resonance, for echo. She touched one jacket, and then the next. Her fingers walked past the pink and the cream and the powder blue and back to the pink. A heathered tweed with flecks of black and white and an unexpected green, like seaweed left out to moulder. She looked at Dinah and smiled and beckoned a finger, then she picked up the pink tweed suit and held it up to the shop manager without even looking at her, as if she were just any other shop girl on the floor. 'Please fetch this in her size,' she said.

'No,' said Dinah. 'I can't.'

Yasuko looked at her, a look that was half-inquiry, half-challenge. 'Of course you can.'

Dinah shook her head again. But she took the hanger. She entered the dressing room.

After some time she pulled aside the curtain in a sort of mute plea.

Yasuko looked at her. She saw the girl turn from Yasuko and back to her own reflection in the mirror. She saw the girl's eyes reach to her own eyes and see herself, hold her own gaze. Strange alchemy. Yasuko smiled. She felt filled with a perverse sadness. How humbling it was, to be reminded, yet again, how powerless one was rendered by love.

The girl looked away from her own reflection, perhaps with some reluctance, and back to Yasuko. Yasuko knew that, even as she stood there in bare feet, even with her tee-shirt beneath the jacket, she had seen something that could not be unseen. She had seen that she was changed, powerful.

It was nothing, in the end, that Yasuko had done. The suit had played its part in the magic, certainly. The seams, the length, the weight, the balance, the shoulders, where the button was placed and how it fell from her back. The colour that did something quite unexpected to her skin. The cut that made the garment a kind of armour. But really the transformation was something that was happening in the girl herself. It had started, and it would be ongoing, and it was extraordinary. She was changing into something quite different than Yasuko had predicted. But perhaps that was always the case. Yasuko felt a rush of something. Pride or disappointment.

She beckoned the girl forward, and Dinah came, lightly. She turned back again to the mirror. She could see the girl struggling with the shift. Yasuko knew exactly what she was feeling, the violent luxury of the silk lining against her thighs, the balance of the garments' weighted hems, their formal, heavy set against the hip and shoulder, the borrowed gravity of their internal structure.

At that moment the shop assistant burst forth from behind Yasuko, exclaiming — the fit, the colour, the girl's natural sense of style. She made a series of tiny adjustments at the lapel and hems. She turned

Dinah with light movements, so that she went round in a clockwise circle. More exclamations, stroking the fabric at the back and seat, until Dinah had turned 360 and was facing where she had started. Behind her, in the mirror, Yasuko raised her eyebrows to draw Dinah's smile. She nodded.

Then they were back on the street. Yasuko felt the girl's daze, her bemusement. She saw that the girl could not comprehend quite what had happened in such a brief space of time. It was interesting to Yasuko that Dinah had reframed the moment, perhaps in a bid to understand it. She was now protesting the generosity of the purchase, the size of it. Her struggle was impotent, of course, but she had latched on to it as some sort of necessary act. Mild protestation, but insistent. 'You can't, Yasuko. I don't understand. It is too much.'

Yasuko laughed. She put her hands up with the fingers fanned, to put a stop to the tiresome argument. 'Don't be ridiculous, my dear. Every young woman needs a suit at some time in her life. And this is your time.'

'But it's too good. It's too much. I couldn't wear it to teach.'

'No,' said Yasuko, affronted. 'Please. Do not wear it to teach. Wear it to the 7-Eleven. Wear it to the supermarket. Wear it to the park if you like, but if you wear it to teach in, I promise that I will never forgive you.'

The girl walked silently next to her.

'I don't know what to say. I don't understand what it's for.'

Yasuko sighed.

'A gift is the right object bestowed for no reason. Otherwise what is the point? Otherwise what is all of this for?'

She looked up. What was it all for? The overpass, painted in its awful, haunted municipal colours. The blue and green that were the same wherever you went in the city — their estrangement from any possible natural occurrence, their implacability. The concrete was so thick, thicker than imagination. And yet she knew that the spirits were sufficiently fierce to penetrate through at any time, even to forgive this entrapment. She saw Dinah look up as they passed beneath. She looked at the invisible blank sky, the ancient, brittle millefeuille of the concrete below.

'However, I know you are a person who values clarity and honesty,' said Yasuko, 'so I will tell you. It is a kind of apology.'

'What for?'

Yasuko smiled. She felt again her gratitude for the girl's innocence, her disingenuity. What strange good fortune to have met her, at this time in her life.

'Each of us has a small flame, a light that is our very own. Wouldn't you agree?'

Dinah murmured an assent.

'Here we all are, sending up this light and warmth. It shouldn't be hard just to leave everyone to get on with it by themselves. But so few people can manage it. They lean. They lean in to your space. You know what I am talking about, don't you?

'For them it's just a normal, everyday transaction. Friends do it. People you barely know. Men in the train. Once a boss stood too close to me and called me "sweetheart". I left that job the same day. None of the other staff members minded him. They just laughed it off. Marriage is very bad for it. Sex also. People, I think, find it very difficult to believe that any other person is fully human. In some deep part of themselves it isn't possible. In my experience, people are either vampires or cattle. The vampires try to drain your light, your warmth; they get a sort of strength from it. The others, the cattle, they are simply ignorant, they trample blindly everywhere. I am not sure which is worse.'

Dinah nodded.

Yasuko turned to her. 'My own flame isn't particularly strong or fierce. Just a homely orangey-yellow. But I do have a special gift.' She lowered her voice here, speaking confidentially. 'Do you want to know what it is?'

'Of course,' Dinah said.

'I have an acute sense of what will compromise me.'

'Yes.'

'Is that the right word?'

'Yes.'

'Wherever I am I can tell the exact moment someone else begins to press upon my flame, when they try to borrow from or bend that little filament. I am almost pathological in my protection of this small flame.' She turned an enquiring look to Dinah. 'And you?'

Dinah was silent. The world with all of its edges folded in upon themselves.

'Me?'

'Do you know what might have the same effect on you?'

'I don't think I can feel it. In myself. The thing you are talking about.'

Yasuko studied her. 'No,' she said. 'But it is still there. That feeling does not mean the flame does not exist. It simply means it is very weak at present. But this time in your life is only temporary. It is brief. I know it feels like forever, but take my word for it, it is passing by already. Soon it will be over, and you will look back and wonder how it was possible. You will forget all about it. If somebody asks you about the friends you had in Japan, you will take a minute to recall them. Perhaps you will even forget our names.'

'No,' said Dinah. 'That is not possible.'

'I have been lucky to meet you. Perhaps I have taken advantage of you. Do you know what makes you special, Dinah?'

'No.'

'When I sit here, right now, with you, there is not a breath of wind to disturb me. There is nothing that leans or pushes or steals. You probably don't know how rare that is. But one day, you will. You have become like a daughter to me.'

They left. They followed a narrow pedestrian street parallel to the station. It was one Yasuko knew well, the roadside shrines, the vending machines, the Print Club booths. She looked for the cats and saw them. Their ginger fur, each with its wound or impediment or scar, their badges of mange and their weeping eyes. A pair of salarymen pushed ahead of them, clutching briefcases and cans of Asahi.

'I hope you'll forgive me my little idiosyncrasy,' said Yasuko. She stopped in her tracks and removed a can of salmon from her handbag.

She had the gratification of hearing the girl laugh aloud. As if she, Yasuko, were a prestidigitator and the girl her eager audience. Canned salmon from Louis Vuitton. Next she would make something vanish.

Yasuko crossed the street and found a spot beside one of the road-side shrines on the pavement. She took a tissue from her purse also and swept the spot clear of dust. Then she removed the lid using the ring pull and used it as a scoop to remove the meat. She placed little piles of the expensive salmon at discrete intervals. The cats purred and yowled and threaded in and out between her feet. She spoke to them, and they walked around her with their heads tilted one way and then another, as if listening.

Finally she took a wet wipe from her purse and cleaned her hands. She stood up and winked at Dinah.

'Who else is there to look after the cats?' she said. 'Here. Let us go this way.'

She pointed to a pedestrian footbridge at the end of the cul-de-sac.

Dinah nodded and they walked. But Yasuko saw the obstacle.

A group of men were gathered there, just before the place the footbridge rose up over the tracks. Yasuko had seen them before, of course. They were a mid-life-crisis club who met there often, but never so many. Ten of them, all wearing full motocross leathers, right down to the fine, webbed gloves and the sponsorship insignia. Their bikes were propped up on spikes and the chrome gleamed cool and expensive in the moonlight. They were taking turns in straddling each other's bikes, inspecting the engines. Occasionally they revved them, then dismounted and tinkered away.

Their voices were so loud, as if they owned the whole street, the buildings around, the smokestack that rose behind the nearby hospital, the tracks, everything. As if they owned the whole night and the sky itself. She saw immediately that if they wished to get past, she must negotiate the threat of their presence, she must lower her eyes, must demur and retreat. She knew — just as quickly — that her pride would not tolerate this.

As they drew close she did something else instead. She laughed at them. Open faced, open mouthed, she made eye contact with the tallest and nearest and laughed with clear, direct insolence. She tipped her head back to do it.

'*That* is what you do when you reach middle age, my dear friend,' she said loudly to Dinah, 'and your wife no longer lets you put your tiny prick inside her. Also when your boss has passed you over for promotion three times.'

The tallest of the three men raised his head and yelled at her. Nothing original. You would not expect it. As she and Dinah walked closer he came out from behind the heavy body of the bike and spat on the concrete.

Yasuko stopped. They were nearly at the footbridge. The bridge was divided in two: one side had steps, the other a slope so that cyclists could wheel their bikes down. You were meant to dismount, and there were signs to that effect, but a kid was riding over with his girlfriend balanced on the handlebar before him. Their hair was flying in the wind, the whole picture a vision of freedom as bright and sharp as lemon at the bottom of a clear glass.

Yasuko turned. She was borne up suddenly with a kind of distilled, levitating glee. She saw Dinah watching her, and saw her half-understanding. Yasuko turned to face the men. When she spoke her voice was still jovial, but it was also dangerously quiet. She spoke rapidly. She cursed them from the depth of her being and she called on the cats to take her revenge. She saw the men's faces change in a slow ripple. It was like watching people observing a natural disaster, caught on film at the exact moment when they realise their vantage point is not invulnerable.

Yasuko retrieved Dinah's arm, where it had fallen, linked it through hers, and stepped her away up the footbridge steps. They stopped at the end to look at the sky. It was beautiful.

One of the station-front hotels on the north side was called Hotel Suica. There was a neon sign that showed a piece of watermelon with a bite taken from it. It pulsed in the night sky.

'What did you say to them?' asked Dinah.

'Nothing much,' said Yasuko. 'I told them their mothers would be ashamed.'

'Did you hear something?' Dinah asked.

'No,' said Yasuko, and she led the way toward the station entrance.

Behind them as they walked, the cats came. They emerged from nowhere and thickened into clots like crystal in a test-tube. They emerged from the shrine house, neatly sidestepping the tiny saucers of salt and the heaped-up piles of expensive salmon. They came from the dead zone between the tracks, and from park benches, and from between cars. They flowed out of the stairwells at the base of the apartment building opposite. They came until they flowed together into a particoloured sea, a sea of mange and fallen nobility, and they came and came until their sea at last broke over the men below, who had not thought to run and were still standing, holding their motorcycles, frozen in disbelief.

12

Beds filled with low dense plants, nestled up to their necks, never having to move. The low hammock of the motorway overbridge. The homeless man who lived there. Out from the shadow and back into the world with its transparent air.

Dinah clutched the black silken thread of the carrier bag. She felt the weight of what was inside it, moving in its exoskeleton of expensive tissue. She felt the glow of transformation still on her, the sense of strange power she had felt in that dressing room.

Down Meiji-dori, things becoming homelier and more anachronistic as they neared her neighbourhood. Past the rusted mechanic's workshop, the hole-in-the-wall pickle vendor. A faded poster of a popular boy band advertising domestic tourism. A shop selling second-hand appliances.

As they walked Dinah had the strange sensation that she was not outside at all, but instead beneath a vast awning. She felt that the evening would continue forever, and that they would walk and walk forever inside it and she would never tire. They were nearing her street, but it was completely different. Everywhere she looked, suddenly, there was life, movement. When she was small there had been a book with black and white pictures. You painted it with water, and colour came up out of black and white like magic.

That was how it was. Everything that had been invisible had begun to flower.

People were emerging from shops and houses. A group of men in short cotton jackets were carrying a portable shrine on their shoulders, and people were following down the street, laughing and cheering. Dinah saw the elderly woman she had seen before, watering her plants. She too was standing and waving at the procession as it passed. A handsome young couple in cotton yukata rode past on a bicycle. The girl sat side-saddle on the front bar, with her feet in their high-heeled sandals gracefully crossed. An old man in a leisure suit walked past with his grandson's hand held in his.

'Where are we going?' Dinah asked. Yasuko smiled and shook her finger.

'Nowhere,' she said. 'Simply walking.'

They passed the school and the paper factory, and then they reached her own park, the park she had spent so many nights of despair alone in.

It was filled with people. She could not understand it.

There were carts and caravans selling small metal clips and badges with flashing lights inside, and fans, and chocolate-covered bananas, and yakisoba, and goldfish in plastic bags. There were knotted pieces of paper tied to the trees. Teenagers in yukata sat on all of the benches. Children ran and shouted. Everything was floating, floating in the light, and Dinah understood at last that everything had been there all along. It was she who had been blind. She had not seen any of it. On and on they walked, going deeper or further in toward the heart of something, though who knew what that might be.

'Tell me, Dinah. Where is your brother now? What is he doing?'

There was no jolt. Dinah did not look up as she moved across the gap of air beneath her. Her legs carried her across and she answered without thinking. The light was moving between day and night. She knew exactly where Michael was, and where she was also, because — after all — they were always to be found together.

'He is lying in bed. I can hear him breathing. Perhaps he is asleep. Our mother is in the kitchen, doing the dishes. As for me, I am still reading. Our lights are off, but I'm reading using the hall light, which is reflecting off the wall and onto the page of my book.'

'Yes.' Yasuko's voice was warm. So warm, so alive, so kind.

The sound of Michael breathing. There was still light coming through the curtains, lighting them like a lantern. She could see the patterns in the curtains and along the walls, the plastered gib, forming and reforming. The outside world was breathing also, and she could hear the in-out of the vast lungs of the wind and the evening air. She could hear the neighbours up the road having a party. Everything was waiting outside for them, but it was soft here and they were protected.

Her phone vibrated deep in her back pocket. It did not pull her out of the dream. She was back there, and Michael also.

'Michael, are you awake?'

'Yes.'

'I can't sleep.'

A sigh. 'Well, what do you want me to do about it?' It was the grudging grumpiness she knew very well and loved almost best of all. There was the sound of him getting up, padding down the hall.

'He is playing,' she said to Yasuko. 'He is playing something to help me sleep.'

13

There was no way she would survive it. There was no way. Dinah lay down.

She couldn't avoid it any longer. She was going to remember whether she liked it or not. She lay on the bed. She kept her eyes open. She allowed it to happen. As if there were any other choice.

There it all was: the beauty of that particular Oamaru day. Horribly beautiful and clear and sunny. The trees came up out of the flat surface of the lawn, piercing it irrationally. The sun shone on every blade of grass, not forgetting a single fucking one.

She had stood with her mother. They had embraced then separated to look at each other in the awful sunlight. It was then that Dinah had seen the calamity.

'Oh no.'

She had left a bright smear on the shoulder of her mother's pale-grey silk blouse. It was lipstick. A smudge. An irremovable mark.

'Oh,' said Dinah. She couldn't breathe. 'I'm sorry. I'm so sorry.'

Her brain froze. She had a sudden sense of calm. A sense of unexpected and thus wonderful reprieve. The funeral could not possibly take place. The car was due in a few minutes and her mother's blouse was irreversibly ruined. There was no other choice. They would have to stand there, forever, unmoving, in that room. She was filled with such clarity. She demonstrated to herself, to her mother, to any god who happened to be watching, how very still she could stand. If they both stood still in this fashion, everything would go away, she knew.

The funeral guests would sit and sit and eventually they would tire of waiting and they would leave, silently, whispering amongst themselves. The sandwiches under their plastic wrap in the hall would dry and curl and succumb to mould. Dust would come with its great kindness.

She looked at her mother without blinking. She hoped her eyes were able to communicate all of this clearly. She hoped for the miracle of her mother's understanding. Michael, of course, would have understood it all without words.

Her mother looked at the stain on her blouse then back at Dinah. She stood silently, gravely, for a while. Dinah thought, without any logic, 'It is working. It is working.' Relief flooded through her. They would stand here. The funeral would not take place. Everything would be alright.

But that was not what had happened.

As she stood and watched, her mother took off the blouse. She unbuttoned it, slowly, from bottom to top, and stood there, half naked, in her bra. She stood for a few seconds, then she went into the bathroom. There was the sound of running water, and after a while she came back out holding the blouse. She put it back on. The shoulder was black with wet. Then her mother picked up the hairdryer and put it on full blast and she dried her shoulder, standing by the window, looking out. She stood there holding the hairdryer until the wetness was dry. Until the stain was gone.

Dinah's eyes filled with tears. It seemed to her that it had been in her mother's power to put a stop to it all, and she had refused. Her mother turned around, then, looked at her, and spoke.

'Darling,' she said. 'I know that you know this, but I am going to say it anyway. You can't blame yourself.'

How could Dinah explain that she was crying with anger, not grief. How could she explain that her whole body was filled with anger? She was so angry that her mother had ignored the miracle, had instead cleaned the stain from the silk blouse, dried it, remained calm. That in this fashion she would go to her son's funeral, make small talk to the people who were there.

From the distance of error, now, Dinah saw it all again. From this distance she saw her mother standing like someone chained, bending over low to lift the next burden. She thought of the mother at the bus stop bowing to her son as he left her. The next burden, at her own son's funeral, had been the labour of making her daughter, Dinah, feel better. What a fucking job. But what else could you do except bend low from the waist and pick it up. What else could you do but allow yourself that grace?

Dinah found her phone. It would be early morning in New Zealand, perhaps too early, but her mother was an early riser.

She sat on the bed, listening to the dial tone. If her mother didn't answer in a few rings, she would hang up so as not to wake her.

'Dinah,' her mother said. Her voice was there and unchanged. 'Darling. Is everything alright?'

Dinah paused. She wasn't able to breathe for a second. The sound of her mother's voice filled her with such a rush of homesickness and self-pity. She wanted to weep, and she wanted to apologise. Most of all she wanted to be absolved of her selfishness, her blindness. She swallowed instead, so that those feelings moved deeper inside her, burrowed in and took up residence, became a known part of her, a grainy texture that she could neither ignore nor resolve.

'Everything's okay. Everything's fine. It's all fine. I just,' she stopped. 'I just wanted to hear your voice.'

14

Because it was office hours she entered through the front entrance of the UN university building. The concourse was all in a white quartz. At its borders there were low quartz-tiled planter boxes filled with small shrubs covered in lime, almost neon, green cones.

She knocked at Jun's door, and he stood aside to let her enter.

'Why did you ask me to come?'

'Because I wanted to see you. And also because I wanted you to meet someone.'

She nodded. They sat down briefly and then there was another knock at the door. Jun got up to answer it.

'I'm sorry,' he said. 'Please forgive me for this.'

Standing at the door was a man who Dinah recognised immediately. He was of middle height and stature, and handsome. He had even eyes, and a salt-and-pepper beard, neatly trimmed. He wore glasses that reflected the light.

'Kinoshita-san, this is Dinah. Dinah, this is my grandfather.'

Dinah shook his hand.

'You are the young woman who my son mentioned,' he said. 'The one who is a friend of my daughter.' He came into the room and looked around. He nodded as if in approval, then turned back to Dinah. Jun pulled up a chair for him, but he waved a hand and continued standing.

Dinah looked at Jun. She felt the strain in her ribs. She could feel each one of them, as if they were a concertina at her sides, each of them. She placed her hand possessively at the bottom of the final row of bones. There was not much holding a person together. She dipped her fingers into the gap of cartilage and muscle experimentally.

Traitor, said her blood. Traitor.

She felt she could not speak.

'Yasuko was right,' she said. She was looking at Jun. 'She was right.'

'About what, my dear?'

Such a serious voice. She turned to look at Yasuko's father. He was broken; she saw it in his face. She ignored him, turned back to Jun. Jun hadn't stopped looking at her. Dinah realised that she was crying.

'He has come to steal you,' she said. 'He is trying to steal you from her.'

Jun shook his head. His face was full of sympathy. He reached across and touched her hand for a second.

'I called him, Dinah. I contacted my grandfather after we last talked. I didn't know who else to speak to.'

Kinoshita nodded.

Dinah looked at him. She shivered. She had come out dressed for the sun, and the air conditioning was very cool.

'Jun tells me that you have been helping Yasuko.'

'We are friends,' said Dinah.

Yasuko's father raised his eyebrows. 'I see.'

She stared at him. 'I have been trying to understand,' she said.

'That is good. That is good of you.' He looked emptied. 'You should know that I have failed at that.'

Dinah said nothing. She looked at him. She was waiting. Suddenly she was very tired.

'I made many mistakes with my daughter. I have to live with it. I did not know any better.'

Dinah felt anger, but she had no desire to use it against this man.

'So many of the hopes I had for myself I put into my daughter. There is no straightforward way to do that. You seek to pass on all your hope and optimism. But what is it really? Is it love or ego? And where does it all go? You put the hope in, the love in, and it emerges as something else altogether. It is the child itself. Each time different. I have begun to think that this is one of the only mysteries we have left in the world.'

Dinah shivered again. She heard an echo of Jun's painstaking, precise speech. He continued.

'I made a mistake. I did not know any better. That is why I did things differently, the next time.'

'What did you do?'

'You must know how wonderful it was having Yasuko and Junichiro with us in Sapporo. It was like a homecoming. Jun was a beautiful boy. Very strong. Big for his age. Very strong-willed.'

Dinah looked across at Jun. Yasuko's father did not seem to be describing the same person.

'He would shout. We all laughed about it. He would open his mouth and shout for his mother. To us it was a beautiful thing, a pure thing. From the mother's perspective, who knows? I remember Junichiro opening his mouth, like a baby bird, and shouting out. Mama! No one else would do. He was hungry all of the time. He would open his mouth wide, wide. He had all his teeth from a very young age, and he would cry or shout to hold her. We were all amused.'

Dinah wrapped her arms around herself. She was very cold. Kinoshita was still speaking. She had never discussed this time with Yasuko. However, she knew very clearly that whatever he remembered and whatever he would explain about Yasuko, about Jun, he understood nothing of any importance. She found that she was not really listening to his speech. His voice was deep and aspirated as if each word required a discrete volume of air blown from a set of bellows.

Dinah imagined Jun as a boy, his mouth opening wide in want, an unschooled, unquenchable want, a hunger that would never be sated. Was Kinoshita's description accurate? And if it was, what did it mean? Dinah's stomach was hollow with her own hunger, right up under her ribcage, stripping it out like a casket of reeds, thinning everything. It was an ugly feeling, it left her estranged, somehow malignant.

'When Junichiro turned three there were signs that Yasuko's illness had returned. It is a tragedy. I had failed her already. I wanted to repair things with her. But our responsibility had also changed. We needed to do what was best for Jun.'

Dinah looked across at Jun. She was not sure if he was hearing this for the first time.

'What did you do?'

'We asked for help.'

'What sort?'

'There was a new clinic, a very good one. Not too far from us. I had made a mistake the previous time, I thought, by keeping her at home. I thought it was the right thing to do.'

He looked at Dinah with a kind of appeal, as if he were hoping for recognition of his impossible choice.

Dinah nodded.

'What happened?'

'She left,' he said. 'She took Jun and they disappeared.'

Dinah sat and looked at the picture on the wall.

Jun showed no sign of contesting this. She realised he had stopped listening. He was looking at something on his phone. His entire demeanour was one of sufferance, like a teenager politely tolerating an adult conversation.

She wished to feel the hot flood of anger she had felt before. She wanted an anger that boiled up and shook things loose. But Yasuko's father was an old man, and she could not feel anger at him. He had been depleted, emptied by his life.

'What will you do?'

'I will go to the apartment. I have the address. I will offer to help again. I will seek to help her.'

'Nothing you can do will be of any help to her,' said Dinah. She thought it was very cruel of her, and she felt a moment of guilt. But then Kinoshita looked up at her. His glasses caught the light and the reflection obscured his eyes and the effect was one of blankness and a steady coldness.

'I understand that you are returning home soon,' said Kinoshita. 'You are a student of literature? You will continue your academic career?'

'I don't know. I haven't decided.'

'Ah, well. You are young. But my advice to you: don't waste too much time on this stage. At your age it feels like time goes on forever. It is only when you reach my age that you realise that this was an illusion.'

Dinah nodded. She looked to her left. Jun looked up, raised his brows.

Dinah was filled with a mixture of irritation and humour. It couldn't be so easy, could it? To reduce it all to such a gesture.

'Junichiro-kun,' said the grandfather. 'I am afraid that I have a meeting. You will escort Dinah-san to the station, won't you? And see her home. Perhaps you children could find a place to eat a nice meal on the way.'

Jun nodded, pale and compliant. 'Of course,' he said. He looked at Dinah, waiting.

15

They were walking side by side along the empty wide pavement. All she needed do was avoid Jun's eyes. And this was reasonably easy. She made her expression as flat and unreadable as his. She didn't know what to think or to feel. She felt as though she had been stripped and examined. She did not know what remained.

'We must warn her,' she said.

'What about?'

'About your grandfather.'

'I don't think Yasuko needs a warning. Anyway, you said you wanted to help her. You said you were worried about her. Are you?'

'Yes,' said Dinah. 'No. I don't know.'

'Do you want something to drink?'

'Yes, okay.'

Jun stopped by a Sunkus convenience store. The feeling of nakedness was still with her. She wondered how long it would be before it faded and she could allow the world to subside back into its place. She found that she did not know what that place was.

Jun opened the beer fridge and retrieved a Kirin tallboy. He stood aside. She had meant to buy a bottle of water but in the end reached in also and took a Sapporo.

They walked and sipped. The quality of the silence had again changed. It had become strangely companionable not to talk, not to be needed in any fashion. She wasn't quite sure of the direction in which they were heading, whether toward the trains or the subway or somewhere else.

'What will we do?' she asked.

'What about?'

'About Yasuko.'

'You know it is not your responsibility, don't you?' Jun said. His voice was surprisingly gentle. 'I know my grandfather suggested we go to a restaurant, but would it be alright with you if we picked up something quickly, to go?'

'I don't need anything. You don't need to escort me either. Just point me in the direction of the subway. I have my phone.'

Jun didn't answer. His attention was diverted. Dinah felt tired. She was, in fact, very hungry, had not eaten since a slice of toast and Bonne Maman many, many hours ago.

'Hold on,' said Jun. He stood and looked. 'I always miss it. It's just over here.' He took her arm and they crossed the street, then they were separate again and he stopped. The storefront was very missable. A tiny green frilled awning. One woman stood behind the high counter. There was no food visible, but Dinah could smell a smell that was both hot and cool; white and green. She looked over the counter. The woman was slicing spring onions as fine as thread. Jun spoke quickly to the woman in Japanese.

Dinah stood by, awkward, unsure if she would also need to order, and how she might do so when she still spoke so little Japanese and had no idea what the woman was selling. Jun did not move away from the counter, so she decided simply to wait. She could always buy something at the station. She went and sat on the wall a few metres away. It was somehow very necessary to sit. A train of ants wended their way along the concrete paver to her left. She thought back to the afternoon in front of the piano teacher's house, when they had discovered that Michael was gifted differently, far from the commonplace fashion in which anyone else was gifted. The busy insect lives were somehow reassuring, as they had been then. It seemed amazing that it had been so many years since her brain had slowed enough to notice them.

'Ready? I know a place where we can sit to eat. Come on.'

Jun's hand was on her forearm again, in a mute, heavy touch. When he released it she allowed the arm to hang down so that their hands almost brushed together. They walked side by side. Jun was carrying a couple of blue plastic carrier bags in his other hand, and she reached across to take one, so that they carried an equal load. The bag clinked as she took it. Inside were two brown bottles he must have purchased from the woman at the hole-in-the-wall joint. They continued walking. Their hands touched silently.

'Here.'

An alley that they walked down, and then a clearing between the low-rise apartment blocks and the backs of restaurants and narrow houses. Not really either a park or a vacant lot, but something in-between. There was a gravel path that ran through it, but the rest was untended grass, long and full of weeds. There were two tall trees at the end of the lot. One had a wooden bench beneath it, the other a milling, turning colony of cats.

Jun walked a little ahead and sat. Dinah followed and sat too. There was space between them for the plastic bags.

'Tell me about your brother,' Jun said.

'We were twins,' said Dinah. 'He built the world, and we both lived inside it. He made it up, and I believed him.'

Jun was listening; his face was without expression.

'He was a pianist. He would have gone on to do postgraduate work, maybe even have a recording career. But he had a breakdown. He lived at home with my mother after that. He got a bit better, he came back to the city I was living in. He was taking his meds. By chance I bumped into him on the street.'

The park was there and not there. Dinah felt her own face sliding around. The tears, something breaking.

'He died later that day. He jumped.' She was crying and it was like an earthquake.

She thought about walking up Victoria Street to catch the bus and seeing him without warning. He was in a pair of blue overalls, standing in the empty, weed-filled car park of the Centra Hotel. When he turned, the sun caught the plane of his cheek and jaw.

283

She remembered the feeling. It was so simple. A burst of joy, a holiday release from all of the heaviness and loneliness of living apart. She called out his name with that in her voice. 'Michael!' There was no one else in the whole world whose name she could call like that, with such abandon, without any need to protect herself.

Her voice rushed out across the street, and she stood waving. They had not seen each other for almost a year. Over that time she had called home every second day. She and her mother had developed a new coded language of pretend hope and practicality. 'The new meds seem to be working well,' was one part of the code. 'He is playing again,' was another.

Michael never came to the phone. Sometimes she heard his voice in the background. His voice asked their mother a question. Did you put milk on the shopping list? Will it rain later? She heard his heavy, flat-footed tread.

'He's doing much better. He's talking about going up to Auckland again.'

'You're not serious. Why?'

'I think to be closer to you.'

And there he was, as close as it was possible to be. There he was, facing her.

It had struck her then not just with the force of a single error, but with the weight of all past errors gathered together to roost and flap. It was Michael, but also it was not. He had fashioned a new body for himself, padded with extra weight. The new body was meant to keep him safe. It was an insulation from the world's sharpness, the way a hawk is hooded, or a horse blinkered so that it doesn't startle. And a punishment, to trap and slow his own younger self, the person who had injured him.

He was carrying a plastic pump with a translucent tank like the spare fuel tank of an old outboard motor. It had a long trigger-handled metal hose and was slung in a strap over his shoulder. He looked across the road to where she was standing waving her arms. Across the traffic of Victoria Street she saw his eyes swing and then come to a stop on her.

She walked out. A motorist leaned on a horn; somebody swore loudly. Then she was on the other side of the street, out of the shade and into the sun. They were standing together. And as though a miracle had occurred while she crossed, he was Michael again. She wouldn't have believed it possible, but there he was. She was so desperate that she almost laughed with relief. His eyes were clear; he unstrapped the pump and put it down so that he could hug her. There was his smile with all of its familiar grace, the Tom Sawyer swagger that made everything he chose — the job, the blue, oil-smeared overalls, his body — somehow the right and enviable thing.

'What on earth are you doing?' she asked. His hands were grained black with oil. 'You look ridiculous.'

As soon as she said it she could have bitten her tongue, but he smiled mildly and nodded as if it were a singular sort of secret.

'Weeds today. Don't laugh. Honestly,' he said, 'it's temporary. But it's kind of great. You won't believe some of the things I'm doing here.' His voice was lighter than she remembered. But he sounded the same. The same cadence, the same rhythms. She put her hands on his shoulders to squeeze them. She wanted to look at his hands, but he was wearing yellow gloves.

'What wouldn't I believe you're doing?'

'Fixing things. Everything,' he said airily. 'Light bulbs, air conditioning, lifts. Painting the skirting boards. Unblocking the urinals.'

She nodded.

'It's a superpower,' he said, pointing at his overalls. 'These things. They make you invisible. I can go anywhere.' He lowered his voice confidentially. 'I'm learning all the time. People are animals, half of them, I swear. They'll do anything for something free. Every hotel room has bottles of body wash and shampoo, right?' Dinah nodded. 'They just refill them from the same big industrial tubs of detergent. The tubs are so old they have dead moths floating in them. And every day people sneak the little bottles home with them like they're getting away with something.'

He had laughed. Taken a small step back. She didn't know what else to do, so she laughed too.

'I like your name badge,' she said ironically. The badge pinned to his chest was made out of plastic but something, perhaps heat, had bent it into an undulating wave, warping his name.

'Oh yes,' he looked down. 'It went through the dryer. They make us wear these.'

He turned and looked back up again at the car-park tower.

'I'd better go,' he said. 'Those weeds won't kill themselves.'

And she laughed again, as if it were a joke.

'But I'll see you tonight, won't I?' he said.

'Tonight?'

'Yes. At home.' He looked confused for a second.

She paused. 'At your flat? I'm busy tonight, but how about Friday? We could go out, just us two? Do you have a phone?'

He nodded, took an old Nokia from one of the pockets on his leg. 'Can you put your number in?' he said, and passed it to her. 'The buttons are tiny.'

She took it, added her number, and sent herself a message, felt the gentle buzz against her hip.

'My number's in there. But I'll call you. Tomorrow. And we'll go out for dinner.'

He nodded, graciously, gently, kindly.

'I'll see you there. Bye, Dinah.'

'See you tomorrow.'

'See you tomorrow.'

Then he was gone, gone, and he would not come back again.

Jun held her shoulder. Dinah looked at his face, and still there was no emotion on it at all. It was like a clearing. As if Jun were looking through a screen at her. He nodded. Nothing in his face — not sympathy. Not pity. He had taken the information that Dinah had given him and it was now something else, existed in a different landscape.

'Did he say that he was going to do this?' he asked. 'When you met him? Was there any clue?'

'No,' said Dinah. She paused.

'And now you are alone?' he said.

Dinah felt as if she were out of breath, as if she had run too far and all of the oxygen in the world had to fight to push its way to her through a too-small space.

'Yes,' she said.

'I understand,' he said.

'I think for half of my childhood I did not know what was real,' Dinah said. 'Michael told me that if you looked through the window in my mother's room, you could see into a different world, a different life. If you looked long enough. It was like a little round orbit, a lens. He went through into that world.'

'Did you tell anyone about it?'

'It was simply our world. The world.'

She was standing in the garden. The taste of soft earth-flavoured water from the garden hose. The bricks and baby tears. The smell of worms and spiders. The saw-toothed leaves of a camellia, curled. Tingling with fear and power.

'Did it ever work for you?' asked Jun. His face was still, cool, nothing in it. 'Did you go through?'

'I don't know,' said Dinah. She felt that she had, surely. But she could not remember. She could not remember.

'Yes,' he said. 'That is how it is. That is how it was for me too.'

'How did you survive?'

Jun shrugged. 'I don't know if surviving is what I am doing. But what I am doing, what I am forcing myself to do, is trying to see the world without her in it. It is very, very dull. There are no short cuts. I don't know how to make anything come alive. But I have to do it.'

The plastic rustled as Jun retrieved the containers.

'I hope you don't mind this,' said Jun. 'I should probably have taken you somewhere nice, but I find I don't much like restaurants anymore. I hate eating in places full of other people. I don't like being watched while I eat.'

'That's okay.'

'This place only makes one thing, negi toro, but it's the best. Have you had it?'

'Spring onion?'

'Yes. With tuna. The leftover fatty meat from along the spine. They make it by scraping down the spine and between the bones with a spoon so they get all of it. Then it's mixed with mayo and the negi.'

The filling rose above the rice and nori like a soft pink cloud flecked with white and green. She took a piece in her fingers and took a bite. The fish was sweet and oily and rich almost like a mousse, but the richness was cut with the acid of the onion. It was so delicious that emotion rose within her. Gratitude. Relief. Who knew? She took another piece. Another sip of beer.

'What are we doing?' she said out loud.

Jun shrugged. 'It doesn't have to be a thing,' he said. 'Not everything has to have a label. Do you like the sushi?'

'Yes, it's really good.'

They ate. For a while it was enough. The heat and the beer and the food and sitting next to Jun were enough.

'Jun?' she said. He didn't answer, but she could hear him listening. 'I'm sorry.'

'Don't worry so much.' On the other side of the park, the cats clustered and milled around their tins of cat food. The mange and dignity, the mottled fur.

'Are you going home after this?' he asked. It wasn't clear if he meant her apartment or home as in New Zealand, halfway across the world. She shrugged.

'You should you know,' he said. 'It's not that there's nothing for you here. But I think maybe you should be with your family.' He moved closer and patted her shoulder. It was a strange action, even endearing, as if she were a dog, or a younger sibling crying inconsolably. He gave off a dappled amber smell, crushed young leaves with a mercurial, animalic odour beneath: ants in hot sun.

'I am going to get ridiculously drunk,' he said. 'Would you care to join me?'

She hesitated. The cats were moving to and fro around the base of the neighbouring tree.

Jun reached down to retrieve the second carrier bag. He took out the bottle. It was brown and looked like the kind of thing that contained cough syrup.

'Shochu. They distil it at the restaurant. It's probably lethal, but what the hell.' He took a long, deep swig and passed it to her.

She drank too. She smiled. It felt surprisingly easy.

'Look,' he said. 'I am not my mother. And you are not your brother. By some miracle we have escaped that fate. Could we, perhaps, not speak about it all for the time being? For a while? This is a free universe, right? You are here, and I am here also. Two people who will probably never see each other again.'

She knew what this meant. Of course she did. She saw Yasuko's face as clear as day, but she could not have both things. Jun stood up so that he was facing her. When he took the bottle again his hand closed next to hers and against her own. She did not release her hand but stood also. They were standing too close. He leaned toward her, not looking at her but instead past her to the moon or to the neighbouring apartment's closed windows. She let go at last, and he drank with a kind of sigh, then placed the bottle on the ground. Then he took her wrists and placed her palms on his chest. They stood for a while. There was a moment when he simply looked at her, as if interested to see what she would do next, and she felt something akin to forgiveness, though whether he were forgiving her or she herself, she didn't know. She slid her hands down until they were resting on his thighs, her thumbs arced over them. She felt the warmth of his skin through the denim. The hard muscle, the separateness of his body.

Dinah felt the arms of the park close her in. With this sensation came the reminder that she could not, could never again be hurt. She had known it for so long and it had not helped her until now. Now she leaned in to Jun so that the lines of their body were adjacent and she felt his cock get hard. The white liquor came to light in her stomach, and she undid his belt. Jun walked her backwards then past the bench and toward the tree until its bark pressed through her clothes. She smelt his amber scent again as he leaned in to her neck and pulled her skirt up. What was surprising was that while they fucked, there were no consequences at all, only the cats milling, turning their heads away from the scene, spilling in and out of the shadow like distillations of the night air.

Yasuko's new apartment was much smaller than her old one, but she had no need for anything more than a studio. She was living in a state of great vision. She felt her father's presence in the city still, but it was hopelessly clumsy. She had evaded him with little effort. She had surpassed him, transcended his knowledge. It is in the nature of things that the child outgrows the parent.

The biggest surprise was how much she missed the girl. She thought of the period in the early evenings of their friendship when she had visited the girl in her mind's eye. She had watched her coming home with thin plastic shopping bags from the local supermarket. Watched her tread up the metal rungs, and the flakes of rust that filtered off into the air. She had watched at dusk when the girl walked to a local park, as if the half-light were a kind of equilibrium that she could endure.

Yasuko thought of her face, its irregularity, the lack of symmetry, the way her skin was made up of many different colours — pink, white, red, yellow, even a sort of olive green. At that time she did not wear make-up, not a scrap of it, and the nakedness of her face had been awful, disturbing. The grief that came off her palpable. Her hair was scraped back into an unflattering ponytail. Down-at-heel sandals, a shapeless cotton skirt. She had taken no care in her appearance. Yasuko thought of her transformation.

Of course she thought of Jun also. But that door remained open. She would never close it. It is open, she said, to the night, turning her face to her son, who was crouched in the wings of the room. Welcome home, she said, in the manner of one greeting the loved one who has returned from a long and arduous journey.

For now, she walked. The sky was pink and full of beauty, and she did not wish to be at home. There was a café with dolls in the window dressed in Noh costume. She noted it, passed another station, followed the road that curved upward and would intersect, she knew, with Ikebukuro, where — she decided — she would catch a taxi home instead.

A hoarder's house covered in ivy. A yakuza mansion with concrete walls garlanded in razor wire. A street with plastic floral decorations on each street lamp.

On the final cross-street before Meiji-dori, there were police and a cordon. She felt and heard it before she saw any detail. The crackle in the air, of despair, of drama — a conflagration. She became quickly a bystander, an observer, shrinking back into her guise of respectable middle-aged woman. She stood demurely next to a policeman who was speaking in agitated tones over his CB radio. There were people gathering; a young foreign couple; an elderly man walking a dog. They had all begun to look upwards. A plane tree stirred its leaves in the golden street light.

There was a young Japanese schoolgirl on the roof.

Yasuko could feel the girl breathing, the way the ceiling of her world had lifted off and each breath was an admission of disbelief. There was pain, and while there was pain there was hope, she thought. Each breath was an act of refusal. Flares going up. As soon as those flares illuminated, as soon as they caught, then it would be too late.

Yasuko stood, was a bystander. She was in two parts. Part of her asked the policeman something, a question about the event. 'Is it someone with a knife or a gun, officer?' she asked, and she was a respectable woman in a Chanel jacket and Gucci heels who earned a polite murmur from the distracted man. 'Nothing like that, Ma'am. Just a girl being foolish. Failed her exams, something like that. If you could move along a little.'

Part of Yasuko, however, was ascending, sensible. There was little she could do, but perhaps there was something.

And this is what she saw: a girl in middy uniform standing on the gravel, almost at the edge. There was blood on her blouse, her own or some-one else's. Her knees were bleeding too, from where she had been crouching on the rough surface and shuffling forward, in order to prove something to herself about pain. Her flesh was alive with the imprint. She was too close to the edge.

Yasuko had arrived too late. The girl's mind was closed to her, after all, a shut box of regret and guilt. Yasuko conceded her failure — this was where work had to start, in any case. But she did what she could, and what she could do was to cast slowness outward and upward toward the girl. It moved in a circle, like a lasso. She saw the girl as a product, distilled, of each of her own private moments. She saw her as a baby — fat dimpled hands stirring at her mother's neck. The favourite clothes that were washed and hung out

292

to dry and washed again. She saw her at six, at seven. At each moment there was all of the time in the world. She saw her earlier that evening, holding her best friend's hair back from her neck. Time moved so slowly that it had all but stopped. Light hung liquid in the air. The policeman's face was a mixture of boredom and sympathy, each pore of it magnified by sweat and slow time.

The girl's eyes widened invisibly, imperceptibly, marking the break of the leash or bond that held her. It had always already been too late, but now, in the syrupy, maple light, the arduous, enduring pink of it, she floated without falling. She was held in Yasuko's pity. Her polycotton blouse lifted out from her body as if underwater. A heavy black leather shoe, half-unlaced, dangled poised from the point of her toe.

And so it was that Yasuko excused herself politely from the fixed gaze of the silent policeman, and followed the road back to Meiji-dori, and home to her supper.

Acknowledgements

Bird Life's epigraph is taken from the English subtitles of the 1970 movie *The Garden of the Finzi-Continis (Il giardino dei Finzi Contini)*, directed by Vittorio De Sica and based on the novel of the same name by Giorgio Bassani (1962).

I wrote this book over several years and could not have finished it without a number of very generous people. Thank you to Creative New Zealand and the estate of Louis Johnson for the grant that enabled me to begin what would ultimately become this novel. Thank you also to the Arts Foundation of New Zealand — your early support of my writing meant a great deal to me and continues to fire my work.

Thanks to my agent, Will Francis, who is both brilliant and exceptionally patient. To all of the team at Scribe, and with particular thanks to my editor Molly Slight, editorial assistant Laura Ali, and copy editor David Golding. I'm profoundly grateful for your vision and belief, and for the questions and ideas that have helped this book find its final form. I also wish to thank the whole team at Te Herenga Waka University Press, particularly Fergus and Ashleigh, for giving the book the perfect home in Aotearoa New Zealand.

Eternal gratitude to the Glen Road Writers for a steady provision of inspiration, advice, cake, support, and true friendship. Sue Orr, Kate Duignan, Ingrid Horrocks, Elizabeth Knox, Sarah Laing, Emma Martin, Kirsten McDougall, Susan Pearce, Rebecca Priestley, and Emily Perkins, I count myself exceptionally lucky to know you and to benefit from your collective wisdom.

Thank you to Ryan Skelton for being an amazing sounding board and checker of facts and words. Thank you to Katie Sweetman for her early and very kind reading of the novel. To Imogen Prickett, friend of my heart, always. And to Sandeep Parmar: I miss you every day — this is dedicated to you.

To my beloved parents, Barbara and Bruce, and to my siblings Esther and Chris and their beautiful families — thank you always for your generosity and kindness and humour and love. Thanks to the Williamses and Walronds for just being the best. And to Dawn and Allan Shuker — without your immense gift of time and kindness, I really could not have written this book.

To Carl: I love you. Thank you for listening and for understanding everything. Thanks for being my first, best reader and my most steady support. And finally, thank you to my darlings, Alexander and Lotte, for being so funny and so strange and so beautiful all at the same time.